P9-CCP-040

Lola

and the

Boy Next Door

Lola
and the
Boy Next Door

Stephanie Perkins

Dutton Books

an imprint of Penguin Group (USA) Inc.

Dutton Books
A member of Penguin Group (USA) Inc.

Published by the Penguin Group | Penguin Group (USA) Inc., 375 Hudson Street, New York, New York 10014, U.S.A. | Penguin Group (Canada), 90 Eglinton Avenue East, Suite 700, Toronto, Ontario M4P 2Y3, Canada (a division of Pearson Penguin Canada Inc.) | Penguin Books Ltd, 80 Strand, London WC2R 0RL, England | Penguin Ireland, 25 St Stephen's Green, Dublin 2, Ireland (a division of Penguin Books Ltd) | Penguin Group (Australia), 250 Camberwell Road, Camberwell, Victoria 3124, Australia (a division of Pearson Australia Group Pty Ltd) | Penguin Books India Pvt Ltd, 11 Community Centre, Panchsheel Park, New Delhi—110 017, India | Penguin Group (NZ), 67 Apollo Drive, Rosedale, Auckland 0632, New Zealand (a division of Pearson New Zealand Ltd.) | Penguin Books (South Africa) (Pty) Ltd, 24 Sturdee Avenue, Rosebank, Johannesburg 2196, South Africa | Penguin Books Ltd, Registered Offices: 80 Strand, London WC2R 0RL, England

Library of Congress Cataloging-in-Publication Data

Perkins, Stephanie.
Lola and the boy next door / Stephanie Perkins.—1st ed.
p. cm.
Summary: Budding costume designer Lola lives an extraordinary life in San Francisco with her two dads and beloved dog, dating a punk rocker, but when the Bell twins return to the house next door Lola recalls both the friendship-ending fight with Calliope, a figure skater, and the childhood crush she had on Cricket.
ISBN 978-0-525-42328-7 (hardcover)
[1. Dating (Social customs)—Fiction. 2. Costume design—Fiction. 3.Fathers and daughters—Fiction. 4. Neighbors—Fiction. 5. Ice skating—Fiction. 6. San Francisco (Calif.)—Fiction.] I. Title.
PZ7.P4317Lol 2011
[Fic]—dc23 2011015533

Published in the United States by Dutton Books,
a member of Penguin Group (USA) Inc.
345 Hudson Street, New York, New York 10014
www.penguin.com/teens
Designed by Irene Vandervoort

Printed in USA | First Edition | 10 9 8 7 6 5 4 3 2 1

For Jarrod, best friend & true love

Lola

and the

Boy Next Door

chapter one

I have three simple wishes. They're really not too much to ask.

The first is to attend the winter formal dressed like Marie Antoinette. I want a wig so elaborate it could cage a bird and a dress so wide I'll only be able to enter the dance through a set of double doors. But I'll hold my skirts high as I arrive to reveal a pair of platform combat boots, so everyone can see that, underneath the frills, I'm punk-rock tough.

The second is for my parents to approve of my boyfriend. They hate him. They hate his bleached hair with its constant dark roots, and they hate his arms, which are tattooed with sleeves of spiderwebs and stars. They say his eyebrows condescend, that his smile is more of a smirk. And they're sick of hearing his music blasting from my bedroom, and they're tired of fighting about my curfew whenever I watch his band play in clubs.

And my third wish?

To never ever ever see the Bell twins ever again. Ever.

But I'd much rather discuss my boyfriend. I realize it's not cool to desire parental approval, but honestly, my life would be so much easier if they accepted that Max is *the one*. It'd mean the end of embarrassing restrictions, the end of every-hour-on-the-hour phone-call check-ins on dates, and—best of all—the end of Sunday brunch.

The end of mornings like this.

"Another waffle, Max?"

My father, Nathan, pushes the golden stack across our antique farmhouse table and toward my boyfriend. This is not a real question. It's a command, so that my parents can continue their interrogation before we leave. Our reward for dealing with brunch? A more relaxed Sunday-afternoon date with fewer check-ins.

Max takes two and helps himself to the homemade raspberry-peach syrup. "Thanks, sir. Incredible, as always." He pours the syrup carefully, a drop in each square. Despite appearances, Max is careful by nature. This is why he never drinks or smokes pot on Saturday nights. He doesn't want to come to brunch looking hungover, which is, of course, what my parents are watching for. Evidence of debauchery.

"Thank Andy." Nathan jerks his head toward my other dad, who runs a pie bakery out of our home. "He made them."

"Delicious. Thank you, sir." Max never misses a beat. "Lola, did you get enough?"

I stretch, and the seven inches of Bakelite bracelets on my right arm knock against each other. "Yeah, like, twenty minutes ago. Come on," I turn and plead to Andy, the candidate most likely to let us leave early. "Can't we go now?"

He bats his eyes innocently. "More orange juice? Frittata?"

"No." I fight to keep from slumping. Slumping is unattractive.

Nathan stabs another waffle. "So. Max. How goes the world of meter reading?"

When Max isn't being an indie punk garage-rock god, he works for the City of San Francisco. It irks Nathan that Max has no interest in college. But what my dad doesn't grasp is that Max is actually brilliant. He reads complicated philosophy books written by people with names I can't pronounce and watches tons of angry political documentaries. I certainly wouldn't debate him.

Max smiles politely, and his dark eyebrows raise a titch. "The same as last week."

"And the band?" Andy asks. "Wasn't some record executive supposed to come on Friday?"

My boyfriend frowns. The guy from the label never showed. Max updates Andy about Amphetamine's forthcoming album instead, while Nathan and I exchange scowls. No doubt my father is disappointed that, once again, he hasn't found anything to incriminate Max. Apart from the age thing, of course.

Which is the real reason my parents hate my boyfriend.

They hate that I'm seventeen, and Max is twenty-two.

But I'm a firm believer in age-doesn't-matter. Besides, it's only five years, way less than the difference between my parents. Though it's no use pointing this out, or the fact that my boyfriend is the same age Nathan was when my parents started dating. This only gets them worked up. "*I* may have been his age, but Andy was thirty," Nathan always says. "Not a teenager. And we'd both had several boyfriends before, plenty of life experience. You can't jump into these things. You have to be careful."

But they don't remember what it's like to be young and in love. Of course I can jump into these things. When it's someone like Max, I'd be stupid not to. My best friend thinks it's hilarious that my parents are so strict. After all, shouldn't a couple of gay men sympathize with the temptation offered by a sexy, slightly dangerous boyfriend?

This is so far from the truth it's painful.

It doesn't matter that I'm a perfect daughter. I don't drink or do drugs, and I've never smoked a cigarette. I haven't crashed their car—I can't even drive, so they're not paying high insurance rates—and I have a decent job. I make good grades. Well, apart from biology, but I refused to dissect that fetal pig on principle. And I only have one hole per ear and no ink. Yet. I'm not even embarrassed to hug my parents in public.

Except when Nathan wears a sweatband when he goes running. Because really.

I clear my dishes from the table, hoping to speed things along. Today Max is taking me to one of my favorite places, the

Japanese Tea Garden, and then he's driving me to work for my evening shift. And hopefully, in between stops, we'll spend some quality time together in his '64 Chevy Impala.

I lean against the kitchen countertop, dreaming of Max's car.

"I'm just shocked she's not wearing her kimono," Nathan says.

"What?" I hate it when I space out and realize people have been talking about me.

"Chinese pajamas to the Japanese Tea Garden," he continues, gesturing at my red silk bottoms. "What *will* people think?"

I don't believe in fashion. I believe in costume. Life is too short to be the same person every day. I roll my eyes to show Max that I realize my parents are acting lame.

"Our little drag queen," Andy says.

"Because that's a new one." I snatch his plate and dump the brunch remains into Betsy's bowl. Her eyes bug, and she inhales the waffle scraps in one big doggie bite.

Betsy's full name is Heavens to Betsy, and we rescued her from animal control several years ago. She's a mutt, built like a golden retriever but black in color. I wanted a black dog, because Andy once clipped a magazine article—he's *always* clipping articles, usually about teens dying from overdoses or contracting syphilis or getting pregnant and dropping out of school—about how black dogs are always the last to be adopted at shelters and, therefore, more likely to be put down. Which is totally Dog Racism, if you ask me. Betsy is all heart.

"Lola." Andy is wearing his serious face. "I wasn't finished."

"So get a new plate."

"Lola," Nathan says, and I give Andy a clean plate. I'm afraid they're about to turn this into A Thing in front of Max, when they notice Betsy begging for more waffles.

"No," I tell her.

"Have you walked her today?" Nathan asks me.

"No, Andy did."

"Before I started cooking," Andy says. "She's ready for another."

"Why don't you take her for a walk while we finish up with Max?" Nathan asks. Another command, not a question.

I glance at Max, and he closes his eyes like he can't believe they're pulling this trick again. "But, Dad—"

"No buts. You wanted the dog, you walk her."

This is one of Nathan's most annoying catchphrases. Heavens to Betsy was supposed to be mine, but she had the nerve to fall in love with Nathan instead, which irritates Andy and me to no end. We're the ones who feed and walk her. I reach for the biodegradable baggies and her leash—the one I've embroidered with hearts and Russian nesting dolls—and she's already going berserk. "Yeah, yeah. Come on."

I shoot Max another apologetic look, and then Betsy and I are out the door.

There are twenty-one stairs from our porch to the sidewalk. Anywhere you go in San Francisco, you have to deal with steps and hills. It's unusually warm outside, so along with my pajama bottoms and Bakelite bangles, I'm wearing a tank top. I've also got on my giant white Jackie O sunglasses, a long brunette wig with emerald tips, and black ballet slippers. *Real* ballet slippers, not the flats that only look like ballet slippers.

My New Year's resolution was to never again wear the same outfit twice.

The sunshine feels good on my shoulders. It doesn't matter that it's August; because of the bay, the temperature doesn't change much throughout the year. It's always cool. Today I'm grateful for the peculiar weather, because it means I won't have to bring a sweater on my date.

Betsy pees on the teeny rectangle of grass in front of the lavender Victorian next door—she always pees here, which I totally approve of—and we move on. Despite my annoying parents, I'm happy. I have a romantic date with my boyfriend, a great schedule with my favorite coworkers, and one more week of summer vacation.

We hike up and down the massive hill that separates my street from the park. When we arrive, a Korean gentleman in a velveteen tracksuit greets us. He's doing tai chi between the palm trees. "Hello, Dolores! How was your birthday?" Mr. Lim is the only person apart from my parents (when they're mad) who calls me by my real name. His daughter Lindsey is my best friend; they live a few streets over.

"Hi, Mr. Lim. It was divine!" My birthday was last week. Mine is the earliest of anyone in my grade, which I love. It gives me an additional air of maturity. "How's the restaurant?"

"Very good, thank you. Everyone asking for beef galbi this week. Goodbye, Dolores! Hello to your parents."

The old lady name is because I was named after one. My

great-grandma Dolores Deeks died a few years before I was born. She was Andy's grandmother, and she was fabulous. The kind of woman who wore feathered hats and marched in civil rights protests. Dolores was the first person Andy came out to. He was thirteen. They were really close, and when she died, she left Andy her house. That's where we live, in Great-Grandma Dolores's mint green Victorian in the Castro district.

Which we'd never be able to afford without her generous bequeathal. My parents make a healthy living, but nothing like the neighbors. The well-kept homes on our street, with their decorative gabled cornices and extravagant wooden ornamentation, all come from old money. Including the lavender house next door.

My name is also shared with this park, Mission Dolores. It's not a coincidence. Great-Grandma Dolores was named after the nearby mission, which was named after a creek called *Arroyo de Nuestra Señora de los Dolores.* This translates to "Our Lady of Sorrows Creek." Because who wouldn't want to be named after a depressing body of water? There's also a major street around here called Dolores. It's kind of weird.

I'd rather be a Lola.

Heavens to Betsy finishes, and we head home. I hope my parents haven't been torturing Max. For someone so brash onstage, he's actually an introvert, and these weekly meetings aren't easy on him. "I thought dealing with one protective father was bad enough," he once said. "But two? Your dads are gonna be the death of me, Lo."

A moving truck rattles by, and it's odd, because suddenly—just that quickly—my good mood is replaced by unease. We pick up speed. Max must be beyond uncomfortable right now. I can't explain it, but the closer I get to home, the worse I feel. A terrible scenario loops through my mind: my parents, so relentless with inquiries that Max decides I'm not worth it anymore.

My hope is that someday, when we've been together longer than one summer, my parents will realize he's *the one,* and age won't be an issue anymore. But despite their inability to see this truth now, they aren't dumb. They deal with Max because they think if they forbade me from seeing him, we'd just run off together. I'd move into his apartment and get a job dancing naked or dealing acid.

Which is beyond misguided.

But I'm jogging now, hauling Betsy down the hill. Something's not right. And I'm positive it's happened—that Max has left or my parents have cornered him into a heated argument about the lack of direction in his life—when I reach my street and everything clicks into place.

The moving truck.

Not the brunch.

The moving truck.

But I'm sure the truck belongs to another renter. It has to, it always does. The last family, this couple that smelled like baby Swiss and collected medical oddities like shriveled livers in formaldehyde and oversize models of vaginas, vacated a week ago. In the last two years, there's been a string of renters, and every time someone moves out, I can't help but feel ill until the new ones arrive.

Because what if *now* is the time they move back in?

I slow down to get a better look at the truck. Is anyone outside? I didn't notice a car in the garage when we passed earlier, but I've made a habit out of not staring at the house next door. Sure enough, there are two people ahead on the sidewalk. I strain my eyes and find, with a mixture of agitation and relief, that it's just the movers. Betsy tugs on her leash, and I pick up the pace again.

I'm sure there's nothing to worry about. What are the chances?

Except . . . there's *always* a chance. The movers lift a white sofa from the back of the truck, and my heart thumps harder. Do I recognize it? Have I sat on that love seat before? But no. I don't know it. I peer inside the crammed truck, searching for anything familiar, and I'm met with stacks of severe modern furniture that I've never seen before.

It's not them. It can't be them.

It's not them!

I grin from ear to ear—a silly smile that makes me look like a child, which I don't normally allow myself to do—and wave to the movers. They grunt and nod back. The lavender garage door is open, and now I'm positive that it wasn't earlier. I inspect the car, and my relief deepens. It's something compact and silver, and I don't recognize it.

Saved. Again. It *is* a happy day.

Betsy and I bound inside. "Brunch is over! Let's go, Max."

Everyone is staring out the front window in our living room.

"Looks like we have neighbors again," I say.

Andy looks surprised by the cheer in my voice. We've never talked about it, but he knows something happened there two years ago. He knows that I worry about their return, that I fret each moving day.

"What?" I grin again, but then stop myself, conscious of Max. I tone it down.

"Uh, Lo? You didn't see them, by any chance, did you?"

Andy's concern is touching. I release Betsy from her leash and whisk into the kitchen. Determined to hurry the morning and get to my date, I swipe the remaining dishes from the table and head toward the sink. "Nope." I laugh. "What? Do they have another plastic vagina? A stuffed giraffe? A medieval suit of armor—what?"

All three of them are staring at me.

My throat tightens. "What is it?"

Max examines me with an unusual curiosity. "Your parents say you know the family."

No. NO.

Someone says something else, but the words don't register. My feet are carrying me toward the window while my brain is screaming for me to turn back. It can't be them. It wasn't their furniture! It wasn't their car! But people buy new things. My eyes are riveted next door as a figure emerges onto the porch. The dishes in my hands—*Why am I still carrying the brunch plates?*—shatter against the floor.

Because there she is.

Calliope Bell.

chapter two

"She's just as beautiful as she is on television." I poke at the complimentary bowl of cookies and rice crackers. "Just as beautiful as she always was."

Max shrugs. "She's all right. Nothing to get worked up over."

As comforted as I am by his state of unimpress, it's not enough to distract me. I sag against the railing of the rustic teahouse, and a breeze floats across the reflecting pool beside us. "You don't understand. She's *Calliope Bell.*"

"You're right, I don't." His eyes frown behind his thick Buddy Holly frames. This is something we have in common—terrible vision. I love it when he wears his glasses. Badass rocker meets sexy nerd. He only wears them offstage, unless he's playing an acoustic number. Then they add the necessary touch of sensitivity. Max is always conscious of his appearance, which some people might find vain, but I understand completely. You only have one chance to make a first impression.

"Let me get this straight," he continues. "When you guys were freshmen—"

"When I was a freshman. She's a year older."

"Okay, when you were a freshman . . . what? She was mean to you? And you're still upset about it?" His brows furrow like he's missing half of the equation. Which he is. And I'm not going to fill him in.

"Yep."

He snorts. "That must have been some pretty bitchy shit for you to break those plates over."

It took fifteen minutes to clean up my mess. Shards of china and eggy frittata bits, trapped between the cracks of the hardwood floor, and sticky raspberry-peach syrup, splattered like blood across the baseboards.

"You have no idea." I leave it at this.

Max pours himself another cup of jasmine tea. "So why did you idolize her?"

"I didn't idolize her then. Only when we were younger. She was this . . . gorgeous, talented girl who also happened to be my neighbor. I mean, we hung out when we were little, played Barbies and make-believe. It just hurt when she turned on me, that's all. I can't believe you haven't heard of her," I add.

"Sorry. I don't watch a lot of figure skating."

"She's been to the World Championships twice. Silver medals? She's the big Olympic hopeful this year."

"Sorry," he says again.

"She was on a Wheaties box."

"No doubt selling for an entire buck ninety-nine on eBay." He nudges my knees with his underneath the table. "Who the hell cares?"

I sigh. "I loved her costumes. The chiffon ruffles, the beading and Swarovski crystals, the little skirts—"

"Little skirts?" Max swigs the rest of his tea.

"And she had that grace and poise and confidence." I push my shoulders back. "And that perfect shiny hair. That perfect skin."

"Perfect is overrated. Perfect is boring."

I smile. "You don't think I'm perfect?"

"No. You're delightfully screwy, and I wouldn't have you any other way. Drink your tea."

When I finish, we take another stroll. The Japanese Tea Garden isn't big, but it makes up for its size with beauty. Perfumed flowers in jewel-toned colors are balanced by intricately cut plants in tranquil blues and greens. Pathways meander around Buddhist statuary, koi ponds, a red pagoda, and a wooden bridge shaped like the moon. The only sounds are birdsong and the soft click of cameras. It's peaceful. Magical.

But the best part?

Hidden nooks, perfect for kissing.

We find just the right bench, private and tucked away, and Max places his hands behind my head and pulls my lips to his. This is what I've been waiting for. His kisses are gentle and rough, spearmint and cigarettes.

We've dated all summer, but I'm still not used to him. Max. *My boyfriend,* Max. The night we met was the first time my parents had let me go to a club. Lindsey Lim was in the bathroom, so I was temporarily alone, perched nervously against Verge's rough concrete wall. He walked straight up to me like he'd done it a hundred times before.

"I'm sorry," he said. "You must have noticed me staring at you during the set."

This was true. His stare had thrilled me, though I didn't trust it. The small club was crowded, and he could've been watching any of the hungry girls dancing beside me.

"What's your name?"

"Lola Nolan." I adjusted my tiara and shifted in my creepers.

"Lo-lo-lo-lo Lo-la." Max sang it like the Kinks' song. His deep voice was hoarse from the show. He wore a plain black T-shirt, which I would soon discover to be his uniform. Underneath it, his shoulders were broad, his arms were toned, and right away I spotted the tattoo that would become my favorite, hidden in the crook of his left elbow. His namesake from *Where the Wild Things Are*. The little boy in the white wolf suit.

He was the most attractive man who'd ever spoken to me. Semicoherent sentences tumbled around in my head, but I couldn't keep up with any of them long enough to spit one out.

"What'd you think of the show?" He had to raise his voice above the Ramones, who'd started blasting from the speakers.

"You were great," I shouted. "I've never seen your band before."

I tried to yell this second part casually, like I had just never seen *his* band before. He didn't have to know it was my first show ever.

"I know. I would have noticed you. Do you have a boyfriend, Lola?"

Joey Ramone echoed it behind him. *Hey, little girl. I wanna be your boyfriend.*

The guys at school were never this direct. Not that I had much experience, just the odd monthlong boyfriend here and there. Most guys are either intimidated by me or think I'm strange. "What's it to you?" I jutted out my chin, confidence skyrocketing.

Sweet little girl. I wanna be your boyfriend.

Max looked me up and down, and the side of his lips curled into a smile. "I see you already need to go." He jerked his head, and I turned to find Lindsey Lim, jaw agape. Only a teenager could look that awkward and surprised. Did Max realize we were still in high school? "So why don't you give me your number?" he continued. "I'd like to see you sometime."

He must have heard my heart pounding as I sifted through the contents of my purse: watermelon bubble gum, movie-ticket stubs, veggie burrito receipts, and a rainbow of nail-polish bottles. I withdrew a Sharpie, realizing too late that only kids and groupies carry Sharpies. Luckily, he didn't seem to mind.

Max held out a wrist. "Here."

His breath was warm on my neck as I pressed the marker to his skin. My hand trembled, but somehow I managed to write it in clear, bold strokes below his tattoos. Then he smiled—that signature smile, using only one corner of his mouth—and ambled away, through the sweaty bodies and toward the dimly lit bar. I allowed myself a moment to stare at his backside. Despite my number, I was sure I'd never see it again.

But he did call.

Obviously, he called.

It happened two days later, on a bus ride to work. Max wanted to meet in the Haight for lunch, and I nearly died turning him down. He asked about the next day. I was working then, too. And then he asked about the next, and I couldn't believe my luck that he was still trying. Yes, I told him. *Yes.*

I wore a pink soda-fountain-style waitress dress, and my natural hair—I'm a brunette, average in color—was in two buns like Mickey Mouse ears. We ate falafel and discovered we were both vegetarians. He told me he didn't have a mother, and I told him I didn't really either. And then, as I wiped the last crumbs from my mouth, he said this: "There's no polite way to ask, so I'm just gonna go for it. How old are you?"

My expression must have been terrible, because Max looked stricken as I struggled to come up with a suitable answer. "Shit. That bad, huh?"

I decided delay was my best tactic. "How old are you?"

"No way. You first."

Delay again. "How old do you think I am?"

"I think you have a cute face that looks deceptively young. And I don't want to insult you either way. So you'll have to tell me."

It's true. My face is round, and my cheeks are pinchable, and my ears stick out farther than I'd like. I fight it with makeup and wardrobe. My curvy body helps, too. But I was going to tell the truth, I really was, when he started guessing. "Nineteen?"

I shook my head.

"Older or younger?"

I shrugged, but he knew where this was headed. "Eighteen? Please tell me you're eighteen."

"Of course I'm eighteen." I shoved the empty plastic food basket away from me. Outside, I was an ice queen, but inside I was freaking out. "Would I be here if I wasn't?"

His amber eyes narrowed in disbelief, and the panic rose inside of me. "So how old are *you*?" I asked again.

"Older than you. Are you in college?"

"I will be." *Someday.*

"So you're still living at home?"

"How old are you?" I asked a third time.

He grimaced. "I'm twenty-two, Lola. And we probably shouldn't be having this conversation. I'm sorry, if I had known—"

"I'm legal." And then I immediately felt stupid.

There was a long pause. "No," Max said. "You're dangerous."

But he was smiling.

It took another week of casual dating before I convinced him to kiss me. He was definitely interested, but I could tell I made him nervous. For some reason, this only made me bolder. I liked Max in a way I hadn't liked anyone in years. Two years, to be exact.

It was in the main public library, and we met there because Max had deemed it safe. But when he saw me—short dress, tall boots—his eyes widened into an expression that I already recognized as an uncustomary display of emotion. "You could get a decent man in trouble," he said. I reached for his book, but I brushed the boy in the wolf suit instead. His grip went loose. "Lola," he warned.

I looked at him innocently.

And that was when he took my hand and led me away from the public tables and into the empty stacks. He backed me against the biographies. "Are you sure you want this?" A tease in his voice, but his stare was serious.

My palms sweated. "Of course."

"I'm not a nice guy." He stepped closer.

"Maybe I'm not a nice girl."

"No. You're a very nice girl. That's what I like about you." And with a single finger, he tilted my face up to his.

Our relationship progressed quickly. I was the one who slowed things back down. My parents were asking questions. They no longer believed I was spending that much time with Lindsey. And I knew it was wrong to keep lying to Max before things went further, so I came clean to him about my real age.

Max was furious. He disappeared for a week, and I'd already given up hope when he called. He said he was in love. I told him that he'd have to meet Nathan and Andy. Parents make him edgy—his father is an alcoholic, his mother left when he was five—but he agreed. And then the restrictions were placed upon us. And then last week, on my seventeenth birthday, I lost my virginity in his apartment.

My parents think we went to the zoo.

Since then, we've slept together once more. And I'm not an idiot about these things; I don't have romantic delusions. I've read enough to know it takes a while for it to get good for girls. But I hope it gets better soon.

The kissing is fantastic, so I'm sure it'll happen.

Except today I can't concentrate on his lips. I've waited for them all afternoon, but now that they're here, I'm distracted. Bells ring in the distance—from the pagoda? from outside the gardens?—and all I can think is *Bell. Bell. Bell.*

They're back. There were three of them this morning, Calliope and her parents. No sign of Calliope's siblings. Not that I'd mind seeing Aleck. But the other one . . .

"What?"

I'm startled. Max is looking at me. When did we stop kissing?

"What?" he asks again. "Where are you?"

My eye muscles twitch. "I'm sorry, I was thinking about work."

He doesn't believe me. This is the problem of having lied to your boyfriend in the past. He sighs with frustration, stands, and puts one hand inside his pocket. I know he's fiddling with his lighter.

"I'm sorry," I say again.

"Forget it." He glances at the clock on his phone. "It's time to go, anyway."

The drive to the Royal Civic Center 16 is quiet, apart from the Clash blasting through his stereo. Max is ticked, and I feel guilty. "Call me later?" I ask.

He nods as he pulls away, but I know I'm still in trouble.

As if I needed another reason to hate the Bells.

chapter three

My supervisor is rearranging the saltshakers. She does this with an alarming frequency. The theater is in a between-films nighttime lull, and I'm using the opportunity to scrub the buttery popcorn feeling from my arm hair.

"Try this." She hands me a baby wipe. "It works better than a napkin."

I accept it with genuine thanks. Despite her neuroticisms, Anna is my favorite coworker. She's a little older than me, very pretty, and she just started film school. She has a cheerful smile—a slight gap between her front teeth—and a thick, singular stripe of platinum in her dark brown hair. It's a nice touch. Plus, she always wears this necklace with a glass bead shaped like a banana.

I admire someone with a signature accessory.

"Where in the bloody hell did that come from?" asks the only other person behind the counter. Or more precisely, on top of the counter, where her ridiculously attractive, English-accented boyfriend is perched.

He's the other thing I like about Anna. Wherever she goes, he follows.

He nods toward the baby wipe. "What else are you carrying in your pockets? Dust rags? Furniture polish?"

"Watch it," she says. "Or I'll scrub *your* arms, Étienne."

He grins. "As long as you do it in private."

Anna is the only person who calls him by his first name. The rest of us call him by his last, St. Clair. I'm not sure why. It's just one of those things. They moved here recently, but they met last year in Paris, where they went to high school. *Paris.* I'd kill to go to school in Paris, especially if there are guys like Étienne St. Clair there.

Not that I'd cheat on Max. I'm just saying. St. Clair has gorgeous brown eyes and mussed artist hair. Though he's on the short side for my taste, several inches shorter than his girlfriend.

He attends college at Berkeley, but despite his unemployment, he spends as much time here at the theater as he does across the bay. And because he's beautiful and cocky and confident, everyone loves him. It only took a matter of hours before he'd weaseled his way into all of the employee areas without a single complaint by management.

That kind of charisma is impressive. But it doesn't mean I want to hear about their private scrubbings. "My shift ends in a half hour. Please wait until I've vacated the premises before elaborating upon this conversation."

Anna smiles at St. Clair, who is removing the giant ASK ME ABOUT OUR MOVIE-WATCHERS CLUB! button from her maroon work vest. "Lola's just jealous. She's having Max problems again." She glances at me, and her smile turns wry. "What'd I tell you about musicians? That bad boy type will only break your heart."

"They're only bad because they're lame," St. Clair mutters. He pins the button to his own outfit, this fabulous black peacoat that makes him look very European, indeed.

"Just because, once upon a time, you guys had issues with someone," I say, "doesn't mean I do. Max and I are fine. Don't—don't do that." I shake my head at St. Clair. "You're ruining a perfectly good coat."

"Sorry, did you want it? It might balance out your collection." He gestures at my own maroon vest. In between the required Royal Theater buttons, I have several sparkly vintage brooches. Only one manager has complained so far, but as I politely explained to him, my jewelry only attracts *more* attention to his advertisements.

So I won that argument.

And thankfully no one has said anything about the vest itself, which I've taken in so that it's actually fitted and semiflattering. You know. For a polyester vest. My phone vibrates in my pocket. "Hold that thought," I tell St. Clair. It's a text from Lindsey Lim:

u wont believe who i saw jogging in the park. prepare yrself.

"Lola!" Anna rushes forward to catch me, but I'm not falling. Am I falling? Her hand is on my arm, holding me upright. "What happened, what's the matter?"

Surely Lindsey saw Calliope. *Calliope* was the one exercising in the park, as a part of her training. Of course it was Calliope! I shove the other possibility down, deep and hard, but it springs right back. This parasite growing inside of me. It never disappears, no matter how many times I tell myself to forget it. It's the past, and no one can change the past. But it grows all the same. Because as terrible as it is to think about Calliope Bell, it's nothing compared to the pain that overwhelms me whenever I think about her twin.

They'll be seniors this year. Which means that despite the no-show this morning, there's no reason why her twin *wouldn't* be here. The best I can hope for is some kind of delay. I need that time to prepare myself.

I text Lindsey back with a simple question mark. *Please, please, please,* I beg the universe. *Please be Calliope.*

"Is it Max?" Anna asks. "Your parents? Oh God, it's that guy we kicked out of the theater yesterday, isn't it? That crazy guy with the giant phone and the bucket of chicken! How did he find your numb—"

"It's not the guy." But I can't explain. Not now, not this. "Everything's fine."

Anna and St. Clair swap identical disbelieving glances.

"It's Betsy. My dog. Andy says she's acting sick, but I'm sure it's prob—" My phone vibrates again, and I nearly drop it in my frantic attempt to read the new text:

calliope. investigation reveals new coach. shes back 4 good.

"Well?" St. Clair asks.

Calliope. Oh, thank God, CALLIOPE. I look up at my friends. "What?"

"Betsy!" they say together.

"Oh. Yeah." I give them a relieved smile. "False alarm. She just threw up a shoe."

"A shoe?" St. Clair asks.

"Dude," Anna says. "You scared me. Do you need to go home?"

"We can handle closing if you need to go," St. Clair adds. As if he works here. No doubt he just wants me to leave so that he can tongue his girlfriend.

I stride away, toward the popcorn machine, embarrassed to have made a public display. "Betsy's fine. But thanks," I add as my cell vibrates again.

u ok?

Yeah. I saw her this morning.

Y DIDNT U TELL ME???

I was gonna call after work. You didn't see . . . ?

no. but im on it. call me l8r ned.

Lindsey Lim fancies herself a detective. This is due to her lifelong obsession with mysteries, ever since she received the Nancy Drew Starter Set (*Secret of the Old Clock* through *Secret of Red Gate Farm*) for her eighth birthday. Hence, "Ned." She tried to nickname me Bess, Nancy's flirty, shop-happy friend, but I wasn't pleased with that, because Bess is always telling Nancy the situation is too dangerous, and she should give up.

What kind of friend says that?

And I'm definitely not George, Nancy's other best friend, because George is an athletic tomboy with a pug nose. George would never wear a Marie Antoinette dress—even with platform combat boots—to her winter formal. Which left Ned Nickerson, Nancy's boyfriend. Ned is actually useful and often assists Nancy during life-threatening situations. I can get down with that. Even if he is a guy.

I picture Lindsey parked in front of her computer. No doubt she went directly to the figure-skating fansites, and that's how she knows about the new coach. Though I wouldn't put it past her to have walked up to Calliope herself. Lindsey isn't easily intimidated, which is why she'll make a great investigator someday. She's rational, straightforward, and unflinchingly honest.

In this sense, we balance each other out.

We've been best friends since, well . . . since the Bells stopped being my best friends. When I entered kindergarten, and they realized it was no longer cool to hang out with the neighbor girl who only spent half days at school. But that part of our history isn't as harsh as it sounds. Because soon I met Lindsey, and we discovered our mutual passions for roly-poly bugs, sea-green crayons, and those Little Debbies shaped like Christmas trees. Instant friendship. And later, when our classmates began teasing me for wearing tutus or ruby slippers, Lindsey was the one who growled back, "Shove it, fartbreath."

I'm very loyal to her.

I wonder if she'll find out anything about the other Bell?

"Pardon?" St. Clair says.

"Huh?" I turn around to find him and Anna giving me another weird look.

"You said something about a bell." Anna cocks her head. "Are you sure you're okay? You've been really distracted tonight."

"I'm great! Honestly!" How many times will I have to lie today? I volunteer to clean the fourth-floor bathrooms to stop incriminating myself, but later, when Andy shows up to take me home—my parents don't like me riding the bus late at night—he eyes me with the same concern. "You okay, Lola-doodle?"

I throw my purse at the floorboard. "Why does everyone keep asking me that?"

"Maybe because you look like . . ." Andy pauses, his expression shifting to barely masked hope. "Did you and Max break up?"

"Dad!"

He shrugs, but his Adam's apple bobs in his throat, a dead giveaway that he feels guilty for asking. Maybe there's hope for Max and my parents after all. Or, at least, Max and Andy. Andy is always the first to soften in difficult situations.

Which, by the way, doesn't make him "the woman." Nothing annoys me more than someone assuming one of my dads is less-than-dad. Yeah, Andy bakes for a living. And he stayed at home to raise me. And he's decent at talking about feelings. But he also fixes electrical sockets, unclogs kitchen pipes, squashes cockroaches, and changes flat tires. And Nathan may be the resident disciplinarian and a tough lawyer for the ACLU, but he also decorates our house with antiques and gets teary during sitcom weddings.

So neither is "the woman." They're both gay men. Duh.

Besides, it's not like all *women* fit into those stereotypes either.

"Is it . . . our neighbors?" Andy's voice is tentative. He knows if it is about them, I won't talk.

"It's nothing, Dad. It was just a long day."

We ride home in silence. I'm shivering as I climb out of the car, but it's not because of the temperature drop. I stare at the lavender Victorian. At the bedroom window across from my own. There's no light on. The cold gripping my heart loosens, but it doesn't let go. I *have* to see inside that room. Adrenaline surges through me, and I jolt up the stairs, into the house, and up another flight of stairs.

"Hey!" Nathan calls after me. "No hug for your dear old pop?"

Andy talks to him in a low voice. Now that I'm at my bedroom door, I'm afraid to go in. Which is absurd. I'm a brave person. Why should one window scare me? But I pause to make sure Nathan isn't coming up. Whatever waits for me on the other side, I don't want interruptions.

He isn't coming. Andy must have told him to leave me alone. Good.

I open my door with false confidence. I reach for the light switch but change my mind and decide to enter Lindsey Lim style. I creep forward in the shadows. The rows of pastel houses in this city are so close that the other window, the one that lines up perfectly with my own, is mere feet away. I peer through the darkness and search for habitation.

There aren't any curtains on the window. I squint, but as far as I can tell, the bedroom is . . . empty. There's nothing in there. I look to the right, into Calliope's room. Boxes. I look down, into their kitchen. Boxes. I look straight ahead again.

No twin.

NO TWIN.

My entire body exhales. I flick on my light and then my stereo—Max's band, of course—and turn it up. Loud. I sling off my ballet slippers, tossing them onto the shoe mountain that blocks my closet, and yank off my wig. I shake out my real hair and throw down my work vest. The stupid short-sleeved, collared shirt they make me wear and the ugly boring black pants follow the vest to the floor. My red silk Chinese pajama bottoms come back on, and I add the matching top. I feel like myself again.

I glance at the empty window.

Oh, yes. I definitely feel like myself again.

Amphetamine blasts from my speakers, and I dance over to my phone. I'll call Lindsey first. And then Max, so that I can apologize for being such a space case at the Tea Garden. Maybe he's even free tomorrow morning. I don't have to work until two, so we could go to brunch on our own terms. Or maybe we could *say* we're going to brunch, but we can *really* go to his apartment.

My eyes close, and I jump and thrash to the pounding drums. I spin in circles and laugh and throw my body. Max's voice is pissed off. His lyrics taunt. The energy of his guitar builds and builds, and the bass thrums through me like blood. I am invincible.

And then I open my eyes.

Cricket Bell grins. "Hi, Lola."

chapter four

He's sitting in his window. Literally sitting in it. His butt is on the windowsill, and his legs—impossibly long and slender—are dangling against the side of his house, two stories above the ground. And his hands are folded in his lap as if spying on his unsuspecting female neighbor was the most natural thing in the world.

I stare, helpless and dumbfounded, and he bursts into laughter. His body rocks with it, and he throws back his head and claps his hands.

Cricket Bell *laughs* at me. And *claps.*

"I called your name." He tries to stop smiling, but his mouth only opens wider with delight. I can practically count his teeth. "I called it a dozen times, but your music was too loud, so I was waiting it out. You're a good dancer."

Mortification strips me of the ability to engage in intelligent conversation.

"I'm sorry." His grin hasn't disappeared, but he visibly squirms. "I only wanted to say hello."

He swings his legs back inside of his bedroom in one fluid motion. There's a lightness to the way he lands on his feet, a certain grace, that's instantly recognizable. It washes me in a familiar aching shame. And then he stretches, and I'm stunned anew.

"Cricket, you're . . . tall."

Which is, quite possibly, the stupidest thing I could say to him.

Cricket Bell was always taller than most boys, but in the last two years, he's added half a foot. At least. His slender body—once skinny and awkward, despite his graceful movements—has also changed. He's filled out, though just slightly. The edge has been removed. But pointing out that someone is tall is like pointing out the weather when it's raining. Both obvious and irritating.

"It's the hair," he says with a straight face. "Gravity has always been my nemesis."

And his dark hair *is* tall. It's floppy, but . . . inverted floppy. I'm not sure how it's possible without serious quantities of mousse or gel, but even when he was a kid, Cricket's hair stood straight up. It gives him the air of a mad scientist, which actually isn't that far off. His hair is one of the things I always liked about him.

Until I didn't like him at all, that is.

He waits for me to reply, and when I don't, he clears his throat. "But you're taller, too. Of course. I mean, it's been a long time. So obviously you are. Taller."

We take each other in. My mind spins as it tries to connect the Cricket of the present with the Cricket of the past. He's grown up and grown into his body, but it's still *him*. The same boy I fell in love with in the ninth grade. My feelings had been building since our childhood, but that year, the year he turned sixteen, was the year everything changed.

I blame it on his pants.

Cricket Bell had always been . . . *nice*. And he was cute, and he was intelligent, and he was older, and it was only natural that I would develop feelings for him. But the day everything fell into place was the same day I discovered that he'd become interested in his appearance. Not in an egotistical way. Simply in a "maybe baggy shorts and giant sneakers aren't the most attractive look for a guy like me" way.

So he started wearing these pants.

Nice pants. Not hipster pants or preppy pants or anything like that, just pants that said he cared about pants. They were chosen to fit his frame. Some plain, some pinstriped to further elongate his height. And he would pair them with vintage shirts and unusual jackets in a way that looked effortlessly cool.

So while the guys in my grade could barely remember to keep their flies zipped—and the only ones who DID care about their appearance were budding homosexuals—here was a perfectly friendly, perfectly attractive, perfectly dressed straight boy who just-so-happened to live next door to me.

Of course I fell in love with him.

Of course it ended badly.

And now here he is, and his dress habits haven't changed. If anything, they've improved. Both his pants and his shirt are still slim-fitting, but now he's accessorized. A thick, black leather watchband on one wrist, a multitude of weathered colorful bracelets and rubber bands on the other. Cricket Bell looks good. He looks BETTER.

The realization is surprising, but the one that follows stuns me even more.

I'm not in love with him anymore.

Instead, looking at him makes me feel . . . hollow.

"How've you been?" I give him a smile that's both warm and cool. One that I hope says, *I'm not that person anymore. You didn't hurt me, and I* never *think about you.*

"Good. Really, really good. I just started at Berkeley, so that's where my things are. You know. In Berkeley. I stopped by to help my parents unpack." Cricket points behind him as if the boxes are right there. He was always a hand-talker.

"Berkeley?" I'm thrown. "As in . . . ?"

He looks down into the alley between our houses. "I, uh, graduated early. Homeschooling? Calliope did, too, but she's skipping the college thing for a few years to concentrate on her career."

"So you're staying there?" I ask, hardly daring to believe it. "In a dorm?"

"Yeah."

YES. OH MY GOD, YES!

"I mean, I'll bring a few things over," he says. "For weekends and school breaks. Or whatever."

My chest constricts. "Weekends?"

"Probably. I guess." He sounds apologetic. "This is all new to me. It's always been the Calliope Parade, you know?"

I do know. The Bell family has always revolved around Calliope's career. This must be the first time in Cricket's life that his schedule doesn't revolve around hers. "I saw her on TV last year," I say, trying not to sound distressed by the idea of seeing him regularly. "World Championships. Second place, that's impressive."

"Ah." Cricket sags against his window frame. He scratches the side of his nose, revealing a message written on the back of his left hand: REVERSE CIRCUIT. "But don't let her hear you say that."

"Why not?" I stare at his hand. It's surreal. He always wrote cryptic reminders there and always in that same black marker. I used to write on mine sometimes just to be like him. My stomach clenches at the memory. Did he notice? Did Calliope tease him about it when I wasn't around?

"You know Cal. It doesn't count if it's not first." He straightens up, on the move again, and holds out both hands in my direction. "But how are you? I'm sorry, I've completely taken over this conversation."

"Great. I'm great!"

I'm great? Two years of revenge fantasies, and *that's* what I come up with? Of course, in my daydreams, I'm never wearing matching pajamas either.

Oh, no. I'm wearing matching pajamas.

And my hair! I have wig hair! It's totally flat and sweaty!

Everything about this moment is wrong. I'm supposed to be dressed in something glamorous and unique. We're supposed to be in a crowded room, and his breath is supposed to catch when he sees me. I'll be laughing, and he'll be drawn toward me as if by magnetic force. And I'll be surprised but uninterested to see him. And then Max will show up. Put his arm around me. And I'll leave with my dignity restored, and Cricket will leave agonizing that he didn't go for me when he had the chance.

Instead, he's staring at me with the strangest expression. His brow has creased and his mouth has parted, but the smile has disappeared. It's his solving-a-difficult-equation face. Why is he giving me his difficult equation face?

"And your family?" he asks. "How are they?"

It's unnerving. That face.

"Um, they're good." *I am confident and happy. And over you. Don't forget, I'm over you.* "Andy started his own business. He bakes and delivers these incredible pies, every flavor. It's doing well. And Nathan is the same. You know. Good." I glance away, toward the dark street. I wish he'd stop looking at me.

"And Norah?" His question is careful. Delicate.

There's another awkward silence. Not many people know about Norah, but there are certain things that can't be hidden from neighbors. Things like my birth mother.

"She's . . . Norah. She's in the fortune-telling business now, reading tea leaves." My face grows warm. How long will we stand here being polite? "She has an apartment."

"That's great, Lola. I'm glad to hear it." And because he's Cricket, he *does* sound glad. This is all too weird. "Do you see her often?"

"Not really. I haven't seen Snoopy at all this year." I'm not sure why I add that.

"Is he still . . . ?"

I nod. His real name is Jonathan Head, but I've never heard anyone call him that. Snoopy met Norah when they were both teenagers. They were also alcoholics, drug addicts, and homeless gutter punks. When he got Norah pregnant, she came to her older brother for help. Nathan. She didn't want me, but she didn't want to get an abortion either. And Nathan and Andy, who'd been together for seven years, wanted a child. They adopted me, and Andy changed his last name to Nathan's so that we'd all have the same one.

But yes. My father Nathan is biologically my uncle.

My parents have tried to help Norah. She's hasn't lived on the streets in years—before her apartment, she was in a series of group homes—but she still isn't exactly the most reliable person I know. The best I can say is that at least she's sober. And I only see Snoopy every now and then, whenever he rolls into town. He'll call my parents, we'll take him out for a burger, and then we won't hear from him again for months. The homeless move around more than most people realize.

I don't like to talk about my birth parents.

"I like what you've done with your room," Cricket says

suddenly. "The lights are pretty." He gestures toward the strands of pink and white twinkle lights strung across my ceiling. "And the mannequin heads."

I have shelves running across the top of my bedroom walls, lined with turquoise mannequin heads. They model my wigs and sunglasses. The walls themselves are plastered with posters of movie costume dramas and glossy black-and-whites of classic actresses. My desk is hot pink with gold glitter, which I threw in while the paint was drying, and the surface is buried underneath open jars of sparkly makeup, bottles of half-dried nail polish, plastic kiddie barrettes, and false eyelashes.

On my bookcase, I have endless cans of spray paint and bundles of hot glue sticks, and my sewing table is collaged with magazine cutouts of Japanese street fashion. Bolts of fabric are stacked precariously on top, and the wall beside it has even more shelves, crammed with glass jars of buttons and thread and needles and zippers. Over my bed, I have a canopy made out of Indian saris and paper umbrellas from Chinatown.

It's chaotic, but I love it. My bedroom is my sanctuary.

I glance at Cricket's room. Bare walls, bare floor. Empty. He acknowledges my gaze. "Not what it used to be, is it?" he asks.

Before they moved, it was as cluttered as my own. Coffee canisters filled with gears and cogs and nuts and wheels and bolts. Scribbled blueprints taped up beside star charts and the periodic table. Lightbulbs and copper wire and disassembled clocks. And always the Rube Goldberg machines.

Rube was famous for drawing those cartoons of complex

machines performing simple tasks. You know, where you pull the string so that the boot kicks over the cup, which releases the ball, which lands in the track, which rolls onto the teeter-totter, which releases the hammer that turns off your light switch? That was Cricket's bedroom.

I give him a wary smile. "It's a little different, CGB."

"You remember my middle name?" His eyebrows shoot up in surprise.

"It's not like it's easy to forget, Cricket *Graham Bell.*"

Yeah. The Bell family is THAT Bell family. As in telephone. As in one of the most important inventions in history.

He rubs his forehead. "My parents did burden me with unfortunate nomenclature."

"Please." I let out a laugh. "You used to brag about it all the time."

"Things change." His blue eyes widen as if he's joking, but there's something flat behind his expression. It's uncomfortable. Cricket was always proud of his family name. As an inventor, just like his great-great-great-grandfather, it was impossible for him not to be.

Abruptly, he lurches backward into the shadows of his room. "I should catch the train. School tomorrow."

The action startles me. "Oh."

And then he bounds forward again, and his face is illuminated by pink and white twinkle lights. His difficult equation face. "See you around?"

What else can I say? I gesture at my window. "I'll be here."

chapter five

Max picks his black shirt off his apartment floor and pulls it on. I'm already dressed again. Today I'm a strawberry. A sweet red dress from the fifties, a long necklace of tiny black beads, and a dark green wig cut into a severe Louise Brooks bob. My boyfriend playfully bites my arm, which smells of sweat and berry lotion.

"You okay?" he asks. He doesn't mean the bite.

I nod. And it *was* better. "Let's get burritos. I'm craving guacamole and pintos." I don't mention that I also want to leave before his roommate, Amphetamine's drummer, comes home. Johnny's a decent guy, but sometimes I feel out of my depth when Max's friends are around. I like it when it's just the two of us.

Max grabs his wallet. "You got it, Lo-li-ta," he sings.

I smack his shoulder, and he gives me his signature, suggestive half grin. He knows I hate that nickname. No one is allowed to call me Lolita, not even my boyfriend, not even in private. I am not some gross old man's obsession. Max isn't Humbert Humbert, and I am not his nymphet.

"That's your last warning," I say. "And you just bought my burrito."

"Extra guacamole." He seals his promise with a deep kiss as my phone rings. Andy.

My face flushes. "Sorry."

He turns away in frustration but says softly, "Don't be."

I tell Andy we're already at the restaurant, and we've just been walking around. I'm pretty sure he buys it. The mood killed, Max and I choose a place only a block away. It has plastic green saguaro lights in the windows and papier-mâché parrots hanging from the ceiling. Max lives in the Mission, the neighborhood beside mine, which has no shortage of amazing Mexican restaurants.

The waiter brings us salty chips and extra-hot salsa, and I tell Max about school, which starts again in three days. I'm so over it. I'm ready for college, ready to begin my career. I want to design costumes for movies and the stage. Someday I'll walk the red carpets in something never seen before, like Lizzy Gardiner when she accepted her Oscar for *The Adventures of Priscilla, Queen of the Desert* in a dress made out of golden credit cards. Only mine will be made out of something new and different.

Like strips of photo-booth pictures or chains of white roses or Mexican *lotería* cards. Or maybe I'll wear a great pair of swashbuckling boots and a plumed hat. And I'll swagger to the stage with a saber on my belt and a heavy pistol in my holster, and I'll thank my parents for showing me *Gone with the Wind* when I had the flu in second grade, because it taught me everything I needed to know about hoop skirts.

Mainly, that I needed one. And badly.

Max asks about the Bell family. I flinch. Their name is an electric shock.

"You haven't mentioned them all week. Have you seen . . . Calliope again?" He pauses on her name. He's checking for accuracy, but, for one wild moment, I think he knows about Cricket.

Which would be impossible, as I have not yet told him.

"Only through windows." I trace the cold rim of my mandarin Jarritos soda. "Thank goodness. I'm starting to believe it'll be possible to live next door and not be forced into actual face-to-face conversation."

"You can't avoid your problems forever." He frowns and tugs on one of his earrings. "No one can."

I burst into laughter. "Oh, that's funny coming from someone whose last album had *three* songs about running away."

Max gives a small, amused smile back. "I've never claimed I'm not a hypocrite."

I'm not sure why I haven't told him about Cricket. The timing just hasn't felt right. I haven't seen him again, but I'm still a mess of emotions about it. Our meeting wasn't as bad as it could have been, but it was . . . unsettling. Cricket's uncharacteristic ease compared to my uncharacteristic *un*ease combined with the knowledge that I'll be seeing him again. Soon.

He didn't even mention the last time we saw each other. As if it didn't matter. More likely, it didn't affect him. I've spent so many dark nights trying to forget about Cricket. It doesn't feel fair that he could have forgotten about me.

It's too much to explain to Max.

And I don't want him to think Cricket Bell means something to me that he doesn't. That chapter of my life is *over.*

It's over, unlike my conversation with Lindsey the next day, the same one we have every time we talk now. "I like Max," I say. "He likes me. What's wrong with that?"

"The law," she says.

It's the last Friday of our summer break, and we're squished together on my tiny front porch. I'm spray-painting a pair of thrift-store boots, and she's scoping out the lavender Victorian. Lindsey supports my relationship for the most part, but she's relentless when it comes to this one sticking point.

"He's a good guy," I say. "And our relationship is what it is."

"I'm not saying he isn't a good guy, I'm merely reminding you that there could be consequences to dating him." Her voice is calm and rational as her eyes perform a quick scan of the neighborhood before returning to the Bell house.

Lindsey never stops examining her surroundings. It's what she does.

My best friend is pretty, bordering on plain. She wears practical clothing and keeps her appearance clean. She's short, has braces, and has had the same haircut since the day we met. Black, shoulder length, tidy bangs. The only thing that might seem out of place is her well-worn, well-loved pair of red Chuck Taylors. Lindsey was wearing them the day she tripped a suspect being chased by the police on Market Street, and they've since become a permanent wardrobe fixture.

I laugh. Sometimes it's the only option with her. "Consequences. Like happiness? Or love? You're right, who'd want a thing like tha—"

"There he is," she says.

"Max?" I swivel mid-spray, barely missing her sneakers in my excitement.

"Watch it, Ned." She slides aside. "Not everyone wants shoes the color of a school bus."

But she's not talking about my boyfriend. My heart plummets to discover Cricket Bell waiting to cross the street.

"Oh, man. You got it on the porch."

"What?" My attention jerks back. Sure enough, there's an unsightly splotch of yellow beside the newspaper I'd spread out to protect the wood. I grab the wet rag I brought outside, for this very purpose, and scrub. I groan. "Nathan's gonna kill me."

"Still hasn't forgiven you for dyeing the grout in his bathroom black?"

The splotch smears and grows larger. "What do you think?"

She's staring at Cricket again. "Why didn't you tell me he was so . . ."

"Tall?" I scour harder. "Unwanted?"

". . . colorful."

I look up. Cricket is striding across the street, his long arms swinging with each step. He's wearing skinny mailman-esque pants with a red stripe down the side seam. They're a tad short—purposely, I can tell—exposing matching red socks and pointy shoes. His movements suddenly become exaggerated, and he hums an unrecognizable tune. Cricket Bell knows he has an audience.

There's a familiar clenching in my stomach.

"He's coming over," Lindsey says. "What do you want me to do? Kick him in the balls? I've been dying to kick him in the balls."

"Nothing," I hiss back. "I'll handle it."

"How?"

I cough at her as he leaps up the stairs with the ease of a gazelle. "Lola!" His smile is ear to ear. "Funny meeting you here."

"Funny that. You being on her porch and all," Lindsey says.

"*Your* house?" Cricket stumbles back down the top steps and widens his eyes dramatically. "They all look so similar."

We stare at him.

"It's good to see you again, Lindsey," he adds after a moment. Now there's a touch of genuine embarrassment. "I just passed your parents' restaurant, and it was packed. That's great."

"Huh," she says.

"What are you doing here?" I blurt.

"I live here. Not here-here, but there-here." He points next door. "Occasionally. On the weekends. Well, my parents told me they set up my bed, so I assume it's a go."

"They did. I saw them move it in yesterday," I say, despite myself. "There still aren't any curtains on your window," I add, not wanting him to think that I've been *purposefully* watching his room.

One hand fiddles with the bracelets on his other. "Now, that's a shame. Promise you won't laugh when you see me in my underwear."

Lindsey's eyebrows raise.

"I cut a pathetic figure undressed," he continues. "Dressed, too, for that matter. Or half dressed. One sock on, one sock off. Just a hat. No hat. You can stop me at any time, you know. Feel free to tell me to shut up."

"Shut up, Cricket," I say.

"Thanks. Did you dye your hair? Because you weren't blond last weekend. Oh, it's a wig, isn't it?"

"Ye—"

"Hey, cool shoes. I've never seen boots that color before. Except rain boots, of course, but those aren't rain boots."

"No—"

The front door opens, and Andy appears in a white apron. He's holding a flour-dusted wooden spoon as if it were an extension of his arm. "Could I persuade you ladies to sample—"

Cricket pops back onto the porch and stretches his lengthy torso between Lindsey and me to shake my dad's hand. "It's nice to see you again, Mr. Nolan. How are you?"

Lindsey mouths, *What's he been smoking?*

I'm as baffled as she is. He's like Cricket times ten.

"I'm good." Andy glances at me, trying to determine if he should throw him off our property. I give my dad the smallest shake of my head, and he turns his attention back to Cricket. Which, frankly, would be impossible not to do, considering the sheer energy radiating off him. "And you? Still inventing mysterious and wondrous objects?"

"Ah." Cricket hesitates. "There's not really a market for that sort of thing these days. But I hear you're running a successful pie operation?"

My father looks flattered that the news has spread. "I was just about to ask the girls if they'd mind testing a new pie. Would you like a slice?"

"I would *love* a slice." And he springs ahead of Andy, who follows him inside.

The porch is silent. I turn to Lindsey. "What just happened?"

"Your father invited the former love of your life in for pie."

"Yeah. That's what I thought."

We're quiet for a moment.

"There's still time for an excuse," she says. "We don't have to go in there."

I sigh. "No, we really do."

"Good. Because that guy demands observation." And she marches inside.

I take another look at the paint splotch and find that it's dried. Crap. I spray the last side of my shoes, move the project where it won't get tripped on, and head inside for whatever torture awaits me. They're standing around one of the islands in our kitchen. We have an unusually large kitchen for the city, because my parents removed the dining room to add space for Andy's business. Everyone already has a plate of pie and a glass of milk.

"Unbelievable." Cricket wipes the crumbs from his lips with his long fingers. "I would have never thought to put kiwi in a pie."

Andy spots me hovering in the doorway. "Better hurry before this one eats it all." He nods toward his guest. Outwardly, my dad is collected, but I can tell that inside he's gloaty beyond belief. How quickly one's allegiance changes under the influence of a compliment. I smile as if none of this is a big deal. But I'm *freaking out.* Cricket Bell. In my kitchen. Eating kiwi pie. And then I take the empty space beside him, and I'm stunned *again* by his extraordinary height. He towers over me.

Andy points his fork at the other half of the green pie. "Have the rest, Cricket."

"Oh, no. I couldn't." But his brightened eyes suggest otherwise.

"I insist." My dad nudges the dish toward him. "Nathan's always complaining that I'm trying to make him fat, so it'll be better if it's gone before he comes home."

Cricket turns to me with his entire body—head, shoulders, chest, arms, legs. There are no half gestures with Cricket Bell. "Another slice?"

I motion toward the piece in front of me, which I haven't even started.

"Lindsey?" he asks.

She shakes her head. "I'm not exactly pie-deprived, visiting here so often."

Why is he here? Isn't there some campus party he should be at? The more I think about it, the more incensed I become. How dare he show up and expect me to be friendly? People can't just *do* that.

"How's your family?" Andy asks.

Cricket swallows. "They're good. My parents are the same. Dad's a little too exhausted, Mom's a little too enthusiastic. But they're good. And Cal is busy training, of course. It's a big year with the Olympics coming up. And Aleck is married now."

"Is he still composing?" Andy asks. Alexander, or Aleck as dictated by the family nickname, is the twins' older brother. He was already in high school when Calliope started training, so he escaped most of the family drama. I never knew him well, but I do vividly recall the complicated piano concertos that used to glide through our walls. All three Bells could be considered prodigies in their fields.

"And teaching," Cricket confirms. "And he had his first child last year."

"Boy or girl?" Lindsey asks.

"A girl. Abigail."

"Uncle . . . Cricket," I say.

Lindsey and Andy both let out an uncontrolled snort, but

Andy instantly looks horrified for doing it. He glares at me. *"Lola."*

"No, it's okay," Cricket says. "It's completely ridiculous."

"I'm sorry," I say.

"No, please. Don't be." But there's a catch in his voice, and he says it so quickly that I look at him in surprise. For the briefest moment, our eyes lock. There's a flash of pain, and he turns away. He hasn't forgotten.

Cricket Bell remembers everything.

My face burns. Without thinking, I push away my plate. "I need to . . . get ready for work."

"Come on." Lindsey grabs my hand. "You'll be late."

Andy glances at the Frida Kahlo wall calendar where I post my schedule. He frowns toward Frida's unibrow. "You didn't write it down."

Lindsey is already pulling me upstairs. "I'm covering for someone!" I say.

"Am I supposed to pick you up?" he hollers.

I lean over the banister and look into the kitchen. Cricket is staring at me, parted mouth and furrowed brow. His difficult equation face. As if *I'm* the problem, not him. I rip away my gaze. "Yeah, the usual time. Thanks, Dad."

Lindsey and I run the rest of the way into my bedroom. She locks my door. "What'll you do?" Her voice is low and calm.

"About Cricket?"

She reaches underneath my bed and pulls out the polyester vest. "No. Work."

I search for the remaining pieces of my uniform, trying not

to cry. "I'll go to Max's. He can drive me to work before Andy gets there."

"Okay." She nods. "That's a good plan."

It's the night before school starts, and I'm working for real this time. Anna and I—and her boyfriend, of course—are inside the box office. The main lobby of our theater is enormous. Eight box-office registers underneath a twenty-five-foot ceiling of carved geometric crosses and stars. Giant white pillars and dark wooden trim add to the historic opulence and mark the building as not originally a chain movie theater. Its first incarnation was a swanky hotel, the second a ritzy automobile showroom.

It's another slow evening. Anna is writing in a battered, left-handed notebook while St. Clair and I argue across the full length of the box office. She just got another part-time job, unpaid, writing movie reviews for her university's newspaper. Since she's a freshman, they're only giving her the crappy movies. But she doesn't mind. "It's fun to write a review if you hate the movie," she told me earlier. "It's easy to talk about things we hate, but sometimes it's hard to explain exactly why we like something."

"I know you like him," St. Clair says to me, leaning back in his chair. "But he's still far too old for you."

Here we go again. "Max isn't *old,*" I say. "He's only a few years older than you."

"Like I said. Too old."

"Age doesn't matter."

He snorts. "Yeah, maybe when you're middle-aged and—"

"Golfing," Anna helpfully supplies, without looking up from her notebook.

"Paying the mortgage," he says.

"Shopping for minivans."

"With side air bags."

"And extra cup holders!"

I ignore their laughter. "You've never even met him."

"Because he never comes in here. He drops you off at the curb," St. Clair says.

I throw up my hands, which I've been mehndi-ing with a Bic pen. "Do you have any idea how difficult it is to park in this city?"

"I'm just saying that if it were Anna, I'd want to meet her coworkers. See where she's spending her time."

I stare at him, hard. *"Obviously."*

"Obviously." He grins.

I scowl back. "Get a job."

"Perhaps I will."

Anna finally looks up. "I'll believe that when I see it." But she's smiling at him. She twirls the glass banana on her necklace. "Oh, hey. Your mom called. She wanted to know if we're still on for dinner tomorrow—"

And they're off in their own world again. As if they don't see each other enough as it is. He stays in her dorm on weekdays, and she stays in his on weekends. Though I do admit that their trade-off is appealing. I hope Max and I share something like it someday. Actually, I hope Max and I share *one* place someday—

"Oy!" St. Clair is talking to me again. "I met your friend today."

"Lindsey?" I sit up straighter.

"No, your old neighbor. Cricket."

The ornamental ceiling tilts and bends. "And how do you know that Cricket Bell was my neighbor?" My question is strangled.

St. Clair shrugs. "He told me."

I stare at him. *And?*

"He lives on my floor in my dorm. We were talking in the hall, and I mentioned that I was on my way to meet Anna, and where she works—"

His girlfriend beams, and I'm struck by a peculiar twinge of jealousy. Does Max tell people about me?

"—and he said he knew someone who worked here, too. You."

One week, and already I can't escape him. It's just my luck that Cricket would live beside my only Berkeley acquaintance. And how does he know where I work? Did I mention the theater? No. I'm positive that I didn't. He must have asked Andy after I left.

"He asked about you," St. Clair continues. "Nice bloke."

"Huh," I finally manage.

"There's a story behind that *huh,*" Anna says.

"There's no story," I say. "There is definitely NOT a story."

Anna pauses in consideration before turning toward St. Clair. "Would you mind making a coffee run?"

He raises an eyebrow. After a moment, he says, "Ah. Of course." He swoops in for a kiss goodbye, and then she watches his backside leave before turning to me with a mischievous smile.

I huff. "You'll just tell him later, when you guys are alone."

Her smile widens. "Yep."

"Then no way."

"Dude." Anna slides into the seat beside me. "You're dying to spill it."

She's right. I spill it.

chapter six

When I was five years old, Cricket Bell built an elevator. It was a marvelous invention made from white string and Tonka truck wheels and a child-size shoe box, and because of it, my Barbies traveled from the first floor of their dollhouse to the second without ever having to walk on their abnormally slanted feet.

The house was built in my bookcase, and I'd desired an elevator for as long as I could remember. The official Barbie Dream House had one made of plastic, but as often as I begged my parents, they wouldn't budge. No Dream House. Too expensive.

So Cricket took it upon himself to make one for me. And while Calliope and I decorated my bookcase with lamp shades made from toothpaste caps and Persian rugs made from carpet samples, Cricket created a working elevator. Pulleys and levers and gears come to him as naturally as breathing.

The elevator had completed its first run. Pet Doctor Barbie was enjoying the second floor and Calliope was pulling down the elevator to fetch Skipper, when I stood on my tiptoes, puckered my lips, and planted one on her very surprised brother.

Cricket Bell kissed me back.

He tasted like the warm cookies that Andy had brought us. His lips were dusted with blue sugar crystals. And when we parted, he staggered.

But our romance was as quick as our kiss. Calliope proclaimed us "grody" and flounced back to their house, dragging Cricket behind her. And I decided she was right. Because Calliope was the kind of girl you wanted to impress, which meant that she was *always* right. So I decided that boys were gross, and I would never date one.

Certainly not her brother.

Not long after the elevator incident, Calliope decided that I was grody, too, and my friendship with the twins ended. I imagine Cricket complied with the arrangement in the easy way of anyone under the sway of someone with a stronger personality.

For several years, we didn't talk. Contact was limited to hearing their car doors slam and glimpsing them through windows. Calliope had always been a talented gymnast, but the day she switched to figure skating, she burst into a different league altogether. Her parents bragged to mine about *potential,* and her life turned into one long practice session. And Cricket, too young to stay at home without a parent, went with her.

On the rare occasions that he *was* at home, he busied himself inside his bedroom, building peculiar contraptions that flew and chimed and buzzed. Sometimes he'd test one in the small space between our houses. I'd hear an explosion that would bring me racing to my window. And then, but only then, would we exchange friendly, secretive smiles.

When I was twelve, the Bell family moved away for two years. Training for Calliope. And when they came back, the twins were different. Older.

Calliope had blossomed into the beauty our neighborhood had expected. Confidence radiated from every pore, every squaring of her shoulders. I was awed. Too intimidated to talk to her, but I chatted occasionally with Cricket. He wasn't beautiful like his sister. Where the twins' matching slenderness made Calliope look ballet-esque, Cricket looked gawky. And he had acne and the peculiar habits of someone unused to socializing. He talked too fast, too much. But I enjoyed his company, and he appeared to enjoy mine. We were on the verge of actual friendship when the Bells moved again.

They returned only a few months later, on the first day of summer before my freshman year. I would be turning fifteen that August, and the twins sixteen that September. Calliope looked exactly as she had before they left.

But, once again, Cricket had changed.

Lindsey and I were on my porch, licking Cherry Garcia in waffle cones, when a car pulled up next door and out stepped Cricket Bell as I'd never seen him before—one beautifully long pinstriped leg after another.

Something deep inside of me *lurched*.

The stirring was as startling and unpleasant as it was thrilling and revolutionary. I already knew that this image—his legs, those pants—would be imprinted in my mind for the rest of my life. The moment was that profound. Lindsey called out a sunny hello. Cricket looked up, disconcerted, and his eyes met mine.

That was it. I was gone.

We held our gaze longer than the acceptable, normal amount of time before he shifted to Lindsey and raised one hand in a quiet wave. His family materialized from the car, everyone talking at once, and his attention jerked back to them. But not without another glance toward me. And then another, even quicker, before disappearing into the lavender Victorian.

I took Lindsey's hand and gripped it tightly. Our fingers were sticky with ice cream. She knew. Everything that needed to be said was spoken in the way I held on to her.

She smiled. "Uh-oh."

Verbal contact happened that same night. The odd thing is that I no longer remember what I wore, but I know I chose it carefully, anticipating a meeting. When I finally pulled aside my curtains, I wasn't surprised to discover him standing before his window, staring into mine. Of course he was. But he was taken aback by my appearance. Even his hair seemed more startled than usual.

"I was . . . getting some fresh air," I said.

"Me, too." Cricket nodded and added a great, exaggerated inhalation.

I'm still not sure if it was a joke, but I laughed. He gave me a nervous smile in return, which quickly broke into his full-wattage grin. He's never had any control over it. Up close, I saw that his acne had disappeared, and his face had grown older. We stood there, smiling like fools. What do you say to someone who is not the same and yet completely the same? Had I changed, too, or had it just been him?

Cricket ducked away first. Some excuse about helping his mom unpack dishes. I vowed to initiate a real conversation the next day, but . . . his close proximity fizzled my brain, tied my tongue. He didn't fare any better.

So we waved.

We'd never waved through our windows before, but it was unavoidably clear that we were aware of each other's presence. So we were forced to acknowledge each other all day and all night, still having nothing to say but wanting to say *everything*.

It took weeks before this torturous situation changed. Betsy and I were leaving the house as he was strolling home, those pinstriped pants and his hair looking like it was trying to touch the sky.

We stopped shyly.

"It's nice to see you," he said. "Outside. Instead of inside. You know."

I smiled so that he'd know I knew. "I'm taking her for a walk. You wouldn't want to join—"

"Yes."

"—us?" My heart thrummed.

Cricket looked away. "Yeah, we could catch up. Should catch up."

I looked away, too, trying to control my blush. "Do you need to drop that off?"

He was carrying a paper bag from the hardware store. "OH. Yeah. Hold on." Cricket shot up his stairs but then stopped halfway. "Wait right there," he added. He bounded inside and came back only seconds later. He held out two Blow Pops.

"It's so lame," he said. "I'm sorry."

"No, I love these!" And then I did blush, for using the word *love.*

Our tongues turned green-apple green, but we talked for so long that by the time we returned home, they were pink again. The feeling inside of me grew. We began bumping into each other at the same time every afternoon. He'd pretend to be running an errand, I'd pretend to be surprised, and then he'd join Betsy and me on our walk.

One day, he didn't appear. I paused before his house, disappointed, and looked up and down our street. Betsy strained forward on her leash. The Bells' door burst open, and Cricket flew down so quickly that he almost toppled into me.

I smiled. "You're late."

"You waited." He wrung his hands.

We stopped pretending.

Cricket defined the hours of my day. The hour I opened my curtains—the same time he opened his—so that we could share a morning hello. The hour I ate my lunch so that I could watch him eat his. The hour I left my house for our walk. The hour I called Lindsey to dissect our walk. And the hour after dinner when Cricket and I chatted before closing our curtains again.

At night, I lay in bed and pictured him lying in his. Was he thinking about me, too? Did he imagine sneaking into my bedroom like I imagined sneaking into his? If we were alone in the dark instead of daylight, would he find the courage to kiss me? I wanted him to kiss me. He was the boy. He was *supposed* to make the first move.

Why wasn't he making the first move? How long would I have to wait?

These feverish thoughts kept me awake all summer. I'd rise in the morning, covered in sweat, with no recollection of when I'd finally fallen asleep and no recollection of my dreams, apart from three words echoing in my head, in his voice. *I need you.*

Need.

What a powerful, frightening word. It represented my feelings toward him, but every night, my dreams placed it inside his mouth.

I needed him to touch me. I was obsessed with the way his hands never stopped moving. The way he rubbed them together when he was excited, the way he sometimes couldn't help but clap. The way he had secret messages written on the back of his left. And his fingers. Long, enthusiastic, wild, but I knew from watching him build his machines that they were also delicate, careful, precise. I fantasized about those fingers.

And I was consumed by the way that whenever he spoke, his

eyes twinkled as if it were the best day of his life. And the way his whole body leaned toward mine when I spoke, a gesture that showed he was interested, he was listening. No one had ever moved their body to face me like that.

The summer sprawled forward, each day more agonizing and wonderful than the last. He began hanging out with Lindsey and my parents, even with Norah, when she was around. He was entering my world. But every time I tried to enter his, Calliope was hostile. Cold. Sometimes she pretended that I wasn't in the room, sometimes she'd even leave while I was speaking. This was the first time he'd chosen someone over her, and she resented me for it. I was stealing her best friend. I was a threat.

Rather than confront her, we retreated to the safety of my house.

But . . . he still wasn't making any moves. Lindsey supposed he was waiting for the right moment, something significant. Maybe my birthday. His is exactly one month after mine, also on the twentieth, so he'd always remembered. That morning, I was heartened to see a sign taped to his glass: HAPPY LOLA DAY! WE'RE THE SAME AGE AGAIN!

I leaned out my window. "For a month!"

He appeared with a smile, his hands rubbing together. "It's a good month."

"You'll forget about me when you turn sixteen," I teased.

"Impossible." His voice cracked on the word, and it shook my heart.

Andy took over Betsy's afternoon walk so that we could

have complete freedom. Cricket greeted me at the usual time, raising two pizza boxes over his head. I was about to say I was still stuffed from lunch when . . . "Are those empty or full?" My question was sly. I had a feeling this wasn't about pizza.

He opened up a box and smiled. "Empty."

"I haven't been there in years!"

"Same here. Calliope and I were probably with you the last time I went."

We took off running down the hill, toward the park at the other end of our street—the one that barely counted because it was tiny and sandwiched between two houses—back up another hill, past the spray-painted sign warning NO ADULTS ALLOWED UNLESS ACCOMPANIED BY CHILDREN, and to the top of the Seward Street slides.

"Oh God." I had a jolt of terror. "Were they always this steep?"

Cricket unfolded the boxes and laid them long and greasy side down, one on each narrow concrete slide. "I claim left."

I sat down on my box. "Sucks to be you. The right side is faster."

"No way! The left side always wins."

"Says the guy who hasn't been here since he was six. Keep your arms tucked in."

He grinned. "There's no way I've forgotten *those* scrapes and burns."

On the count of three, we took off. The slides are short and fast, and we flew to the bottom, holding in our screams so as not to disturb the Seward Witch, the mean old lady who shouted obscenities at people enjoying themselves too loudly and just another reason why the slides were so much fun. Cricket's feet flew off first, followed quickly by his bottom. He hit the ground with a *smack* that had us rolling with laughter.

"I think my ass is actually smoking," he said.

I bit down the obvious comment, that his pants had made this fact abundantly clear in June.

We stayed for half an hour, sharing the slides with two guys in their twenties who were high and a playgroup of moms and preschoolers. We were waiting behind the moms, about to go down for the last time, when I heard snickering. I looked over my shoulder and discovered the arrival of three girls from school. My heart sank.

"Nice dress," Marta Velazquez said. "Is it your mommy's?"

I was wearing a vintage polka-dot swing dress—two sizes too large that I'd tightened with safety pins—over a long-sleeved striped shirt and jeans rolled greaser-style. I wanted to look pretty for my birthday.

I no longer felt pretty.

Cricket turned around, confused. And then . . . he did something that changed everything. He stepped deliberately in front of them and blocked my view. "Don't listen to them. I like how you dress."

He liked me just as I was.

I sat down quietly on my pizza box. "It's our turn."

But what I ached to say was, *I need you.*

On the walk home, he had me joking and laughing about the people who'd tormented me for years. I finally realized how absurd it was that I'd worried so much about what my classmates thought about me. It's not like I wanted to look like *them*.

"Cricket!" Andy said, when he saw us approaching. "You're coming over for the birthday dinner, right?"

I looked at Cricket hopefully. He put his hands in his pockets. "Sure."

It was simple and perfect. My only guests were Nathan, Andy, Lindsey, and Cricket. We ate Margherita pizza, followed by an extravagant cake shaped like a crown. I ate the first piece, Cricket ate the biggest. Afterward, I walked my friends outside. Lindsey gave me a nudge in the back and disappeared.

Cricket shuffled his feet. "I'm not great with gifts."

My heart leaped. But instead of a kiss, he removed a fistful of watch parts and candy wrappers from his pocket. Cricket sifted through the pile until he found a soda-bottle cap, metallic pink. He held it up. "Your first."

Perhaps most girls would've been disappointed, but I am not most girls. We'd recently seen a belt made out of bottle caps in a store window, and I'd said that I wanted to make one. "You remembered!"

Cricket smiled in relief. "I thought it was a good one. Colorful." And as he placed it in my open palm, I reread the message scrawled onto the back of his hand for the hundredth time that day: FUSE NOW.

This was the moment.

I gripped the cap and stepped forward. His breathing quickened. So did mine.

"You promised you'd be there!"

We jumped apart. Calliope was on the porch next door, seemingly on the verge of tears. "I needed you, and you weren't there."

An unmistakable flash of panic in his eyes. "Oh God, Cal. I can't believe I forgot."

She was wearing a delicate cardigan, but the way she crossed her arms was anything but soft. "You've been forgetting a lot of things lately."

"I'm sorry. It slipped my mind, I'm so sorry." He tried to shake the wrappers and watch parts back into his pocket, but they spilled onto my porch.

"Smooth, Cricket." She looked at me and scowled. "I don't know why you're wasting your time."

But she was still talking to *him*.

"Thanks for dinner," he mumbled, shoving everything back into his pockets. "Happy birthday." He left without looking at me. From their porch, Calliope was still glaring. I felt slapped in the face. Ashamed. I didn't have anything to be ashamed about, but she had that effect. If she wanted you to feel something, you would.

Later, Cricket told me that he was supposed to have gone to some meeting. He was vague about it. After that, it was as if we'd taken a small step backward. We started school. He hung out with Lindsey and me, while Calliope made new friends. There was a quiet tension between the twins. Cricket didn't talk about it, but I knew he was upset.

One Friday after school, he showed me a video of the

Swiss Jolly Ball—a mechanical wonder he'd seen while visiting a museum in Chicago. I hadn't been inside his house since Calliope's icy behavior at the beginning of summer. I'd hoped this was an excuse to go into his bedroom, but his laptop was in the living room. He sat on one side of a love seat, leaving space to sit beside him. Was it an invitation? Or a gesture of kindness, in that he was offering me the room's larger couch?

WHY WAS THIS SO HARD?

I took a chance and sat beside him. Cricket pulled up the video, and I scooted closer, under the guise of seeing it better. I couldn't concentrate, but as the machine's silver ball shot through tunnels, set off whistles, and zoomed across tracks, I laughed in delight anyway. I inched closer until I was in the dip between the cushions. I smelled the faintest twinge of his sweat, but it wasn't bad. It was very far from bad. And then the side of my hand brushed the side of his, and my heart *collapsed*.

He was very still.

I cleared my throat. "Are you doing anything special for your birthday tomorrow?"

"No." He moved his hand into his lap, flustered. "Nothing. I'm not doing anything."

"Okay . . ." I stared at his hand.

"Actually, Calliope has some skating thing. So it'll be another afternoon of bad rink food, skating vendors, and squealing girls."

Was that an excuse to avoid me? Had I been wrong this whole time? I went home upset and called Lindsey. "No way," she said. "He likes you."

"You didn't see him. He's been acting so weird and cagey."

But the next morning, I met up with Lindsey to find a present for him. I wasn't ready to give up. I *couldn't* give up. I knew he needed an obscurely sized wrench for a project, and I also knew he was having trouble finding it online. We spent the entire day hunting the city's specialty shops, and as I walked home that night so proud of procuring one, I felt a nervous hope again. And then I saw it.

A party in full swing.

The Bell house was loud and packed, and there were strings of tiki lights hanging in their bay windows. This wasn't a party that happened at the last second. It was a planned party. A planned party that I had not been invited to.

I froze there, devastated, holding the tiny wrench and taking in the spectacle. A pack of girls rushed past me and up the stairs. How had the twins made so many new friends so quickly? The girls knocked on the door, and Calliope opened it and greeted them with happy laughter. They moved past her and into the house. And that's when she saw me, staring up from the sidewalk.

She paused, and then made a face. "So what? Too good for our party?"

"Wh-what?"

"You know, after spending so much time with my brother, it seems like the least you could do is pop your head in and wish him a happy birthday."

My mind reeled. "I wasn't invited."

Calliope's expression changed to surprise. "But Cricket said you couldn't come."

Explosion. *Pain.* "I . . . he didn't ask. No."

"Huh." She eyed me nervously. "Well. Bye."

The lavender door slammed shut. I stared at it, burning with hurt and humiliation. Why didn't he want me at his party? I stumbled inside my house, yanked my curtains closed, and burst into racking sobs. What happened? What was wrong with me? Why didn't he like me anymore?

His light turned on at midnight. He called my name.

I tried to focus on the catastrophic blow inside my chest. He called my name again. I wanted to ignore him, but how could I? I opened my window.

Cricket stared at his feet. "So, um, what did you do tonight?"

"Nothing." My voice was curt as I threw back his own words. "I didn't do anything."

He looked upset. It only made me despise him more, for trying to make *me* feel guilty. "Good night." I started to close my window.

"Wait!" He yanked at his hair, pulling it taller. "I—I just found out that I'm moving."

It felt as if I'd been knocked in the skull. I blinked, startled to discover fresh tears. "You're leaving? Again?"

"Monday."

"Two DAYS from now?" Why couldn't I stop crying? I was such an idiot!

"Calliope is going back to her last coach." He sounded helpless. "It's not working out here."

"Is *everything* not working out here?" I blurted. "There's *nothing* you want to say to me before you leave?"

Cricket's mouth parted, but it remained silent. His difficult equation face. A full minute passed, maybe two. "At least we have that in common," I finally said. "There's nothing I want to say to you either."

And I slammed my window closed.

chapter seven

He was doing it right there in the open!" I say. "I'm serious, Charlie was admiring your derriere in chemistry."

Lindsey brushes it off. "Even if he was, which I sincerely doubt, you know my policy. No guys—"

"Until graduation. I just thought that since it was Charlie . . . and since his eyes *did* follow you across the room . . ."

"No." And she takes a ferocious bite of her almond-butter-and-jelly sandwich to end the conversation. I hold up my hands in a gesture of peace. I know better than to keep arguing, even if she has had a silent crush on Charlie Harrison-Ming ever since he won twice as many points as her in last year's Quiz Bowl.

Our first week as juniors at Harvey Milk Memorial High has been as expected. The same boring classes, the same nasty mean girls, and the same perverted jerks. At least Lindsey and I have lunch together. That helps.

"Hey, Cleopatra. Wanna take a ride down my Nile?"

Speaking of jerks. Gregory Figson bumps knuckles with a muscled friend. I'm wearing a long black wig with straight bangs, a white dress I made from a bedsheet, chunky golden jewelry, and—of course—ancient Egyptian eyes drawn in kohl.

"No," I say flatly.

Gregory grabs his chest with both hands. "Nice pyramids," he says, and they swagger away, laughing.

"Just when I thought he couldn't get any more disgusting." I set down my veggie burger, appetite eliminated.

"And as if I needed another reason to wait," Lindsey says. "High school boys are morons."

"Which is why I don't date high school boys. I date men."

Lindsey rolls her eyes. Her main reason for waiting to date is that she believes it'll get in the way of her agenda. *Agenda* is her term, not mine. She thinks guys are a distraction from her educational goals, so she doesn't want to date until she's firmly settled in post-high-school life. I respect her decision, even though I'd rather wear sweatpants in public than give up my boyfriend.

Or give up my first opportunity to attend the winter formal. It's for upperclassmen only, and it's still months away, but I'm thrilled about my Marie Antoinette dress, which I've already started collecting materials for. Shimmering silk dupioni and crisp taffeta. Smooth satin ribbon. Delicate ostrich feathers and ornate crystal jewelry. I've never attempted a project this complex, this huge, and it'll take my entire autumn to create.

I decide to begin when I get home. It's Friday, and for once I don't have to work. Also, Amphetamine is playing in a club tonight that doesn't accept anyone under twenty-one. And won't allow Max to sneak me in.

From everything I've read online, I need to start with the undergarments.

I've already bought a ton of fabric for the dress, but the costume still has to be built from the inside out so that when I take the measurements for the actual gown, I can take them over the bulky stays (an eighteenth-century word for corset) and the giant panniers (the oval-shaped hoop skirts Marie and her ladies wore).

I search for hours for instructions on making historically accurate panniers and come up with zilch. Unless I want to make them with hula hoops, and I don't, I'll have to go to the library for more research. Searching for stays brings more success. The diagrams and instructions are overwhelming, but I print out several pages and begin taking measurements and creating a pattern.

I've been sewing for three years, and I'm pretty decent. I started with the small stuff, like everyone does—hemming, A-line skirts, pillowcases—but quickly moved on to bigger items, each more complex than the last. I'm not interested in making what's easy.

I'm interested in making what's beautiful.

I lose myself in the process: tracing out patterns on tissue paper, fitting them together, retracing, and refitting. Nonsewers don't realize how much problem solving goes into garment making, and beginners often quit in frustration. But I enjoy the puzzle. If I looked at this dress as one massive *thing*, it would be too overwhelming. No one could create such a gown. But by breaking it into tiny, individual steps, it becomes something I can achieve.

When my room finally grows too dark, I'm forced to rise from the floor and plug in my twinkle lights. I stretch my sore muscles and stare at my window.

Will he come home this weekend?

The idea fills me with unease. I don't understand why he's been asking Andy and St. Clair questions about me. There are only three possible solutions, each more improbable than the last. Maybe he's not making friends at school and, for some twisted reason, has decided I'd make a decent pal again. I mean, he's come home for the last two weekends. Obviously no one is interesting enough to keep him in Berkeley. Or maybe he feels bad about how things ended between us, and he's trying to make up for it. Clear his conscience.

Or . . . maybe . . . he likes me. In that other way.

I was fine before he came back, perfectly happy without this complication. It would've been better if he'd ignored me. Calliope and I haven't talked yet; there's no reason why Cricket and I should have to either. I drift toward my window, and I'm surprised to discover striped curtains hanging in his room.

And then his light turns on.

I yank my curtains closed. My heart pounds as I back against the wall. Through the gap between curtain fabrics, I watch a silhouette that is undeniably Cricket Bell toss two bags to his floor—one shoulder bag and one laundry bag. He moves toward our windows, and dread lurches inside of me. What if he calls my name?

There's a sudden brightness as he pulls back his own curtains. His body changes from a dark shadow into a fully fleshed human. I slink back farther. He pauses there, and then startles as another figure enters his room. I can barely hear the sound of a girl talking. Calliope.

I can't hide forever. My curtains are thick, and I need to trust them. I take a deep breath and step away, but I trip backward over my project and tear a pattern. I curse. Laughter comes from next door, and for one panicked second, I think they've witnessed my clumsy maneuver. But it's paranoia talking. Whatever they're laughing about has nothing to do with me. I hate that they can still get to me like that.

I know what I need. I call him, and he picks up just before his voice mail.

"HEY," Max says.

"Hi! How is it tonight? When are you guys going on?" The club is loud, and I can't hear his response. "What?"

"[MUFFLE MUFFLE] AFTER ELEVEN [MUFFLE]."

"Oh. Okay." I don't have anything to add. "I miss you."

"[MUFFLE MUFFLE MUFFLE. MUFFLE.]"

"What? I'm sorry, I can't hear you!"

"[MUFFLE MUFFLE] BAD TIME [MUFFLE]."

I assume he's saying he has to go. "Okay! I'll see you tomorrow! Bye!" A click on the other end, and he's gone. I should have texted him. But I don't want to now, because I don't want to bother him. He doesn't like talking before shows.

The call leaves me feeling more cold than comforted. The laughter continues next door, and I resist the urge to throw my sewing shears at Cricket's window to make them shut up. My phone rings, and I answer eagerly. "Max!"

"I need you to tell Nathan to come get me."

Not Max.

"Where are you?" I'm already hustling downstairs. Nathan is crashed in front of the television, eyes half closed, watching *Antiques Roadshow* with Heavens to Betsy. "Why can't you tell him yourself?"

"Because he's gonna be pissed, and I can't deal with pissed right now." The voice is cranky and exhausted.

I stop dead in my tracks. "Not again."

"Landlord changed my locks, so I was forced to break into my apartment. My *own* apartment. They're calling it an incident."

"Incident?" I ask, and Dad's eyes pop open. I thrust out my phone to him without waiting for a response, disgusted. "Norah needs you to bail her out."

Nathan swears and grabs my cell. "Where are you? What happened?" He pulls answers from her as he collects his car keys and throws on his shoes. "I'm taking your phone, okay?" he says to me. "Tell Andy where I'm going." And he's out the door.

This is not the first time my birth mother has called us from a police station. Norah has a long record, and it's always for stupid things like shoplifting organic frozen enchiladas or refusing to pay fines from the transit authority. When I was young, the charges were usually public intoxication or disorderly conduct. And believe me, a person has to be pretty darn intoxicated or disorderly to get arrested in this city.

Andy takes the news silently. Our relationship with Norah is hard on everyone, but perhaps it's hardest on him. She's neither his sister nor his mother. I know a part of him wishes we could ditch her entirely. A part of me wishes that, too.

When I was little, the Bell twins asked me why I didn't have a mom. I told them that she was the princess of Pakistan—I'd overheard the name on the news and thought it sounded pretty—and she gave me to my parents, because I was a secret baby with the palace gardener, and her husband, the evil prince, would kill us if he knew I existed.

"So you're a princess?" Calliope asked.

"No. My mom is a princess."

"That means you're a princess, too," Cricket said, awed.

Calliope narrowed her eyes. "She's not a princess. There's no such thing as evil princes or Pakistan."

"There is, too! And I am!" But I still remember the hot rush of blood I felt when they came back later that afternoon, and I realized I'd been caught.

Calliope crossed her arms. "We know the truth. Our parents told us."

"Does your mom really not have a house?" Cricket asked. "Is that why you can't live with her?"

It was one of the most shameful moments of my childhood. So when my classmates began asking, I kept it simple: "I don't know who she is. I've never met her." I became a regular adoption story, a boring one. Having two fathers isn't an issue here. But a few years ago, Cricket and I were watching television when he turned to me and unexpectedly asked, "Why do you pretend like you don't have a mom?"

I squirmed. "Huh?"

Cricket was messing with a paper clip, bending it into a complicated shape. "I mean, she's okay now. Right?" He meant sober, and she had been for a year. But she was still Norah.

I just *looked* at him.

And I could see him remembering the past. The Bells had heard my screaming birth mother for years, whenever she'd show up wasted and unannounced.

He lowered his eyes and dropped the subject.

I'm grateful that my genetics don't bother Max. His father is a mean drunk who lives in a dangerous neighborhood of Oakland, and he doesn't even know where his mother lives. If anything, Norah makes my relationship with Max stronger. We understand each other.

I leave Andy and head back upstairs. Through my window, I notice Calliope has left Cricket's bedroom. He's pacing. My torn pattern mocks me. The sumptuous, pale blue fabrics stacked on my sewing table have lost their luster. I touch them gently. They're still soft. They still hold the promise of something better.

I'm determined to make up for last night. "Today is all about sparkling."

Heavens to Betsy cocks her head, listening but not understanding. I place a rhinestone barrette in my pale pink wig. I'm also wearing a sequined prom gown that I've altered into a minidress, a jean jacket covered in David Bowie pins, and glittery false eyelashes. I scratch behind Betsy's ears, and then she trots behind me out of my room. We run into Andy on the stairs, carrying up a basket of clean laundry.

"My eyes!" he says. "The glare!"

"*Très* funny."

"You look like a disco ball."

I smile and push past. "I'll take that as a compliment."

"When is Max bringing you home?"

"Later!"

Nathan is waiting at the bottom. "When, Dolores? A specific time would be helpful."

"Your hair is doing the swoopy thing." I set down my purse to fix it. Nathan and I have the same hair—thick, medium brown, and with a strange wave in the front that never behaves. No one ever doubts that Nathan and I are related. We also share the same wide brown eyes and childish grin. When we allow ourselves to grin. Andy is more slender than Nathan and keeps his prematurely gray hair cropped short. Still, despite his hair and despite his additional nine years on this planet, everyone thinks Andy is younger because he's the one who's always smiling. And he wears funny T-shirts.

"When?" Nathan repeats.

"Um, four hours?"

"That's five-thirty. I'll expect you home no later."

I sigh. "Yes, Dad."

"And three phone-call check-ins."

"Yes, Dad." I don't know what I did to deserve the world's strictest parents. I must have been seriously hardcore evil in a past life. It's not like I'm Norah. Nathan didn't get home until after midnight. Apparently, her lock was changed because she hasn't been paying rent, and she caused a scene by smashing in her front window with a neighbor's deck chair to get back inside. Nathan is going to visit her landlord today to discuss back payments. And that whole broken window situation.

"All right, then." He nods. "Have a good time. Don't do anything I wouldn't do."

I hear Andy as I'm walking out the front door. "Honey, that threat doesn't work when you're gay."

I laugh all the way down to the sidewalk. My heavy boots, tattooed with swirls of pink glitter to match my wig, leave a trail of fairy dust as I tramp. "You're like a shooting star," a voice calls from the porch next door. "Sparkly."

My cheer is immediately rendered null and void.

Cricket leaps down his stairs and joins me on the sidewalk.

"Going somewhere special?" he asks. "You look nice. Sparkly. I already said that, didn't I?"

"You did, thanks. And I'm just going out for a few hours." It's not like he's earned full truths or explanations. Of course, now I feel ashamed for thinking that, so I add with a shrug, "I might hit up Amoeba Records later."

Why does he make me feel guilty? I'm not doing anything wrong. I don't owe him anything. I shake my head—more at myself than at him—and move toward the bus stop. "See ya," I say. I'm meeting Max in the Upper Haight. He can't take me, because he's picking up a surprise first. *A surprise.* I have no idea what it is; it could be a gumball for all I care. The fact that I have a boyfriend who brings me surprises is enough.

I feel Cricket's stare. A pressure against the back of my neck. Truthfully, I wonder why he's not following me. I turn around. "What are you doing today?"

He closes the distance between us in three steps. "I'm not doing anything."

I'm uncomfortable again. "Oh."

He scratches his cheek, and the writing on his hand instructs him to CARPE DIEM. Seize the day. "I mean, I have some homework. But it won't take long. Only an hour. Two at the most."

"Right. Homework." I'm about to say something else equally awkward when I hear the grunt of my approaching bus. "That's me!" I sprint away. Cricket shouts something, but I can't hear it over the blast of exhaust as the bus sags against the curb. I grab a seat next to a bony woman in a paisley smock reading *The Tibetan Book of the Dead*.

I glance out the window. He's still watching me. Our eyes lock, and this time, his smile is shy. For some reason . . . it makes me smile back.

"Ooo," the woman beside me says. "You're sparkly."

chapter eight

I should've wished for the gumball.

"It'll be great for gigs," Max says, with more animation than usual. "You know how bad it was, loading our stuff into three separate cars. The parking in this city, for one thing. Impossible."

"Excellent! Right! Exactly!"

It's a van. Max bought a van. It's big, and it's white, and it's a *van.* As in, it's not a '64 Chevy Impala. As in, my boyfriend traded in his car to buy a van.

He walks around it, admiring its . . . what? Wide expanse? "You know we've wanted to tour the coast. Craig knows some guys in Portland, Johnny knows some guys in L.A. This is what we needed. We can do it now."

"Touring! Wow! Great!"

TOURING. Extended periods of time without Max. Sultry, slinky women in other cities flirting with my boyfriend, reminding him of my inexperience. TOURING.

Max stops. "Lola."

"Hmm?"

"You're doing the girl thing. Saying you're happy, when you're not." He crosses his arms. The spiderwebs tattooed onto his elbows point at me accusingly.

"I'm happy."

"You're pissed, because you think when I leave, I'll meet someone. Someone older."

"I'm not angry." I'm *worried*. And how much do I hate that we've had this conversation before, so he knows exactly what I'm thinking? "I'm . . . surprised. I just liked your old car, that's all. But this is good, too."

He raises a single brow. "You liked my car?"

"I loved your car."

"You know." Max backs me into its side. The metal is cool against my spine. "Vans are good for other things."

"Other things?"

"Other things."

Okay. Maybe this whole van situation isn't a *complete* loss. My hands are in his yellow-white bleached hair, and our lips are smashed against each other, when there's a loud, rude "Got any change, man?"

We break apart to find a guy in head-to-toe dirty patchwork corduroy glaring at us.

"Sorry," I say.

"No need to be sorry." He glowers at me underneath his white-boy dreadlocks. "I'm only fucking starving."

"ASSHOLE," Max shouts as the guy slumps off.

San Francisco is positively crawling with homeless. I can't walk from home to school without running into a dozen. They make me uneasy, because they're a constant reminder of my origins, but usually I can ignore them. Look past them. Otherwise . . . it's too exhausting.

But in the Haight, the homeless are passive-aggressive jerks.

I don't like coming here, but Max has friends who work in the overpriced vintage clothing boutiques, head shops, bookstores, and burrito joints. Despite the psychedelic graffiti and the bohemian window displays, Haight Street—once the mecca of sixties free love—is undeniably rougher and dirtier than the rest of the city.

"Hey. Forget that guy," Max says.

He sees that I need cheering, so he leads me to the falafel place where we had our first date. Afterward, we wander into a drag shop to try on wigs. He laughs as I pose in an absurd purple beehive. I love his laugh. It's rare, so whenever I hear it, I know I've earned it. He even lets me put one on his head, a blond Marilyn. "Wait till Johnny and Craig see you," I say, referring to his bandmates.

"I'll tell them I decided to grow it out."

"Rogaine works," I say in my best Max voice.

"Is that another old man joke?" Max laughs again as he tosses back my pale pink wig. "We should go. I told Johnny I'd meet him at three-thirty."

I tuck my real hair underneath it. "Because you don't see him enough at home."

"*You* rarely see him," Max says.

Johnny Ocampo—Amphetamine's drummer, Max's roommate—works at Amoeba Records, the one thing I do love about this neighborhood. Amoeba is a vast concrete haven of rare vinyl, band posters, and endless rows of CDs in color-coded genre tabs. There's still something to be said for music you can hold in your hands.

"I was only teasing. Besides," I add, "you never hang out with Lindsey."

"Come on, Lo. She's nosy and immature. It's weird between us."

His words are true, but . . . ouch. Sometimes lying is the polite thing to do. I frown. "She's my best friend."

"I'd just rather spend time with you." Max takes my hand. "Alone."

We're quiet as we enter Amoeba. Johnny, a pudgy but muscled Filipino, is in his usual place behind the information desk, which is raised as if the guys behind it hold the end-all truth about Good Musical Taste and Knowledge. Johnny and Max exchange jerks of the head in acknowledgment as Johnny finishes up with a customer. I wave hello to Johnny and disappear into the merchandise.

I listen mainly to rock, but I browse everything, because I never know when I'll discover something that I didn't know I liked. Hip-hop, classical, reggae, punk, opera, electronica. Nothing grabs my attention today, so I wander over to rock. I'm browsing the *Ps* and *Qs*, when the small, invisible hairs on the back of my neck rise. I look up.

And there he is.

Cricket Bell is standing front and center, searching for something. Someone. And then his gaze locks onto mine, and his face alights like the stars. He smiles—a full smile that reaches all the way to his eyes—and it's sweet and pure and hopeful.

And I know what is about to happen.

My palms break into a sweat. *Don't say it. Oh, please God, don't say it.* But this traitorous prayer follows: *Say it. Say it.*

Cricket weaves easily around the other customers as if we're the only two people in the store. The music over the loudspeakers changes from a sparse pop song into a swelling rock symphony. My heart pounds faster and faster. How badly I once wished for this moment. How badly I wish it would end now.

How badly I wish it would continue.

He stops before me, tugging at his bracelets. "I—I hoped I'd find you here."

Blood rushes to my cheeks. NO. This feeling isn't real. It's an old emotion, stirred up to torment and confuse me. I hate that. I hate him!

But it's like I only hate Cricket because I *don't* hate Cricket. I cut my eyes away, down to the Phoenix album in my hands. "I told you I was coming."

"I know. And I couldn't wait any longer, I have to tell you—"

The panic rises, and I grip the French band tighter. "Cricket, please—"

But his words pour forth in a torrent. "I can't stop thinking about you, and I'm not the guy I used to be, I've changed—"

"Cricket—" I look back up, feeling faint.

His blue eyes are bright. Sincere. Desperate. "Go out with me tonight. Tomorrow night, every ni—" The word cuts off in his throat as he sees something behind me.

Cigarettes and spearmint. I want to die.

"This is Max. My boyfriend. Max, this is Cricket Bell."

Max jerks his head in a small nod. He heard everything, there's no way he didn't.

"Cricket is my neighbor." I turn to Max. "Was my neighbor. Sort of is again."

My boyfriend squints, almost imperceptibly, as his mind sorts this information. It's the exact opposite of Cricket, who is at a complete loss to hide his emotions. His face is stricken, and he's backing up. I doubt he even realizes he's doing it.

Max's expression changes again, just slightly. He's figured out who Cricket is. He knows Cricket Bell must be related to Calliope Bell.

And he knows that I've purposely excluded him from our conversations.

Max places an arm around my shoulders. The gesture probably looks casual to Cricket, but Max's muscles are strained. He's jealous. The thought should make me happy, but I only see Cricket's embarrassment. I wish I didn't care what he thought.

Does this mean we're even? Is this what being even feels like?

The air between us is as thick as bay fog. I have to act, so I give Cricket a warm smile. "It was nice running into you. See you later, okay?" And then I lead Max away. I can tell my boyfriend wants to say something, but as usual, he's keeping his thoughts to himself until they're formed in the exact way he wants them. We walk stiffly, hand in hand, past his friend at the information desk.

I don't want to look back, but I can't help it.

He's staring at me. Staring *through* me. For the first time ever, Cricket Bell looks small. He's disappearing right before my eyes.

chapter nine

It's embarrassing to admit, but whenever Max and I are on a date, I want to stay out longer, walk farther, talk louder, so more people will see us together. I want to run into every classmate who's ever teased me for wearing pointed elf shoes or beaded moccasins, because I know they'll take one look at Max with his dark eyebrows, inked arms, and bad attitude and know that I'm doing *something* right.

Usually, I'm bursting with pride. But as we trudge back to his new van, I don't notice the face of anyone we pass. Because Cricket Bell asked me out. *Cricket Bell asked me out.* What am I supposed to do with that information?

Max unlocks the passenger-side door and holds it open for me. Neither of us has spoken since we left Amoeba. I mumble a thanks and get in. He climbs in the driver's side, turns the key in the ignition, and then says, "I don't like him."

The flatness of his tone makes my stomach turn. "Cricket? Why?"

"I just don't."

I can't reply. I don't know what I'd say. He doesn't break the silence again until we pass the Castro Theatre's landmark neon sign, only blocks from my house. "Why didn't you tell me about him?"

I look at my hands. "He's not important."

Max waits, jaw tense.

"He just hurt me, that's all. It was a long time ago. I don't like talking about him."

He turns to me, struggling to stay calm. "He hurt you?"

I sink into my seat, wanting anything *but* this conversation. "No. Not like that. We used to be friends, and we had a falling-out, and now he's back, and I'm running into him everywhere—"

"You've run into him before." He's staring at the road again. His knuckles tighten on the steering wheel.

"Just . . . in the neighborhood. He's not important, okay, Max?"

"Seems like a glaring omission to me."

I shake my head. "Cricket means nothing to me, I swear."

"He wants to take you out *every night,* and you expect me to believe there's nothing going on?"

"There's not!"

The van jerks to a halt in front of my house, and Max pounds on the steering wheel. "Tell me the truth, Lola! Why can't you tell me the truth for once?"

My eyes sting with tears. "I *am* telling the truth."

He stares at me.

"I love you." I'm getting desperate. He has to believe me. "I don't love him, I don't even like him! I love *you*."

Max closes his eyes for what feels like an eternity. The muscles in his neck are tense and rigid. At last, they relax. He opens his eyes again. "I'm sorry. I love you, too."

"And you believe me?" My voice is tiny.

He tilts my chin toward his and answers me with a kiss. His lips press hard against mine. I push back even harder against his. When we break apart, he looks deep into my eyes. "I believe you."

Max speeds away in his van, the Misfits blasting in a musical cloud of dust behind him. I slump. So much for my day off.

"Who was that?"

I startle at the sharp voice behind me. And then I turn to face her for the first time in two years. Her dark hair is pulled back into a tight ponytail, and she's wearing warm-up clothes. Yet she still manages to look more beautiful than I ever will.

"Hey, Calliope."

She stares at me as if to say, *Why haven't you answered my question?*

"That was my boyfriend."

Calliope looks surprised. "Interesting," she says, after a moment. And I can tell she is, in fact, interested. "Did my brother find you? He went out looking for you."

"He did." I speak the words cautiously. She's waiting for more, but I'm not giving it to her. I don't even know what *more* would be. "Nice seeing you again." I move toward the stairs.

I'm halfway to my front door when she says, "You look different."

"And you look the same."

I shut the door, and Nathan is waiting on the other side. "You didn't call."

Oh, no.

He's furious. "You were supposed to check in over an hour ago. I called five times, and it went straight to your voice mail. Where have you been?"

"I forgot. I'm sorry, Dad, I forgot."

"Was that Max's van? Did he get a new car?"

"You were WATCHING?"

"I was worried, Lola."

"SO YOU DECIDED TO SPY ON ME?"

"Do you know why guys buy vans? Do you?"

"TO HOLD THEIR GUITARS AND DRUMS? To go on TOUR?" I storm past him, upstairs and into my bedroom.

My dad pounds up the stairs behind me. "This conversation isn't over. We have an agreement when you go out with Max. You check in with us."

"What do you think will happen? Why don't you trust me?"

I rip off the pink wig and throw it across my room. "I'm not getting drunk or doing drugs or breaking windows. I'm not *her.* I'm not Norah."

I've taken it too far. At the mention of his sister, Nathan's face grows so hurt and twisted that I know I've hit bull's-eye. I brace for him to tear into me. Instead, he turns without a word. Which, somehow, is worse. But it's his fault for punishing me for things that I haven't done, for things SHE'S done.

How did this day get so awful? When did this happen?

Cricket.

His name explodes inside of me like cannon fire. I move toward our windows. His curtains are open. The bags he brought home are still on his floor, but there's no sign of him. What am I supposed to say the next time we see each other? Why won't he stop ruining my life?

Why does he have to ask me out *now*?

And Max knows about him. It shouldn't matter, but it does. Max isn't the type to keep bringing it up, but he is the type to hold on to it. Save it for when he needs it. Did he believe me when I told him that I love him? That I don't even like Cricket?

Yes, he did.

And I'm in love with Max. So why don't I know if the other half was a lie?

I'm not the only one with guy problems. Lindsey has been remarkably distracted this week. She didn't notice when our math teacher misused the quadratic formula on Monday. Or when Marta Velazquez, the most popular girl in school, forgot to peel the size sticker off her jeans on Tuesday. Her leg said: 12 12 12 12 12. How could Lindsey not notice that when she sat behind it for *an entire hour* in American history?

It's not until Thursday at lunch when Charlie Harrison-Ming walks past us and says, "Hi, Lindsey," and she stutters her "Hey, Charlie" back, that I realize the issue. And then I realize they're wearing the exact same red Chucks. Lindsey's great at solving other people's problems, but her own? Hopeless.

"You could say something about the shoes," I suggest.

"You're the clothes girl," she says miserably. "I sound dumb talking about that stuff."

Today I'm wearing cat-eye glasses and a cheetah-print dress I made last spring. I've pinned oversize red brooches like bullet wounds to the front of the dress, and I have bloodred ribbons tied up and down my arms and throughout my natural hair. I'm protesting big-game hunting in Africa.

"You never sound dumb," I say. "And I'm not the one wearing his sneakers."

"I told you, I don't want to date." But she doesn't sound so convinced anymore.

"I'll support you no matter what you choose. You know that, right?"

Lindsey plants her nose inside a hard-boiled detective novel, and our conversation is over. But she's not reading it. She's staring through the pages. The look gives me a familiar jolt—the expression on Cricket's face the last time I saw him. He never came back home last weekend. His curtains are still open, and his bags are still on his floor. I've been strangely fascinated by the shoulder bag. It's an old, brown leather satchel, the kind that should be worn by a university professor or a jungle explorer. I wonder what's in it. Probably just a toothbrush and a change of underwear.

Still. It looks lonely. Even the mesh laundry bag is sad, only half full.

My phone vibrates once against my leg, through the backpack at my feet, signaling a text. Whoops. We're supposed to have them turned off at school. But who'd text me now, anyway? I bend over to reach for it, and my glasses—a vintage pair that doesn't fit well—clatter to the cement. They've got to be right beneath me, but I can't see them. I can't see anything. I hear the loud prattle of a mob of girls heading our way.

"Oh crud, oh crud, oh crud—"

Lindsey swipes up my glasses just before the girls hit. They buzz past, a swarm of perfume and laughter. "Did your vision get worse again?"

I slide them on, and the world comes back into focus. I frown. "Please. It gets worse every year. At this rate, I'll be blind by twenty."

She nods at my glasses. "And how many pairs do you own now?"

"Only three." I wish they weren't so expensive. I order them online for a discount, but they still eat up entire paychecks. My parents pay for my contacts, but I like variety. I'd prefer *more* variety. I peek at my phone, and I'm thrilled to find the text is from Max:

saw two fallen branches in the shape of a heart. thought of you.

I grin like an idiot.

"Who was it?" Lindsey asks.

"Max!" But then I catch the look on her face. I shrug and turn off my phone. "It's nothing. He saw . . . something."

She flips her novel back open. "Oh."

And then I have it: the perfect solution to her problem. Charlie is totally interested in her, Lindsey just needs someone there to guide her through those first difficult steps. She needs *me* there. A double date! I'M A GENIUS! I'm . . . dating Max. Who would never agree to such a thing. I glance at my best friend, who is staring through her mystery novel again. Trying to solve her own mystery. I cradle my phone in my hands and keep my mouth shut.

And I feel so disloyal to her.

I have an early shift on Saturday. I closed last night. It feels like I never leave, like I should just get it over with and put my old Disney Princess sleeping bag underneath the seventh-floor concessions counter. When I arrive at the theater, I'm surprised to find St. Clair behind the box office. Anna isn't scheduled to work today. I'm further surprised when I notice what he's wearing.

"What's with the uniform?" I ask.

He shrugs. It's a slow, full-bodied shrug that makes him seem . . . more European. "One of the managers said I spent so much time here, I ought to be working. So I am."

"Wait. You got a job here?"

"Yeah, but don't tell anyone. It's a secret." He widens his eyes, joking.

"You. Working?" St. Clair never discusses it, but everyone knows his family is rolling in it. He doesn't need to work. Nor does he strike me as someone who'd want to.

"You don't think I can handle ripping tickets?"

"My exhausted feet say it's a little more than that."

St. Clair grins, and my heart skips a beat. He really IS attractive. What's my problem? I must be more tired than I thought. And I'm not interested in Anna's boyfriend—he's too short, too cocky—but the fact that I'm noticing him bothers me. I dive into work on another floor to distract myself from increasingly uncomfortable thoughts. But St. Clair approaches me a few hours later, once we've calmed down from a rush. "My feet feel dandy," he says. "In fact, I'm considering forming a dance troupe. Would you be interested?"

"Oh, bite me." I'm still irritated. The six people who complained to me about our parking garage didn't help the situation. "Seriously, why did you get a job?"

"Because I thought it would build character." He hops onto my concessions counter. "Because all of my teeth have fallen out, and I can't afford dentures. Because—"

"Fine. Whatever. Be a dillhole."

"I should be doing something productive, shouldn't I?" St. Clair hops back down and grabs a broom from the supply closet. "All right, all right. I'm saving for our future."

"Our future?" I give him a coy smile. "I'm flattered, really, but that's unnecessary."

He pokes my back with the tip of the broom.

"And is Anna aware that you're saving for your future together?"

"Of course." St. Clair sweeps the fallen popcorn around my ankles while I take someone's Diet Coke–and–soft-pretzel order. When I'm done, he continues. "Do you think I'd get a job and not discuss it with her first?"

"No. But still, I thought . . . you know . . ." He looks confused, and I'm forced to finish the thought out loud. "I thought you had money."

St. Clair bursts out laughing as if I've said something foolish. "My father has money. And I'd like to keep him out of my future."

"That sounds . . . ominous."

The European shrug again. This time, to change the subject. "And it'd be nice to have a bit of spending cash so that I could take her out. We tend to dine mainly in our dormitory cafeterias." He frowns. "Come to think of it, we've *always* dined mainly in school cafeterias."

"In Paris?"

"In Paris," he confirms.

I sigh. "You have no idea how lucky you are."

"Actually, I'm confident that I do." St. Clair props the broom against the wall. "So why do *you* work? To support your unhealthy costuming habit? And what IS your hair about today?"

"I wanted to see what it'd look like in tiny buns. And then I added the feathers, because they looked like nests." He's right. That *is* why I work. Plus, my parents said when I turned sixteen I had to get a part-time job to learn about responsibility. So I did.

St. Clair examines my hair closer. "Spectacular."

I back away. "Exactly how far into the future are you planning?"

"Far."

The word hangs between us, loaded with strength and meaning. Max and I talk about running away to Los Angeles and starting a new life together—me designing elaborate costumes by day, him destroying rock clubs by night—but I get the sense that St. Clair's conversations with Anna are more serious than the ones I have with Max. The thought makes me uneasy. I stare at St. Clair. He's not that much older than me.

How can he be so confident?

"When it's right, it's simple," he says to my unasked question. "Unlike your hair."

chapter ten

The moon is fat, but half of her is missing. A ruler-straight line divides her dark side from her light. She hangs low over the bustling Castro, noticeably earlier than the night before. Autumn is coming. For as long as I can remember, I've talked to the moon. Asked her for guidance. There's something deeply spiritual about her pale glow, her cratered surface, her waxing and waning. She wears a new dress every evening, yet she's always herself.

And she's always there.

Since my shift was early, I rode the bus and train home. I'm not sure why I'm so relieved to be back in my neighborhood. It's not like the work itself was hard. But the familiarity of Castro Street comforts me—the glitter in the sidewalks, the chocolate-chip warmth radiating from Hot Cookie, the groups of chattering men, the early Halloween display in the window of Cliff's Variety.

I'm lucky to live in a place that's doesn't have to hide what it is. Businesses like the Sausage Factory (restaurant), Spunk (hair salon), and Hand Job (manicures) are clear about the residents, but there's a genuine sense of love and community. It's a family. And like a family, everyone knows everyone's business, but I don't think it's a bad thing. I like that the guys at Spike's Coffee wave as I pass by. I like that the guys at Jeffery's know Betsy needs the large container of fresh Lamb, Yams & Veggies. I like—

"LOLA!"

A stab to my gut. With dread, I turn to find Cricket Bell performing a spin move around an elderly couple entering Delano's grocery as he's exiting. He's carrying a carton of free-range eggs in each hand. "Are you headed home? Do you have a minute?"

I can't meet his eyes. "Yeah. Yeah, of course."

As he jogs to catch up, I keep moving forward. He's wearing a white dress shirt, a black vest, and a black tie. He'd look like a waiter, except he's also wearing his colorful bracelets and rubber bands.

"Lola, I want to apologize."

I freeze.

"I feel like a jerk, a total ass for . . . for putting you in that situation last week. I'm sorry. I should have asked if you had a boyfriend, I don't know why I didn't ask." His voice is pained. "Of course you'd have a boyfriend. You've just always been this cool, gorgeous girl and seeing you again brought up this whole wreck of emotions and . . . I don't know what to say, but I messed up, and I'm sorry. It won't happen again."

I'm shocked.

I don't know what I expected him to say, but it certainly wasn't this. Cricket Bell thinks I'm cool and gorgeous. Cricket Bell thinks I've *always* been cool and gorgeous.

"And I hope this doesn't make things even weirder," he continues. "I just want to clear the air. I think you're amazing, and being your friend that summer was the happiest summer of my life, and . . . I just want to be a part of your life. Again."

I can hardly think straight. "Right."

"But I'd understand if you don't want to see me—"

"No," I say quickly.

"No?" He's nervous. He doesn't understand how I mean it.

"I mean . . . we can still hang out." I proceed carefully. "I'd like that."

Cricket droops with relief. "You would?"

"Yeah." I'm surprised by how obvious it is. Of course I want him back in my life. He's always been a part of my life. Even when he was gone, some fragment of his spirit lingered behind. I felt it in the space between our windows.

"I want you to know that I've changed," he says. "I'm not that guy anymore."

His body energetically turns to face mine, and the movement startles me. I trip toward him and smack into his chest, and one of the egg cartons drops from his hand and topples toward the sidewalk. Cricket swiftly grabs it before it lands.

"Sorry! I'm so sorry!" I say.

The place where his chest touched mine *burns.* Every place where his body touched mine feels alive. What kind of guy did he think he was, and who is he now?

"It's okay." He peeks inside the carton. "No harm done. All eggs accounted for."

"Here, let me take that." I reach for a carton, but he holds it above his head. It's *way* out of my reach.

"It's okay." He smiles softly. "I have a much better grip on things now."

I make for the other carton. "The least I can do is carry one."

Cricket starts to lift the other one up, too, but something solemn clouds his eyes. He lowers them and gives one to me. The back of his hand reads: EGGS. "Thanks," he says.

I look down. Someone has drawn a game of hopscotch onto the sidewalk in pink chalk. "You're welcome."

"I'll need them back, though. My mom was craving deviled eggs, and she asked me to pick those up. Very important mission."

Silence.

This is the moment. Where I either make things permanently awkward or I make genuine on our friendship. I look up—and then up again, until I reach his face—and ask, "How's college?"

Cricket closes his eyes. It's only for a moment, a breath, but it's enough to show me how thankful he is for my question. *He wants to be in my life.*

"Good," he says. "It's . . . good."

"I sense a *but.*"

He smiles. "But it's been a while since that whole surrounded-by-other-students thing. I guess it takes time to get used to."

"You said you were homeschooled? After you moved?"

"Well, we moved so often that it was easier than enrolling over and over, always taking the same classes. Always being the new kid. We'd done it before, and we didn't want to do it again. Plus, it allowed us to work around Cal's schedule."

The last sentence sticks to me in an unpleasant way. "What about your schedule?"

"Ah, it's not as bad as it sounds. She only has so long to do this. She has to make a run for it while she can." I must look unconvinced, because he adds, "Another five years, and it'll be my turn in the family spotlight."

"But why can't it be your turn now, too? Maybe I'm being selfish, because I'm an only child—"

"No. You're right." And I catch the first glimpse of tiredness between his forehead and his eyes. "But our circumstance is different. She has a gift. It wouldn't be fair for me not to do everything I can to support her."

"And what does she do to support you?" I ask before I can stop myself.

Cricket's expression grows sly. "She does the dishes. Takes out the trash. Leaves the cereal box out for me on weekends."

"Sorry." I look away. "I'm being nosy."

"It's okay, I don't mind." But he doesn't answer my question.

We walk in silence for a minute, when something strikes me. "Today. Today is your birthday!"

His face turns away from mine as fast as a reflex.

"Why didn't you say something?" But I know the answer before I finish asking the question. Memories of the last time I saw him on his birthday fill me with instant humiliation.

Cricket fidgets with his bracelets. "Yep. Eighteen."

I follow his lead to keep the conversation moving forward. "An adult. Officially."

"It's true, I feel incredibly mature. Then again, maturity has always been my greatest strength."

This time, his usual self-deprecation makes me flinch. He *was* always more mature. Except, perhaps, around me. "So . . . you're here to visit Calliope?" I shake my head as the embarrassment continues. "Of course you are. It's her birthday, too. I'm just surprised to see you since it's Saturday night. I assumed you'd be at some party across the bay, chugging beer in the handstand position."

He scratches the side of his neck. "Cal would never admit this, but it's been a rough adjustment for her. Me being away while she's still at home. Not that I wouldn't have come home tonight otherwise, of course I would. And I actually *did* drop by one of those parties for a minute as a favor to someone, but . . . perhaps you didn't notice." Cricket adjusts his tie. "I'm not the kegger type."

"Me neither." I don't have to explain that it's because of Norah. He knows.

"What about your boyfriend?" His voice betrays a forced cool.

I'm embarrassed he'd assume it, but I can't deny that Max looks the type. "He isn't a party guy either. Not really. I mean, he drinks and smokes, but he respects my feelings. He never tries to get me to join him or anything."

Cricket ducks underneath a pink-flowered branch in our path. Our neighborhood blooms year-round. I walk below it without having to bend. "What do your parents think about you dating someone that old?" he asks.

I wince. "You should know that I'm really tired of having that conversation."

"Sorry." But then like he can't help it, "So, uh . . . how old is he?"

"Twenty-two." For some reason, admitting this to him feels uncomfortable.

A long pause. "Wow." The word is slow and heavy.

My heart sinks. I want to be his friend, but on what planet would that work? There's too much history between us for friendship. We quietly climb our street's hill until we reach my house. "Bye, Cricket." I can't meet his eyes again. "Happy birthday."

"Lola?"

"Yes?"

"Eggs." He points. "You have my eggs."

Oh.

Embarrassed, I hold out the carton. His long fingers reach for it, and I find myself bracing for the physical contact. But it doesn't come. He takes the carton by its edge. It's a cautious, deliberate move. It reminds me that I shouldn't be with him.

And it reminds me that I can't tell Max.

chapter eleven

The more I think about our conversation, the more frustrated I get. Cricket says he's changed, but changed *what*? A willingness to speak his mind? To finally say he likes me? Or is there something else? Toward the end of our friendship, he grew so strange and distant until he cut me off completely by not inviting me to that stupid party. Which he still doesn't want to talk about. And now he wants to be friends again, but then he leaves early the next morning and doesn't come home for TWO WEEKS?

Whatever.

"Lola can't play today." Andy is banging around among his pots and pans, which is why we hadn't heard Cricket knock on our front door. We left it open to let the heat escape, because our kitchen gets hot when all of the ovens are running. "She's on pie duty. There was a huge, emergency, last-minute change to an order this morning."

"*Dad.* He didn't come over to *play.*"

Cricket holds up a box. "This was delivered to our house. It's yours."

Andy looks up.

"Lola's," Cricket clarifies. He places it on the floor outside the kitchen while Betsy runs in circles around him. She's always loved Cricket.

"Thanks." I say the word cautiously, a warning if he's listening for it. I set down a bag of flour and move to examine the package. "Cool! It's the boning for my stays."

"Stays?"

"Corset," Andy says distractedly. "Lola, get your butt back in here."

Cricket reddens. "Oh."

Point number two for Andy in today's embarrassment department. Cricket leans over to pet Betsy, who collapses belly-up, and I pretend not to notice his blush. Though I'm not sure he's earned that particular favor. Or my dog's belly.

"It's for a dress," I explain.

Cricket nods without looking at me. "Pie emergency?" A final rub, and then he enters the kitchen, rolling up his sleeves and removing his bracelets. "Need a hand?"

"Oh, no." I'm alarmed. "Thanks, but we've got it."

"Grab an apron, they're in the top drawer there." Andy points across the room.

"You can't ask him to help," I say. "It's not his job."

"He didn't ask." Cricket ties a long, white apron around his waist. "I volunteered."

"See?" Andy says. "The boy makes sense. Unlike some teenagers I could mention."

I narrow my eyes at him. It's not my fault I'd rather spend my only weekend day off with Lindsey. I had to cancel our plans for sushi and shopping in Japantown. When I asked if she wanted to come over and help, she said, "No thanks, Ned. I'll make new plans." And I get that. But if she doesn't hang out with me, she'll just stay in and watch a marathon of *CSI* or *Veronica Mars.*

Which makes her happy. But still.

"Those pumpkins need to be seeded before I can toss them into the oven. Put the seeds and strings on that pile for compost," Andy says.

"Pumpkins. Got it." Cricket washes his hands and grabs the biggest pumpkin.

I resume weighing flour for two dozen crusts. When you bake in large quantities, scales are required, not measuring cups. "Really, we're okay. I'm sure you have homework."

"It's no problem." Cricket shrugs. "Where's the other Mr. Nolan?"

Andy closes his eyes. Cricket tenses, realizing he's said something wrong. "Nathan is with Norah today," I explain.

"Is . . . everything all right?" he asks.

"Peachy," Andy says.

"It's just some financial stuff." I hand Cricket our largest knife for slicing open the pumpkins, along with an apologetic look for Andy's snippiness. Cricket gives me a discreet smile back. He knows my dad isn't normally like this.

Andy's voice is the only one we hear for the next hour as he guides us through production. The original order was for six pies total, but now we're making six of each: classic pumpkin, vegan apple crumble, pear ginger, and sweet potato pecan. I've been helping him bake for years, so I'm pretty good in the kitchen. But I'm surprised by how quickly Cricket adapts. Andy explains that baking is actually a science—leavening and acids, proteins and starches—and Cricket *gets* it. Of course he's a natural. Good chemists are good bakers.

But why is he spending his Saturday making pies when he doesn't have to? Is it that nice-guy thing? Or does he think by spending time with me, I might fall for him? But he doesn't even try to flirt. He stays away from me, focused on his work. It's maddening how someone so easy to read can be so impossible to understand.

When the timer rings at noon, Andy lets out a funny noise of surprise. "We're making good time. We can do this." And he smiles for the first time all day.

Cricket and I exchange relieved grins across the counter. Andy flips on the radio to a station that plays classics from the fifties, and the kitchen relaxes. Cricket slices apples with rhythm and precision to the beat of "Peggy Sue," while Andy and I roll out dough in perfect synchronization.

"We could put this routine on ice and take it to Nationals," Cricket says.

At the mention of ice, Andy pauses. My dad loves figure skating. It is—and I don't use this expression lightly—the gayest thing about him. When I was little, he took me to see *Stars on Ice*. We cheered for the skaters with the prettiest spins and we licked blue cotton candy from our fingers and he bought me a program filled with photographs of beautiful people in beautiful costumes. It's one of my happiest memories. When Calliope started figure skating, I wanted to do it, too. We weren't friends, but I still thought of her as someone worthy of admiration. Which meant copying.

"This is okay," I said after my first lesson. "But when do I get a costume?"

Andy pointed at my plain pink leotard. "That IS your costume, until you're more experienced."

I lost interest.

My parents were peeved. The lessons were expensive, so they made me finish out the season. Thus, I can state that figure skating is *hard*. Andy talked me into another *Stars on Ice* when I was thirteen, but my daydreams of doing triple axels in sequined skirts were long gone. I still feel bad that I didn't even try to enjoy it. He's never asked again.

Andy must have inquired about Calliope, because Cricket is talking about her schedule. "It's a busy year, because of the Olympics. It just means more: more practices, more promotion, more stress."

"When will she know if she's made the Olympic team?" Andy asks.

"If she places in Nationals, she'll go. That's in January. Right now she's working on her new programs, which she'll take to a few of the early Grand Prix competitions. This year, she's doing Skate America and Skate Canada. Then it's Nationals, Olympics, Worlds." He ticks them off on his fingers.

"Do you go to *all* of those?" I ask.

"Most of them. But I doubt I'll make it to Canada. It's during a busy school week."

"You've seen a lot of figure skating."

Cricket pulls the softened pumpkin flesh from the ovens. "Oh, have I? Is that unusual?" He keeps a straight face, but his eyes spark.

I resist throwing a dish towel at him. "So what's the deal with her and second place? You said on your first night back—"

"Cal's been the most talented ladies' figure skater for years, but she's never skated two clean programs in a row in a major competition. She's convinced that she's cursed. It's why she's always switching coaches, and it's why she'd rather get third than second. When she gets third, at least she's happy to have placed. But second. That's too close to first."

I've stopped working again.

"Second hurts." He stares at me for a moment before lowering his head back to the pumpkins.

Andy has been rolling piecrusts slowly, following our conversation with interest. He sets down his rolling pin and dusts the flour from his PRAISE CHEESES! shirt. "What have you been up to, Cricket? What are you studying at Berkeley?"

"Mechanical engineering. Not very cool, is it?"

"But it's perfect for you," I say.

He laughs to himself. "Of course it is."

"I *meant,* it's perfect because you've always built, you know, mechanical things. Contraptions and robots and—"

"Automaton," he corrects. "It's like a robot but completely useless."

The negative tone that's crept into his voice is disconcerting. It's a rare thing from Cricket Bell. But before I can say anything, he shakes it off with a smile. "But you're right. It suits me."

"I've never seen anyone do what you can do," Andy says. "And from such a young age. I'll never forget when you fixed our toaster with that coat hanger when you were, what, five years old? Your parents must be so proud of you."

Cricket shrugs uncomfortably. "I guess."

Andy's head tilts. He studies Cricket for a long moment.

Cricket has returned to work, and it reminds me to return to mine. I begin mashing sweet potatoes. The repetition is actually soothing. As much as I hate losing a day off, I love my father's business. He stumbled into it accidentally when he baked a classic cherry pie with a lattice top for a dinner party, and everyone freaked out. They'd never tasted a homemade piecrust before.

Someone there asked him to make one for another party, and then someone at *that* party asked him to make several for another. It was a business in the blink of an eye. Nathan jokingly called it City Pie Guy, and the name stuck. The logo is a retro-looking man with a mustache and a gingham apron, winking and holding out a steaming pie.

As the drop-off hour approaches, we talk less and less. By the time the last pies are out of the oven and into their boxes, Andy is on edge again. We're all sweating. My dad races outside to open the car doors, and I grab two boxes and run out behind him. We've just tucked the pies safely inside when the front door opens.

Andy gasps.

I look up to find Cricket holding six boxes . . . in each hand. And flying down the stairs. "Ohmygod, ohmygod, ohmygod," Andy whispers. I grip his arm in horror, but Cricket bounds easily onto our driveway.

"Ready for these?" he asks.

The pies are still perfectly stacked.

Andy pauses for a moment. And then he bursts into laughter. "Into the car."

"What?" Cricket asks me as my dad walks away.

"Maybe carry a few less the next time you take a jog down our stairs?"

"Oh." He grins.

"You'd be an excellent circus juggler."

He gestures to his legs. "Wouldn't even have to rent the stilts."

I notice the opening for a question I've had, but I hesitate. "I hope this isn't rude—"

"Then it definitely is."

But he's teasing, so I continue. "Exactly how tall *are* you?"

"Ah, the height question." Cricket rubs his hands together. There's a mathematical equation written there today. "Six four." He grins again. "Not including hair."

I laugh.

"And being thin makes me look even taller."

"And your tight pants," I add.

Cricket makes a startled choking noise.

OH DEAR GOD. WHY WOULD I SAY THAT?

Andy reappears, slaps him on the back, and then we throw ourselves into the welcome distraction of loading the remainder of the pies. I climb into the backseat to keep them steady. Cricket follows in behind me, and even though he doesn't have to be here, it feels natural that he should come along for the delivery. Our neighborhood's traffic is predictably sluggish, but Andy speeds the rest of the way to Russian Hill, past views of Alcatraz and cable cars, and into the area of some of the city's most expensive real estate.

We find parking at the bottom of the famous part of Lombard Street, the steep hill with switchback curves nicknamed "The Crookedest Street in America." The narrow, zigzag road is paved with red bricks and bursting with vibrant flowers. We grab the pies—I'm amazed when Andy stacks most of them on Cricket's arms, trusting him—and run to make the delivery two blocks away.

"You're ten minutes late, Pie Guy." A harsh woman with slicked-back hair opens the door for us. "Put them in there. Wipe your feet," she adds to Cricket as he crosses the threshold, blinded by his pies.

He backs up, wipes them, and moves forward.

"Dirt," she says. "Again."

I look at her rug. Cricket isn't tracking in dirt. He repeats the process one more time, and then we set down the boxes beside an array of crystal decanters in her dining room. She's glaring at Cricket and me as if she doesn't like what she sees. That teenagers had anything to do with her party. We stand in uneasy silence as she writes Andy a check. He folds it once and places it in his back pocket.

"Thank you." He glances in our direction before continuing. "And never call me again. Your business isn't welcome."

And then he walks away.

The woman is stunned with indignation. Cricket's eyebrows pop to his forehead, and I'm barely keeping my laughter under control as we file past her and out the door.

"Hag," Andy adds, when we join him. "You busted your asses for her."

Cricket examines himself. "I should have covered my gang tattoos."

"I wouldn't let you in my house," Andy says.

I hug my stomach from laughing so hard.

"Speaking of appearances." Cricket turns to me. "I'd almost forgotten what you look like."

The laughter stops dead in my mouth. There wasn't time for anything fun when Andy woke me up this morning, so I threw on a pair of jeans and a plain black T-shirt. It's one of Max's. I'm not wearing makeup, and my hair is hanging loosely. I didn't think I'd see anyone but my parents today.

"Oh." I cross my arms. "Uh, yeah. This is me."

"It's a rare occurrence to see Lola in the wild," Andy says.

"I know," Cricket says. "I haven't seen the real Lola since my first night back."

"I like being different."

"And I like that about you," Cricket says. "But I like the real you best."

I'm too self-conscious to reply. The car ride home is unbearable. Andy and Cricket do the talking, while I stare out my window and try not to think about the boy beside me. His body takes up so much room. His long arms, his spindly legs. He has to hunch so that his head won't hit the ceiling, though his hair still does.

I scoot closer to my window.

When we get home, we're greeted by a wagging Heavens to Betsy and the sugary warmth of baked goods. I throw my arms around her and breathe in her doggie scent. It's safer to focus on Betsy. Cricket offers to help with the dishes, but Andy refuses as he reaches for his wallet. "You've already done too much today."

Cricket is surprised. "That's not why I helped."

Andy holds out a few twenties. "Please, take something."

But Cricket puts his hands in his pockets. "I should get home. I just came over to deliver your package." He nods to the box addressed to me, which is still on the floor outside the kitchen.

Alarm dawns across Andy's features. "Did you call your parents? Do they know where you are?"

"Oh, it's fine. They had a big day with Cal planned. I doubt they noticed I was gone."

But Andy doesn't look reassured. Something is bothering him.

"See you around." Cricket reaches for the doorknob.

Andy steps forward. "Would you like to go with us to Muir Woods next Sunday? We're having a family outing. I'd be honored if you joined us, it's the least I can do."

Muir Woods? A family outing? *What is he talking about?*

"Uh." Cricket glances at me nervously. "Okay."

"Great!" Andy says. He's already talking about picnic baskets and avocado sandwiches, and my mind is going haywire. Not only is this the first mention of a day trip, but . . . Max.

"What about Sunday brunch?" I interrupt. Betsy squirms as I hold her tighter.

Andy turns back to me. "It's still on for tomorrow."

"No. Next Sunday."

"Oh," Andy says, as if the thought has just occurred to him. Even though it hasn't. "We'll have to skip it next week."

I'm dumbfounded as they say goodbye and Cricket leaves. My parents would NEVER ask Max to join us. And Max is my BOYFRIEND. And Cricket is . . . I don't know what Cricket is! How am I supposed to explain the cancellation to Max? I can't tell him that *I'm going on an outing with Cricket Bell.* I open my mouth in outrage, but I'm too furious for words.

Andy locks the door and sighs. "Now, why couldn't you date a boy like that?"

chapter twelve

"Andy said that?" Lindsey asks. "Kiss of death."

"I know. As if I'd ever go for him now that *my dad* wants me to date him."

"As if you'd ever go for him again, period."

"Right . . . right."

There's a weighty pause on the other end of the line. "Lola Nolan, please tell me you are not thinking about Cricket Bell in that way."

"Of course I'm not!" And I'm not. I'm definitely not.

"Because he broke your heart. We've spent two good years hating him. Remember that sixteen-page letter you buried in my backyard? And the ceremonial tossing of the pink bottle cap into the surf at Ocean Beach?"

Yeah. I remember.

"And your boyfriend? You do remember your boyfriend? Max?"

I frown at his picture beside my bed. His picture frowns back. "Who's leaving me to go on tour."

"He's not leaving you. Stop being such a drama queen, Ned."

Except he is. Max announced at brunch this morning that Johnny had already secured a show in Southern California. The miracle is that it's for next Saturday night, so he couldn't have made it to our next brunch anyway. So there was no need to invent an excuse for canceling it.

"I don't wanna talk about guys anymore," I say. "Can't we just rehash *Alias* instead?"

There's only one type of television show that Lindsey and I agree on: shows that involve solving crimes while wearing cool disguises. *Alias, Pushing Daisies, Dollhouse, Charlie's Angels,* and *The Avengers* are our favorites. My best friend is happy to comply, so we don't talk about ANY guy for the rest of the week. But they're on my mind.

My boyfriend. Cricket. My boyfriend. Cricket.

How could Andy put me in this position? How could he make up a dumb family outing on the spot like that? And I'm frustrated because since the Bells moved back, every important event seems to happen on weekends. School has always dragged, but it's nothing compared to now. Endless.

And work? Forget it. I lose count of how many wrong tickets I print, wrong soft drinks I pour, wrong theaters I sweep. Even Anna—my most good-natured supervisor, someone I've begun to consider one of my few friends—finally loses it on Saturday when I come back from my dinner break twenty minutes late.

"Where have you been? I'm dying out here." She gestures with her head toward the packed box-office lobby as she hands someone their change and takes the ticket order of the person behind them.

"I'm sorry, I lost track of time. There's this thing tomorrow—"

"You did it yesterday, too. You left me hanging. There were, like, sixty people in the lobby with these screaming children and bad hair, and this one lady projectile sneezed all over my window, and it was totally on purpose, and—"

"I'm so sorry, Anna."

She holds up a hand in panicked frustration, like she doesn't want to hear any more, and I feel terrible. I went to a Turkish coffee shop down the block for a pick-me-up and ended up lost in my thoughts. I don't feel picked up at all.

By the time my shift ends and Andy brings me home, the Bell house is dark. Did Cricket come home? His curtains haven't moved. If he doesn't show up tomorrow, will I be relieved? Or disappointed?

I plan my outfit. If this is going to happen, I need to look better than the last time I saw him, but I can't look *too* interesting. I don't want to encourage him. I choose a red-and-white checked top (cute) with jeans (boring). But by morning I've decided it's hopelessly lame, and I change my shirt twice and my pants three times.

I settle on a similarly checked red-and-white halter dress, which I made from an actual picnic blanket for the last Fourth of July. I add bright red lipstick and tiny ant-shaped earrings for theme, and my big black platform boots because walking will be involved. They're the sportiest shoes I own. I smooth my dress, erect my posture, and parade downstairs.

No one is there.

"Hello?"

No reply.

My shoulders sag. "What's the point of a staircase if no one is here to watch my entrance?"

Behind me, a slightly breathless "hi."

I spin around to find Cricket Bell sitting in my kitchen, and for some reason, the sight of him makes me slightly breathless, too. "I— I didn't know you were there."

Cricket stands, almost knocking over his chair in a rare moment of clumsiness. "I was having some tea. Your parents are loading the car. They were giving you three more minutes." He glances at his watch. "You had thirty seconds left."

"Oh."

"It was good entrance," he says.

Nathan bursts into the room. "There you are! With twenty seconds to spare." He wraps me in a hug, but quickly pulls away and looks me up and down. "I thought you understood we were going into *nature* today."

"Ha ha."

"A dress? Those boots? Don't you think you should change into something less—"

"It's not worth the fight." Andy pops in his head. "Come on. Let's go."

I follow him outside to avoid further chastising from Nathan. Cricket walks several steps behind me. It's a careful distance.

I wonder if he's looking at my butt.

WHY DID I JUST THINK THAT? Now my butt feels COLOSSAL. Maybe he's looking at my legs. Is that better? Or worse? Do I want him looking at me? I hold on to the bottom of my dress as I climb into the backseat and crawl to the other side. I'm sure he's looking at my butt. He has to be. It's huge, and it's right there, and it's huge.

No. I'm acting crazy.

I glance over, and he smiles at me as he buckles his seat belt. My cheeks grow warm.

WHAT IS WRONG WITH ME?

As always, he chats easily with my parents. The more relaxed everyone else gets, the more worked up I am. We're already approaching the Golden Gate Bridge, so we've been driving for . . . fifteen minutes? How can that be?

"Lola, you're awfully quiet," Nathan says. "Do you feel okay?"

"Is it motion sickness?" Andy asks. "Because you haven't had that in years."

"WE AREN'T EVEN OUT OF THE CITY. IT'S NOT MOTION SICKNESS."

There's a shocked silence.

"Maybe it's motion sickness," I lie. "Sorry. I have . . . a headache, too." I cannot believe I'm screaming about motion sickness a foot away from Cricket Bell.

Deep breaths. Take deep breaths. I adjust my dress, but the fabric sticks to my leg, and I accidentally flash Cricket my thigh. This time, I catch him looking. His fingers are messing with his bracelets and rubber bands. Our eyes lock.

A rubber band snaps and shoots into the windshield.

Nathan's and Andy's heads jolt back in fright, but they laugh when they realize what happened.

Cricket's body shrinks up in his seat. "Sorry! Sorry."

And I'm strangely relieved to know that I'm not the only one freaking out.

chapter thirteen

It's been years since I've been here, but Muir Woods still makes me feel as if I've stepped into a fairy tale. It's an enchanted forest, I'm sure of it. Amid the trees are devilish wood sprites and red mushroom caps with white spots and faeries tempting mortals with golden fruit. The redwoods have the same soothing effect on me as the moon. They seem as old as the moon. Ancient and beautiful and wise.

And I need that right now.

The remainder of the drive was restless, but at least it passed quickly. The park is only forty minutes from home. After strolling the trail for a while, we split up. Nathan and Andy, Cricket and me. We'll meet back at the car in a few hours, and because it's not Max, my parents don't ask me to check in with them. If I didn't know any better, I'd swear they're trying to set me up.

Wait. Are my parents trying to set me up?

No, they know I have a boyfriend. And Nathan hates the idea of me dating *anyone*. They must see Cricket as the trustworthy friend he is. Right?

"Is it okay if I eat this in front of you?" Cricket sounds hesitant.

We're sitting beside the creek that runs through the park, half of the picnic spread before us. He holds up the sandwich Andy made for him. It's smoked salmon with cream cheese and sliced avocado.

"Of course. Why wouldn't it be?"

He points at my hummus wrap. "You're still a vegetarian, right?"

"Oh. Yeah. But it doesn't bother me to see other people eating meat, I just can't stomach the thought for myself." I pause. "Thanks for asking. Most people don't ask."

Cricket turns toward the bubbling creek and stretches out his legs. His pants are well-worn, faded pinstripes and frayed hems. It's appropriate for the outdoors as far as his wardrobe is concerned, and once again, I find myself admiring his sense of style.

God, he has good taste.

"I just don't want to offend you." He sets down his sandwich but picks at the poppy seeds on the bread. "I mean, any more than I already have."

A lump forms in my throat. "Cricket. You've never *offended* me."

"But I hurt you." His voice grows quiet. "I wish that I hadn't."

The words are tumbling out before I can stop them. "We were so close, and then you just dropped me. I felt like such an idiot. I don't understand what happened."

He stops flicking poppy seeds. "Lola. There's something I need to tell you."

The acceleration of my heartbeat is sudden and painful. "What is it?"

Cricket faces me with his entire body. "When we talked at our windows that last night," he says, "I knew something was wrong. I could tell you were hurt, when I thought *I* was the one who was supposed to be hurt. But I was so upset about the moving thing that it took me weeks to put the pieces together."

I draw back from him. Why should he be the hurt one? *He'd* excluded *me.*

There's an excruciating pause as his fingers tense and flex. "My sister lied. I didn't know about the party until we got home and a crowd of people jumped out and yelled 'surprise.' Cal told me that she'd invited you, and that you'd turned her down. I believed her. It wasn't until later that I realized you were hurt because she hadn't."

Anger swells inside of me. "Why would she do that?"

He looks ashamed. "She dodged the question, but it's obvious, isn't it? She claimed she was trying to do something nice—throw a party for me, not for her or for the both of us. Sometimes . . . I get overlooked. But she did it out of fear, because she thought she was losing me."

"You mean, she did it out of spite, because she's a bitch." My own fury startles me.

"I know it seems that way, but it's not. And it is." Cricket shakes his head. "It's been the two of us for so long. Her career hasn't given her much of an outside life. She was scared of being left behind. And I'm just as guilty; I let her get away with acting like that, because she was all I had, too."

No. She wasn't.

He stares at his hands. Whatever word he wrote there, it's been crossed off. There's only a black box. "Lola, you were the *only* person I wanted there that night. I was crazy about you, but I didn't know what to do. It was paralyzing. There were so many times when I wanted to take your hand, but . . . I couldn't. That one small move felt impossible."

Now I'm staring at my hands, too. "I would have let you take it."

"I know." His voice cracks.

"I had a present for you and everything."

"I'm sure I would have loved it. Whatever it was." He sounds heartbroken, and the sound breaks mine. "I had something for you, too."

"On *your* birthday?" That's so like him. There's another sharp pain in my chest.

"I made this mechanism that could run between our windows, and I thought we could use it to send each other letters or gifts. Or whatever. It sounds stupid now, I know. Something a little kid would think up."

No. It doesn't sound stupid.

"It was supposed to be ready on your birthday, but I wanted it to be perfect. At least, that's what I kept telling myself. But I was stalling. I blew it. I messed up everything."

I rip off the end of my hummus wrap. "*Calliope* messed up everything."

"No. She never would have been a problem if I'd told you how I felt. But I didn't, not even when I knew we were moving—"

"You knew you were moving?" I'm shocked. For some reason, this news is worse than Calliope's betrayal. How could he keep that from me?

"I couldn't tell you." His body twists in misery. "I thought you'd give up on me. And I kept hoping the move wouldn't actually happen, but it was confirmed that night."

He waits for me to look at him. Somehow, I do. I'm overwhelmed by sadness and confusion. I can't take any more. I want him to stop, but he doesn't. "I'll only say this once more. Clearly, so there's no chance of misinterpretation." His eyes darken into mine. "I like you. I've always liked you. It would be wrong for me to come back into your life and act otherwise."

I'm crying now. "Cricket . . . I have a boyfriend."

"I know. That sucks."

It surprises me, and I give a choked laugh. Cricket pushes a napkin toward me to blow my nose. "I'm sorry," he says. "Was it wrong for me to say that?"

"No."

"Are you sure?"

"No."

We're able to laugh as I wipe away my mascaraed tears, but our lunch is resumed in agonizing silence. The distance between us feels too close, too far, too close. It's warmer than it should be underneath this green canopy. My mind throbs. *I've always liked you*. What would my life have been like had I known this unquestionably?

He still would have moved away.

I've always liked you, I've always liked you, I've always liked you.

But maybe we would have stayed in contact. Maybe we'd even be together now. Or maybe I would have lost interest. Am I only fixated on Cricket because of our traumatic history? Because he was my first crush? Or does something about him transcend that?

He's polishing the skin of a golden apple against his arm. Faeries. Temptation.

"Remember that day I made you the elevator?" he suddenly asks.

I give him a faint smile. "How could I forget?"

"That was the day I had my first kiss."

My smile fades.

"I'm better now." He sets the apple beside me. "At kissing. Just so you know."

"Cricket . . ."

He holds my gaze. His smile is sad. "I won't. You can trust me."

I try not to cry again. "I know."

Despite this complication—knowing he liked me then, knowing he likes me now, and knowing he never purposefully hurt me—as we walk through the woods, the smoky haze between us lifts. The air is tender but clear. Am I that selfish? Did I just need to feel desired? But when I study him on the drive home . . . I can't help but notice his eyes.

There's something about blue eyes.

The kind of blue that startles you every time they're lifted in your direction. The kind of blue that makes you ache for them to look at you again. Not blue green or blue gray, the blue that's just blue.

Cricket has those eyes.

And his laugh. I'd forgotten how easy it is. The four of us are laughing about something dumb in that silly way that happens when you're exhausted. Cricket tells a joke and turns to see if I'm laughing, if I think he's funny, and I want him to know that I *do* think he's funny, and I want him to know that I'm glad he's my friend, and I want him to know that he has the biggest heart of anyone I've ever known. And I want to press my palm against his chest to feel it beat, to prove he's really here.

But we cannot touch.

Everyone laughs again, and I'm not sure why. Cricket looks for my reaction again, and I can't help but laugh. His eyes light up. I have to look down, because I'm smiling so hard back. I catch my parents in the rearview mirror. They have a different kind of smile, like they know a secret that we don't.

But they're wrong. I know the secret.

I close my heavy eyes. I dream about reaching across the backseat and touching his hand. Just one hand. It closes slowly, tightly around mine, and the sensation of his skin against mine is *astounding.* I've never felt anything like it before.

I don't wake until I hear his voice. "Who's that?" he asks sleepily.

Some people claim to know when something bad is about to happen, right before it actually occurs. I feel dread at his question, though I can't say why. His tone was innocent enough. Maybe it's the silence in the front seat that's so deafening. I open my eyes as the car stops in front of our house. And I discover the deep feeling in my gut is right. It's always right.

For there, passed out on the front porch, is my birth mother.

chapter fourteen

Skin and bones. I haven't seen Norah in months. I don't know how it's possible, but she's lost more weight. For as long as I can remember, Norah has been too skinny. Now—body propped against the porch railing, sweater balled into a pillow to support her head—she looks like a pile of twigs wrapped in hippie rags.

Is she just asleep? Or has she been drinking again?

I flush with shame. *That's my mother.* I don't want Cricket to recognize her, even though it's obvious the pieces have been put together, now that the question hangs in the air. Nathan is rigid. He pulls the car into our driveway and turns off the engine. No one gets out. Andy swears under his breath.

"We can't leave her there," he says, after a minute passes.

Nathan climbs out, and Andy follows. I turn in my seat to watch them prod her, and she immediately startles awake. I release a breath that I didn't realize I'd been holding. I get out of the car, and I'm blasted by the stench of body odor. Cricket is beside me, and he's talking, but his words don't reach my ears.

Because it's my mother.

Smelling.

On my porch.

I duck away from him and push up the stairs, past Norah and my parents. "I fell asleep waiting for you to come home," she snaps to them. "I'm not drunk. Just evicted." But I focus on my key in my hand, my key in the lock, my feet to my bedroom. I collapse in bed, but a voice says something about a curtain, it won't stop talking about a curtain, so I haul myself up to shut it and then I'm back down. I hear them in the living room.

"Eighteen months?" Nathan asks. "You told me it'd been twelve since your last payment. I thought we'd worked this out. What do you expect me—"

"I DON'T NEED YOUR HELP. I JUST NEED A PLACE TO CRASH."

The whole neighborhood can hear that. It takes nine long minutes before she lowers her voice. I watch the clock on my phone.

Lindsey calls. I stare at her name, but I don't answer.

When I was little, I thought my parents were just best friends who lived together. I wanted to live with Lindsey when I grew up. It took a while for me to understand that the situation was more complicated than that, but by the time it happened, it didn't matter. My parents were my parents. They loved each other, and they loved me.

But there's always been this nag in the darkest corner of my mind.

I was right for Nathan and Andy, like they were right for me. Why wasn't I right for Norah? I know she wasn't in any condition to take care of me, but why wasn't I enough for her to *try*? And why aren't we—the three of us, her family—enough for her to try now? She may not be on the streets anymore, but . . . well, this time, she *is*. Why is it so impossible for her to be a normal adult?

My phone buzzes. Lindsey has sent a text:

i heard. what can i do? xoxo

My heart falls like a stone. She heard? How long was Norah outside? How many people saw her? I imagine what my classmates will say when they find out that I have *loser* wired into half of my genetic code. *Figures. It's the only explanation for someone* that *screwed up. She must have been wasted while Lola was in the womb.* But that's not even true. I'm not half loser. I'm one hundred percent. I was created from street trash.

Andy knocks on my door. "Lo? Can I come in?"

I don't reply.

He asks again, and when I don't answer, he says, "I'm coming in." My door opens. "Oh, honey." His voice is heartbroken. Andy sits on the edge of my bed and places a hand on my back, and I burst into tears. He picks me up and holds me, and I feel small and helpless as I cry all over his sleeve.

"She's so embarrassing. I hate her."

He hugs me harder. "Sometimes I do, too."

"What's gonna happen?"

"She'll stay here for a while."

I pull back. "For how long?" I've left a puddle of red eye shadow on his shoulder. I try to wipe it away, but he gently takes my hand. The shirt doesn't matter.

"Only a week or two. Until we can find a new apartment for her."

I stare at my red fingertips, and I'm angry that Norah has made me cry again. I'm angry that she's in *my* house. "She doesn't care about us. She's only here because she doesn't have any other options."

Andy sighs. "Then we don't have any option but to help her, do we?"

It grows dark outside. I call Lindsey.

"Thank God! Cricket called two hours ago, and I've been so worried. Are you okay? Should I come over? Do you want to come over here? How bad is it?"

An explosion in my mind. "Cricket told you?"

"He was concerned. I'm concerned."

"*Cricket* told you?"

"He called the restaurant and gave my parents his number, and then told them to tell me to call him. He said it was an emergency."

I grip my phone harder. "So you didn't see her, then? Or hear her? Or hear about it from anyone else?"

Lindsey realizes what the issue is. Her voice softens. "No. I haven't heard anything, neighborhood-wise. I don't think anyone noticed her."

And I'm relieved enough to let the sadness and frustration flood back in. After nearly a minute of silence, Lindsey asks again if I'd like to stay with her. "No," I say. "But I might take you up on it tomorrow."

"She wasn't . . . was she?"

It's easy enough to fill in her blank. "Not wasted, not high. Just Norah."

"Well," she says. "At least there's that."

But it's humiliating that she had to ask. There's a beep on the other line. Max. "I have to go." I switch calls with dread. A vision of my boyfriend at brunch with Norah flashes through my head. This is bound to put an even bigger strain on his relationship with my family. What will he think of her? Will it change his opinion about me? And what if . . . what if he finds something of myself in Norah?

"I missed you," he says. "You coming to the show tonight?"

I'd forgotten about it. I've been so fixated on last night's show that I didn't remember he'd be back here for another one tonight. "Um, I don't think so." The tears are already building. *No, no, no. Don't cry. I'm sick of crying today.*

I practically hear him sitting up. "What's going on?"

"Norah is here. She's staying with us."

Silence. And then, "Fuuuuck." He says it like an exhale. "I'm sorry."

"Thanks. Me, too," I add.

He gives a small, understanding snort of laughter, and then I'm surprised by how angry he gets when I tell him the full story. "So she expects you guys to bail her out of this?"

I roll onto my side, still on my bed. "Like we always do."

"It's messed up your dads are letting her take advantage of them again."

The thought has occurred to me many times over the years, but I still don't know if it's true. Are they—Nathan, especially—enabling her? Or would she be even more lost without them? "I don't know," I say. "She doesn't have anyone else to turn to."

"Listen to yourself. You're defending them. If I were you, I'd be pissed. I'm not you, and I'm *still* pissed."

His anger refuels my own. It's getting easier to talk about it, to talk about everything. We go for another hour until he needs to pack the van for his show. "Do you want me to pick you up?" he asks.

I tell him yes.

I get dressed with a fury I haven't felt in years. I find a gauzy black dress that I've never liked in the back of my closet, and I rip the hem shorter. Orange-and-yellow makeup. Red wig. Boots that lace to my knees.

Tonight, I'm fire.

I storm downstairs. My parents are talking quietly in the kitchen. I have no idea where Norah is, and I don't care. I throw open the front door, and there's a loud, "HEY!" but I'm already blazing down to the sidewalk. Where's Max? Where *is* he?

"Dolores Nolan, get your ass back in here," Nathan says from the doorway.

Andy is behind him. "Where do you think you're going?"

"I'm going to Max's show!" I yell back.

"You aren't going anywhere in that mood OR dressed like that," Nathan says. A familiar white van turns the corner and speeds up our hill. Andy swears, and my parents push out the door but block each other in the process. The van jerks to a halt. Johnny Ocampo slides the door open.

"Do *not* get in that van," Nathan shouts.

I give Johnny my hand. He pulls me inside and slams the door. I crash into a folded cymbal stand as the van lurches forward, and I shriek in pain. Max lets out a rapid string of profanity at the sight of blood running down my arm. The van jerks to another stop as he leans back to make sure I'm okay.

"I'm fine, I'm fine! Go!"

I look out the window to see my parents on the sidewalk, frozen in disbelief. And behind them, sitting on the steps of the lavender Victorian—as if they've been there for a long, long time—are Cricket and Calliope Bell.

The van roars away.

chapter fifteen

I shouldn't have come here.

It takes the band forever to set up, and I'm left alone the entire time. I didn't bring my phone, so I can't call Lindsey. The club is cold and unfriendly. I cleaned the blood off my arm in the bathroom, but it was only a scratch. I'm restless. And I feel stupid. My parents will be enraged, Norah will still be in my house, and the twins were witness to another foolish act. The memory of their expressions is almost too much to bear: the scorn of Calliope, the hurt of Cricket, the shock of my parents.

I'm in so much trouble.

As always, my mind returns again and again to Cricket Bell. Muir Woods seems like a lifetime ago. I remember *what* I felt, but I can no longer remember *how.*

"Lola?"

WHAT'S THAT? WHO'S HERE? Who did my parents send? I'm almost surprised they haven't showed up themselves—

"We thought it was you." It's Anna.

"Hard to tell sometimes." And St. Clair.

They're holding hands and smiling, and I'm so relieved that I fall back against the club's brick wall. "Ohthankgod, it's you."

"Are you *drunk*?" she asks.

I straighten and hold up my chin. "NO. What are you doing here?"

"We're here to see Max's band," St. Clair says slowly.

"Since you invited us? Last week? Remember?" Anna adds at my confusion.

I don't remember. I was so worried about Max touring and the day trip with Cricket that I could have invited the editor of *Teen Vogue* and forgotten about it. "Of course. Thanks for coming," I say distractedly.

They don't buy it. And I end up spilling another private story to them: the story of my birth parents. Anna grasps the banana on her necklace as if the tiny bead is a talisman. "I'm sorry, Lola. I had no idea."

"Not many people do."

"So Cricket was with you when you found her on your porch?" St. Clair asks.

His question snags my full attention. I'd purposefully left Cricket out of the story. I narrow my eyes. "How did you know that?"

St. Clair shrugs, but he looks self-chastised. Like he said

something he shouldn't have. "He mentioned something about taking a road trip with you. That's all."

He knows.

St. Clair knows that Cricket likes me. I wonder if they've already talked this evening, if St. Clair already knew what happened with my mother. "I don't believe it," I say.

"Pardon?" he says.

"Cricket told you. He told you about all of this, about my mother." Anger rises inside of me again. "Is that why you're here? Did he send you to check up on me?"

St. Clair's countenance hardens. "I haven't spoken with him in two days. You invited Anna and myself here, so we came. You're welcome."

He's telling the truth, but my temper is already boiling. Anna grabs my arm and walks me forward. "Fresh air," she says. "Fresh air would be good."

I throw her off and feel terrible at the sight of her wounded expression. "I'm sorry." I can't look at either of them. "You're right. I'll go alone."

"Are you sure?" But she sounds relieved.

"Yeah. I'll be back. Sorry," I mumble again.

I spend a miserable fifteen minutes outside. When I come back, the club is packed. There's hardly standing room. Anna has snagged a wooden bar stool, one of the few seats here. St. Clair stands close to her, facing her, and he smoothes the platinum stripe in her hair. She pulls him even closer by the top of his jeans, one finger tucked inside. It's an intimate gesture. I'm embarrassed to watch, but I can't look away.

He kisses her slowly and deeply. They don't care that anyone could watch. Or maybe they've forgotten they aren't alone. When they break apart, Anna says something that makes him fall into silly, boyish laughter. For some reason, that's the moment that makes me turn away. Something about their love is painful.

I turn toward the bar for a bottle of water, but Anna calls out to me again. I head back, feeling irrationally aggravated that they're here.

"Better?" St. Clair asks, but not in a mean way. He looks concerned.

"Yeah. Thanks. Sorry about all that."

"No problem." And I think we're leaving it at that when he adds, "I understand what it's like to be ashamed of a parent. My father is not a good man. I don't talk about him either. Thank you for trusting us."

His serious tone throws me, and I'm touched by this rare glimpse into his life. Anna squeezes his hand and changes the subject. "I'm looking forward to this." She nods toward the band onstage. Max's guitar is slung low as he adjusts something on his amplifier. They're about to start. "You'll introduce us to him afterward, right?"

Max has been too busy to come out and say hello. I feel bad about this. I feel bad about *everything* tonight. "Of course. I promise."

"You neglected to mention that he's much cooler than us." Worry has crept into her voice.

St. Clair, back to himself, is clearly ready with a catty reply, and I'm pleased that the moment he opens his mouth is the same moment Amphetamine explodes into their set. His words—all words but my boyfriend's—are lost.

The intensity radiating from Max mirrors what I feel burning inside of myself. His lyrics are by turn tender and sweet, scathing and cruel. He sings about falling in love and breaking up and running away, and it's nothing that hasn't been sung before, but it's the way he sings it. Every word is saturated in bitter truth.

Johnny and Craig push an aggressive rhythm, and Max attacks his guitar with string-breaking ferocity. The songs become openly malicious, as if even the assembled crowd is to be distrusted, and when it's time for the acoustic number, his usual soul-searching turns belligerent and cynical. His amber eyes lock with mine across the room, and I'm filled with his vicious attitude. I know it's wrong, but it only makes me want him more. The crowd is fevered and delirious. It's the best performance he's ever given.

And it's for me.

When it's over, I turn to my friends for their reaction. Anna and St. Clair look shocked. Impressed but . . . definitely shocked.

"He's good, Lola. He's *really* good," Anna says at last.

"Has he considered therapy?" St. Clair asks, and Anna elbows him in the ribs. "Ow." I glare at him, and he shrugs. "It was incredible," he continues. "I'm merely pointing out the presence of untempered rage."

"How can you—"

"I need the bathroom," Anna says. "Please don't kill my

boyfriend while I'm gone. And don't leave until I've met Max!"

He's weaving his way toward us now. People are clapping him on the back and trying to engage him in conversation, but Max's eyes are only on mine as he brushes past them. My heart beats faster. The dark roots of his bleached hair and his black T-shirt are sweaty. I'm reminded of the night we met, and there's a flare inside of me that's near animalistic.

Max stiffens as he reaches for an embrace. He's noticed St. Clair. Max's jaw tightens as he sizes him up, but St. Clair slides in an easy introduction. "Étienne St. Clair. My girlfriend Anna"—he points to her retreating figure—"and I work with Lola at the theater. You must be Max."

My boyfriend relaxes. "Right." He shakes St. Clair's outstretched hand, and then he's already pulling me away. "Come on. Let's get out of here."

Max. Yes, I want to be with Max.

"Thanks for coming. Tell Anna bye for me, okay?"

St. Clair looks royally pissed. "Yeah. Sure."

Max leads me down the block to his van. He opens the door, and I'm surprised to discover it's still empty. We climb in. "The next band is using Johnny's drums. I asked the guys to wait a few minutes before loading the rest."

I slam the door, and we're on top of each other. I want to forget everything. I kiss him hard. He pushes back harder. It doesn't take long.

We collapse.

I close my eyes. My temples are still throbbing with the sound of his music. I hear the flick of Max's lighter, but the smell that greets me isn't cigarette smoke. It's sweet and sticky. He nudges me in a silent offer. I refuse. The contact high is enough.

Max drops me off around two in the morning. I forget my wig in his van. I feel like a disaster. Once again, I'm racked with guilt and anger and confusion. I drag myself inside, and my parents are there, as if they've been waiting by the door since I left. They probably have. I brace myself for their wrath.

It doesn't come.

"Thank God." Andy crumples onto our chaise longue.

My parents are both on the verge of tears, and the sight makes me cry for the hundredth time today, huge embarrassing hiccuping sobs. "I'm sorry."

Nathan embraces me in an iron-tight hug. "Don't you *ever* do that again."

I'm shaking. "I won't. I'm sorry."

"We'll talk about this tomorrow, Dolores." Nathan leads me upstairs, and Andy trails behind. I'm closing my bedroom door when Nathan says, "You smell like pot. We'll talk about that tomorrow, too."

I open my window and look into the night sky. "I need your help."

The moon is thin, a sliver of a waning crescent. But she's listening.

It's four in the morning. I can't sleep, so I tell her about my last twenty-four hours. "And I don't know what to do," I say. "It's all happening at once, but everything I do seems to be wrong. *What am I supposed to do?*"

Cricket's window slides open. I dive for my closest pair of glasses so that I can see him. His hair is puffy from sleep, even taller than usual, and his eyes are half shut. "You still talk to the moon?" His question isn't condescending, it's curious.

"Pretty dumb, huh?"

"Not at all."

"Did I wake you up? Did you hear me?"

"I heard you talking, but I didn't hear what you said."

I let out a slow exhale of relief. I need to be more careful. It doesn't escape my attention that it's nice to know when someone is telling the truth. "What are you doing here?" I ask. "It's Sunday night, you should be in your dorm."

Cricket is quiet. He's deciding how to answer. A car with thumping club music cruises down our street, looking for parking. When the bass fades away, he says, "I wanted to make sure you were okay. I was waiting for your light to come on. I fell asleep." He sounds guilty.

"Oh."

"I'll leave early in the morning." Cricket glances across his room at a clock. He sighs. "In two hours, actually."

"Well, I'm here. I made it. Barely."

He stares at me. It's so intense that it's almost invasive. I look down at the alley between our houses, and a stray cat is wandering through Andy's compost pile. "You didn't have to do that," I say.

"I probably shouldn't have. I'm not the right person for you to talk to."

"Is that why you called Lindsey?"

He shrugs uncomfortably. "Did you talk with her? Before you left?"

"Yeah."The cat jumps onto our recycling bin. It looks up, and its haunted eyes flash at me through the darkness. I shiver.

"You're cold," Cricket says. "You should go to bed."

"I can't sleep."

"Do you feel better?" he blurts. "Did Max help?"

I'm filled with shame. "I don't know," I whisper.

We're silent for several minutes. I turn my head and watch the street, the moon, the street. I feel him watch me, the stars, me. The wind is biting. I want to go inside, but I'm afraid to lose his company. Our friendship is teetering on the verge of extinction again. I don't know what I want, but I do know that I don't want to lose him.

"Cricket?"

"Yeah?"

I peel my gaze from the sky to meet his eyes. "Will you come home next weekend?"

He closes them. I get the strangest sense he's thanking someone.

"Yes," he says. "Of course."

chapter sixteen

Nathan wakes me up early so we can talk before school. Also as punishment, I assume. I've only had three hours of sleep. As I'm getting dressed, I peek through my curtains and discover that Cricket has left his open. His usual leather satchel and laundry bag are gone.

There's a pang in the hollow of my chest.

I drag myself downstairs. Andy is awake—he's never awake this early—and he's making scrambled eggs. Nathan is checking his email at the table in one of his nicest suits. There's no sign of Norah. She's probably on the foldout couch in Nathan's office.

"Here." Andy slides a mug of coffee toward me. He doesn't approve of me drinking coffee, so this is serious. We take seats beside Nathan, and he sets aside his phone.

"Lola, we understand why you left last night," he says.

I'm shocked. I'm also relieved that I'm Lola, not Dolores.

Nathan continues, "But it doesn't excuse your behavior. You scared us to death."

Now that sounds about right.

The lecture I'd expected follows. It's painful, it's extensive, and it ends with me receiving a month of grounding. They don't believe me when I tell them I didn't smoke the pot, which they know was Max's, and I can't convince them otherwise on either point. I get a lengthy side lecture about the hazards of drug use, to which I could just as easily point to the closed office door and say, "Duh."

But I don't.

My walk to school is long, my day at school even longer. Lindsey tries to entertain me with stories about the twitchy man her parents hired to help in the restaurant. She's convinced he has a dark secret like a hidden identity or the knowledge of a government cover-up. But all I can think about is tonight. I don't have work. I don't have a date with Max, and I *won't* have one apart from Sunday brunch—if he'll even show up anymore—for another month. And . . . no Cricket.

At least the next month will give me plenty of time to work on my dress.

The thought doesn't cheer me. The stays are progressing faster than expected, and I've even started the wig, but the panniers are frustrating. I still can't find any satisfying instructions. I spend my afternoon doing homework, chatting online with Lindsey, and adding chicken wire to the top of my white base wig. Marie Antoinette wore ENORMOUS wigs. The wire will give it the necessary height without drastically increasing the weight. I'll cover it later with matching fake hair.

Norah is talking with Andy in the kitchen. They picked up her things today, and the boxes have covered Nathan's antiques and taken over our entire living room. The cardboard smells like incense and grime. Norah's voice is weary, and I wince and turn up my music. I still haven't seen her. I'll have to soon, but I'm putting it off as long as possible. Until dinner, I guess.

The doorbell rings at six-thirty.

I pause—my pliers on the wire, my ears perked. Cricket?

But then I hear Max's deep and gravelly voice. My pliers drop, and I'm skidding downstairs. *There's no way, there's no way, there's no way.* Except . . . there he is. He's even abandoned his usual black T-shirt for a striped button-up. His tattoos poke out of the bottom of his sleeves. And he's wearing his glasses, of course.

"Max," I say.

He smiles at me. "Hey."

Andy looks as surprised as I feel. He's clueless about what to do next. I throw my arms around Max. He hugs me back tightly but pulls away after only a moment. *"Wanted to make sure you're surviving,"* he whispers.

I squeeze his hand and don't let go. I had no idea how much I needed to see him again, to know everything is okay between us. I'm not sure why I thought things would be different, other than last night *felt* different. He's apologizing to my father. I know it must be killing him to do this. He states his words calmly and briefly.

"Thank you for saying that, Max." Andy hesitates, despising what he knows has to come next. "Won't you stay for dinner?"

"Thank you. I'd love to."

Max knew my parents would be out to get him, and he's called them on it by showing up tonight. He's so smart.

"So you're the boyfriend."

Max, Andy, and I grow rigid as Norah leans against the door frame between our living room and the kitchen. Even though Nathan is several years older than his sister, Norah looks at least a decade older. In their childhood, she shared the same round face as Nathan and me, but time and substance abuse have left her frail and worn. Her skin hangs as loose as her straggled hair. At least she's had a shower.

"Max. Meet Norah," I say.

He nods at her. She stares back, her expression dead.

"You have a *lot* of nerve showing up here."

Everyone freezes again at the sound of Nathan's voice. Still holding hands, Max and I turn around. My father sets down his briefcase beside the front door. The muscles in Max's hand twitch, but he keeps his speech devoid of the emotion I know he feels. "I came to apologize. It was irresponsible for me to take Lola away last night. She was upset, and I wanted to help her. It was the wrong way."

"Damn straight it was the wrong way."

"Dad."

"Nathan," Andy says quickly. "Let's talk in the office."

The wait is unbearable before Nathan removes his glare from Max and follows Andy. The office door shuts. I'm sweating. I let go of Max's hand and realize my own is shaking. "The worst is over," he says.

"I'm grounded for a month."

He pauses. "Shit."

There's a rude snort in the kitchen doorway, and I'm about to completely lose it.

"I'm sorry." Now Max *does* sound pissed off. "I didn't realize this conversation was any of your business."

Norah gives a cruel smile. "You're right. What would I know about a teenage girl running away and getting into trouble with her boyfriend?"

"I didn't run away," I protest as Max says, "You're out of line."

She strolls into the kitchen and out of sight. "Am I?" she calls out.

I want to die. "I'm so sorry. For all of this."

"Don't apologize." He's harsh. "I'm not here for them. I'm here for you."

The office door bangs open, and Nathan marches straight upstairs to their bedroom without looking at us. Andy gives a tense, fake smile. "Dinner in ten minutes."

Nathan has changed out of his work clothes. He's trying, but barely. I didn't know it was possible to pass a dish of vegetarian lasagna with such hostility. "So. Max. How was the show in L.A.? We didn't realize you'd be back so soon."

Could this get any worse?

"It was in Santa Monica, and it went well. We've booked two more shows there."

Yes. It *could* get worse.

"Do you plan on doing a lot of touring?" Andy asks. I can't decide if he sounds hopeful or skeptical.

"We'd like to do more. I don't want to read meters for the rest of my life."

"So you think this is a valid career choice?" Nathan asks. "You think it's reasonable to expect success?"

"OH MY GOD," I say.

Nathan holds up his hands in apology, but he doesn't say anything. Max stews silently beside me. Norah stares out the window, no doubt longing to be anywhere but here. I scrape the spinach lasagna across my plate without picking it up.

"I only mentioned the show," Nathan says a minute later, "because it was unfortunate that it meant you had to miss our trip. We went to Muir Woods with—"

"A picnic basket!" I say.

Nathan gives me a smug expression. It was a test. He was testing *me,* to see if Max knew about the trip with Cricket.

"You didn't miss anything," I say. "Besides the food. Of course."

Max smells the lie, though he doesn't dare approach it in front of my parents. But I feel the wall build between us.

"Hey, I have an idea," I say. "Let's talk about Norah."

"Lola," Andy says.

She snaps her head toward me as if coming out of a trance. "What?" And then she blinks. "What are you wearing?"

"Excuse me?"

"What is that? What are you supposed to be?"

I'm in a dress with rainbow tulle poking out from underneath, and my hair is in two long braids that I've gelled with glitter. I glare at her. "Me. I'm *me*."

Norah frowns her disapproval, and Nathan turns to her. "Enough. Back off."

"Of course she has the right to complain about my wardrobe." I gesture to her saggy sweater, the one she's had forever that's the color of oatmeal left in the sink. "She's clearly on the cutting edge of fashion."

Max smirks.

"O-kaaaay!" Andy jumps up. "Who wants pie?"

"Wait until you see my dress for the winter formal," I tell Norah. "It's big and it's lavish and it's beautiful, and you're just going to *love* it."

Norah jerks her face back toward the window. Like she has any right to feel hurt after attacking me. Max stiffens again, and Nathan can't resist pouncing upon it. "What will you wear to the dance, Max?"

"He'll wear a tux," I snap. "I wouldn't make him wear a matching costume."

Max stands. "I gotta go."

I burst into tears. Nathan looks shamed. Max takes my hand and walks me to the front door. We step outside. I don't care that I'm grounded. "I'm s-sorry."

This time he doesn't tell me not to apologize. "That was messed up, Lola."

"I know."

"So tell me, did Nathan approve of Norah's 'career choice' as a fortune-teller?"

I feel sick. "It won't be that bad on Sunday."

"Sunday." Max lifts a dark brow. "Brunch. Right." He drops my hand and puts his own in his pockets. "So are you serious about that dance?"

I'm startled. I've talked about my dress a hundred times before. I wipe the tears from my cheeks, wishing I had something other than my fingers. "What?"

"Lola. I'm twenty-two." Max reacts quickly to my crushed expression. He reaches for both of my hands this time, and he draws me into and against his body. "But if it makes you happy, I'll do it. If I can survive these stupid meals, I can survive one stupid dance."

I hate that it sounds like a punishment.

chapter seventeen

"Ta-da!" St. Clair bursts into the lobby with the flourish of a magician. He's showing off for Anna as he always does. It's Thursday, and he isn't scheduled to work, but of course he's here anyway. Though tonight is different.

He's brought someone.

Here's the thing about Cricket Bell. You can't NOT notice him when he walks into a room. The first thing that registers is his height, but it's quickly followed by recognition of his energy. He moves gracefully like his sister, but with an enthusiasm he can't quite seem to control—the constantly moving body, hands, feet. He's been subdued the last few times I've seen him, but he's fully revived now.

"Anna," St. Clair says. "This is Cricket."

Cricket dwarfs St. Clair. They look like Rocky and Bullwinkle, and the comfortable manner between them makes it appear they've been friends just as long. I suppose when one overly kind person and one overly outgoing person become friends, it's easy like that.

Anna smiles. "We keep missing each other in the dorm. It's nice to finally meet you."

"Likewise," Cricket says. "I've heard nothing but good things. In fact, if I weren't standing next to your boyfriend, I'd be tempted to ask you out myself."

She blushes, and St. Clair bounds inside the box office and wrestles her into a hug. "Miiiiiiiine!" he says. The couple buying tickets from me eyes him warily.

"Cut it out." Anna pushes him off, laughing. "You'll get fired. And then I'll have to support your sorry *arse* for the rest of our lives."

The rest of their lives.

Why does this always make me uneasy? I'm not bothered that *they're* happy, am I? He hops into his usual sitting position on the counter, and they're already laughing about something else. Cricket waits on the other side of the glass, looking amused. I hand the couple their change. "So . . . what are you doing in the city on a weekday?" I ask him.

"I ran into St. Clair an hour ago, and he talked me into coming along. He said we'd see a movie," he adds loudly.

"RIGHT," St. Clair says. "That moving-pictures thing. Let's do it." But he returns to his conversation with Anna.

Cricket and I exchange smiles. "Come in." I nod at the box-office door. A man in a fuzzy chartreuse sweater approaches my window, but even that's not enough to distract me from watching Cricket as he moves toward the door. Those long, easy strides. My chest swells with both heartache and heartbreak. He enters, and I jerk away my gaze.

"Enjoy the show," I tell the sweater man. Cricket waits behind me while I print tickets for two more people. It's impossible to concentrate with him standing there. The lobby empties again, and he takes the chair beside me. His hems rise and reveal his socks. Blue and purple stripes. On his left hand is a list: CH 12, SHAMPOO, BOX.

"How are you?" he asks. It's not a casual question.

I remove my glasses for a moment to rub my tired eyes. "Surviving."

"But she won't be there for much longer." He fidgets with his watch. "Will she?"

"Her credit is shot, and she's failed the background check for every potential apartment."

He grimaces. "In other words, she's not leaving tomorrow."

"The break-in charges from when she tried to get back inside her apartment aren't helping either." I cross my arms. "She wants Nathan to sue to have the charges against her dropped, but he won't. Not when she was in the wrong."

Cricket's frown deepens, and I realize that he doesn't know about Norah's recent arrest. I fill him in, because . . . he already knows everything else.

"I'm sorry." His voice turns to anguish. "Is there anything I can do to help?" There's a certain restraint in his muscles as he struggles to keep from reaching out to me.

"What's box?" I blurt.

He's thrown. "What?"

I point at his hand. "Read chapter twelve and buy shampoo, right? What's box?"

His right hand absentmindedly covers his left. "Oh. Uh, I need to find one."

I wait for more.

He looks away, and his body follows him. "And I did. Find one. I'm moving some stuff back into my parents' house. My room at school is crowded. And my other bedroom is empty. It has lots of space. For things."

"You . . . you *do* spend a lot of weekends there."

"Andschoolbreaks andsummers." The words tumble out, and his face darkens as if shamed by his eagerness. No conversation is safe anymore. St. Clair interrupts with timing so perfect that he must have been listening. "Hey, did you know that *Cricket Bell* is related to *Alexander Graham Bell*?"

"Everyone who knows Cricket knows that," I say.

"Really?" Anna looks genuinely interested. "That's cool."

Cricket rubs his neck. "No, it's dumb trivia, that's all."

"Are you joking?" St. Clair says. "He's one of the most important inventors in the entire history of the world. Ever! And—"

"It's nothing," Cricket interrupts.

I'm taken aback, but then I remember that first night he was home, when I mentioned his middle name and our conversation grew awkward. Something has changed. But what?

"Forgive his enthusiasm." Anna grins at her boyfriend. "He's a history nerd."

I can't resist bragging. "Cricket happens to be a brilliant inventor himself."

"I'm not." Cricket squirms. "I mess around. It's not a big deal."

St. Clair looks enraptured. "Just think. You're the direct descendant of the man who invented"—he pulls out his cell—"this!"

"He didn't invent that," Cricket says drily.

"Well, not *this,*" St. Clair says. "But the idea. The first one."

"No." This is the most frustrated I've ever seen Cricket. "I mean he didn't invent the telephone. Period."

The three of us blink at him.

"Anna confused," Anna says.

"Alexander Graham Bell didn't invent the telephone, a man named Elisha Gray did. My great-great-great-grandfather stole the idea from him. And Gray wasn't even the first. There were others, one before Alexander was even born. They just didn't realize the full implications of what they'd created."

St. Clair is fascinated. "What do you mean, he stole the idea?"

"I mean, Alexander stole the idea, took credit for it, and made an unbelievable sum of money that shouldn't have been his." Cricket is furious now. "My family's entire legacy is based on a lie."

Well. That would explain the change.

St. Clair looks guilty for unintentionally goading Cricket into telling us. He opens his mouth to speak, but Cricket shakes his head. "Sorry, I shouldn't let it get to me."

"When did you learn this?" I ask quietly.

"A couple of years ago. There was a book."

I don't like the expression on his face. Further memories of his reluctance to talk about his inventions creep into my mind. "Cricket . . . just because he stole the idea doesn't mean what *you* do is—"

But he launches toward St. Clair. "Movie?"

Anna and I stare at him in concern, but St. Clair easily takes over again. "Yes, if you ladies no longer require our services, I believe we're off." Cricket is already halfway to the door. My heart screams in surprised agony.

He halts. It's as if he's physically stopped by something we can't see. "Will you be here later?" he asks me. "When the movie gets out?"

My throat dries. "I should be here."

He bites his bottom lip. And then they're gone.

"He's so into you," Anna says.

I rearrange a stack of quarters and try to calm my thumping chest. What just happened? "Cricket's a nice guy. He's always been like that."

"Then he's always been into you."

Yes. He has.

Anna whisks out the glass cleaner and sprays a smudge that

St. Clair left behind on the window. Her smile fades as she grows deeper in thought. "What's the matter?" I ask. I'm desperate for a topic change.

"Me? Nothing, I'm fine."

"No way," I say. "It's your turn. Spill it."

"It's . . . my family is coming to visit." She sets down the cleaner, but her hand tightens on the nozzle. "They met Étienne at our graduation last year, and they liked him, but my mom is pretty freaked out by how fast we're moving. This visit could be *so* uncomfortable."

I pry the cleaner away from her. "Do you think you're moving too fast?"

Anna loosens and smiles again, love-struck. "Definitely not."

"Then you'll be fine." I nudge her. "Besides, everyone loves your boyfriend. Maybe your mom has just forgotten how gosh darn *charming* he is."

She laughs. Another patron comes to my window, and I print his ticket. When he leaves, Anna turns back to me and asks, "What about you? How are things with Max these days?"

I'm struck by a terrible realization. "Oh, no. You wanted to meet him. We left!"

"You had a bad night." She shrugs. "Don't worry about it."

"Yeah, but—"

"It's okay, I swear. Everyone makes mistakes." Anna stands and grabs her work keys. "The important thing is to not make the same mistake twice."

My guilt deepens. "I'm sorry about last week. When I came back from dinner late."

She shakes her head. "That's not what I was thinking about."

"Then what?"

Anna looks at me carefully. "Sometimes a mistake isn't a what. It's a who."

And she goes to rip tickets down the hall, leaving me with thoughts as jumbled as ever. Does she mean Max? Or Cricket? An hour later, Franko wanders in. He's about thirty, and his hair is unevenly shorn. Like, he has random bald spots.

"Heeeeeey, Lola. Have you seen the thing?"

"What thing?"

"You know . . . the thing with . . . our schedules on it and stuff?"

"You mean our schedule?"

"Yeah. Have you seen it?"

I glance around. "Not in here. Sorry." But Franko is already sifting through a pile of papers on the counter. He knocks the phone off its hook, and I grab it. "Careful!"

"Did you find it?" Franko spins around as I'm coming up. His elbow jams into my face and knocks my glasses to the floor. "Whoops. I got it, Lola."

There's a sickening crunch of plastic.

"FRANKO!" My world has turned into blobs of color and light.

"Whoa. Sorry, Lola. Were those real?"

Anna rushes in. "What? What happened? Oh." She bends over to pick up what I assume are my glasses. Her voice doesn't sound promising. "Dude."

"What is it?" I ask.

"You can't see?" She holds them closer to my face. Pieces. Many, many pieces.

I moan.

"Sorry," Franko says again.

"Will you please go back to second-floor concessions?" Anna asks. He leaves. "Do you have another pair? Contacts? Anything?" she asks. I moan again. "Okay, no problem. Your shift is almost over. Your dad will be here soon to pick you up."

"I was supposed to take Muni." Of course tonight is the night my parents are busy and leave me to public transportation.

"But you can still take it, right?"

"Anna, you're two feet away, and I can't tell if you're smiling or frowning."

"Okay . . ." She sits down to think but immediately jumps back up. "Étienne and I will take you home! You're only a quick detour from my school."

"You don't have—"

"It's not a question," she interrupts. And I'm relieved to hear her say it. I'm useless for the remainder of my shift. We're ready to leave when the guys return, and Anna approaches the St. Clair–shaped blob. "We're taking Lola home."

"Why? What happened?" the Cricket-shaped blob asks.

I stare toward my shoes as I explain the situation.

"You can't see me?" St. Clair asks. "You have no idea what I'm doing?"

"Stop it," Anna says, and they laugh. I don't know what's happening. It's humiliating.

"I'll take you home," Cricket says.

St. Clair protests. "Don't you have—"

"I'm next door. It's not out of my way."

I'm ashamed of my own helplessness. "Thank you."

"Of course." The sincerity behind this simple statement tugs at me. He's not teasing me or making me feel bad about it. But Anna sounds worried as she hands me my purse. "Are you sure you'll be okay?"

The implied question: *Are you sure you'll be okay with Cricket?*

"I'm fine." I give her a reassuring smile. "Thanks." And it's true until we step outside, and I trip over the sidewalk.

Cricket grabs me.

And I collapse again from the shock of his touch. He lifts me up, and despite the coat between us, my arm is buzzing like a fire alarm. "The sidewalks here are the worst," he says. "The earthquakes have buckled them into land mines." Cricket removes his hand. I blink at him, and he cautiously offers his arm.

I hesitate.

And then I take it.

And then we're so close that I smell him. I *smell* him.

His scent is clean like a bar of soap, but with a sweet hint of mechanical oil. We don't speak as he leads me across the street to the bus stop. I press against him. Just a little. His other arm jumps, and he lowers it. But then he raises it again, slowly, and his hand comes to rest on top of mine. It scorches. The heat carries a message: *I care about you. I want to be connected to you. Don't let go.*

But then . . . he does.

He sits me on the bus stop's fold-down seats, *and he lets go,* and he won't look at me. We wait in agitated silence. The distance between us grows with each passing minute. Will he take my arm again, or will I have to take his? I steal a glance, but, of course, I can't see his expression. Our bus exhales against the curb, and the door whooshes open.

Cricket reaches for me.

I look at the yellow glow in the sky that can only be the moon. *Thank you.*

We climb aboard, and before I can find my Muni pass, he's paid for my ticket. The bus is empty. It rumbles forward, not waiting for us to sit, and he grabs me tighter. I don't need to hold on to him, but I do anyway, with both hands. We lower ourselves into a seat. Together. I'm clutching his shirt, and his heart is pounding like a drum.

"Hi," I whisper.

He peels off my hands and turns toward the aisle. "Please don't make this any harder than it already is," he whispers back.

And I feel like the world's biggest jerk.

"Right." I sink as far away from him as possible. "Sorry. No."

Max's ghost takes a seat between us. It spreads out its legs territorially. The bus is cold, and the ride to the station is short. This time, I have to take his arm. He leads me robotically. Our trip from Van Ness to the Castro is bleak. The train rocks back and forth through the dark tunnels, and my humiliation grows bigger and bigger with each forced jostle against his shoulder. I need out. NOW. The doors open, and I race through the station and out the turnstile. He's on my heels. I don't need him.

I don't need him, I don't need him, I don't need him.

But I trip on the sidewalk again, and his arm is around my waist, and when I pull from his grasp, he only tightens it. There's a silent struggle between us as I try to wriggle my way out. "For a skinny guy, your arms are like a steel trap," I hiss.

Cricket bursts into laughter. His grip loosens, and I break away, stumbling forward.

"Oh, come on, Lola." He's still laughing. "Let me help you."

"I'm never going anywhere again without a backup vision plan."

"I should hope not."

"And I'm only accepting your help because I don't want to run into something and accidentally rip this glorious polyester uniform."

"Understood."

"And *none* of this has changed *anything* between us." My voice shakes.

"Also understood," he says softly.

I take a deep breath. "Okay."

Neither of us moves. He's leaving it up to me. I tentatively reach for him again. He extends his arm, and I take it. The gesture of one friend helping another. There's nothing more, because as long as there's Max, there can't be anything more. And I love Max.

So that's that.

"So," Cricket says, one quiet block later. "Tell me about this famous dress."

"What dress?"

"The one you're making the stays for. It sounds important."

My conversation with Max rushes back in, and I'm embarrassed. Dances are such feminine affairs. I can't bear to hear scorn from Cricket, too. "It's for my winter formal," I say. "And it's *not* important."

"Tell me about it."

"It's . . . just a big dress."

"Big like a parachute? Big like a circus tent?"

As always, he makes me smile when I'm determined not to. "Big like Marie Antoinette."

He whistles. "That *is* big. What are those things called? Hoop skirts?"

"Sort of. In that period, they were called panniers. They went out to the side, rather than around in a perfect circle."

"Sounds challenging."

"It is."

"Sounds fun."

"Maybe it would be if I had any idea what I was doing. Panniers are these giant, structural contraptions. Making them isn't sewing; it's construction. And I have illustrations, but I can't find decent instructions."

"Do you want to show me the illustrations?"

My brow creases. "Why?"

He shrugs. "Maybe I could figure it out."

I'm about to say I don't need his help, when I realize . . . he's *exactly* the right person for the job. "Um. Yeah. That'd be nice, thanks." We've reached my steps. I gently squeeze his arm and let go. "I've got this part."

"I've taken you this far." His voice becomes unsteady. "I can take you that much farther." And he reaches for me one last time.

I brace myself for the contact.

"Cricket!" A call from between our houses, and his arm drops like an anchor. She must have been taking out the trash. Calliope hugs him from behind, and I can't really see her, but she sounds like she's about to cry. "Practice was a nightmare. I can't believe you're here, you said you couldn't come. God, it's good to see you. I'll make hot cocoa and tell you all— Oh. Lola."

Cricket is oddly petrified into silence.

"Your very kind brother walked me home from work," I explain. "My glasses broke, and I'm completely blind."

She pauses. "Where is it you work again? The movie theater?"

I'm surprised she knows. "Yeah."

Calliope turns back to Cricket. "You went to the movies? What about that huuuge project due tomorrow? I thought that's why you couldn't come home. How *strange*."

"Cal—" he says.

"I'll be in the kitchen." She stalks away.

I wait until she's inside. "You have a project due tomorrow?"

He waits a long time before answering. "Yes."

"You weren't coming home tonight, were you?"

"No."

"You came home for me."

"Yes."

We're quiet again. I take his arm. "Then take me home."

chapter eighteen

I'm encouraging him. And I can't stop.

Why can't I stop?

I press my palm against the front door, and my forehead comes to rest against it, too. I listen to his footsteps descend on the other side. They're slow, unhurried. I'm the one making our lives harder. I'm the one making this friendship difficult. *But he's the one who won't stop coming back.* He's smarter than that. He should know it's time to move on and to stay away from me.

I don't want him to stay away.

What DO I want? The answers are murky and unreadable, though it's clear I don't want another broken heart. Not his and certainly not mine. He needs to stay away.

I don't want him to stay away.

"That Bell boy grew up well," Norah says.

I startle. She's in the turquoise chaise longue that rests against the front bay window. How long has she been here? She must have seen us. Did she hear us? She watches him, until I assume his figure disappears, before turning her attention to me.

"You look tired, Lola."

"Speak for yourself."

"Fair enough."

But she's right. I'm exhausted. We stare at each other. Norah is blurry, but I can see enough. Her gray shirt hangs loosely against her chest, and she's wearing one of Andy's grandmother's old quilts wrapped around her for warmth. Her long hair and her thin arms are limp. Everything about her hangs. It's as if her own body has rejected her.

I wonder what she sees when she looks at me.

"You know what we need?" she asks.

I don't like her use of the word *we*. "What?"

"Tea. We need tea."

I sigh. "I don't need tea. I need to go to bed."

Norah pulls herself up. She groans as if her joints are sore, as if they were as old as the blanket around her shoulders. She takes my arm, and I flinch. The warm, comforting feeling of Cricket's hand disappears and is replaced by hers, clammy and sharp. She leads me into the kitchen, and I'm too worn out to stop her.

Norah pulls out a chair at the table. I sag into it.

"I'll be right back," she says. I hear her climb the stairs, followed by the sound of my bedroom door being opened.

Before I can get worked up, my door shuts again. She returns and hands me another pair of eyeglasses.

I'm surprised. "Thanks."

"What happened to the pair you left in?"

"They got stepped on."

"Someone stepped on your glasses?" Now she sounds pissed.

"Not on purpose. Jeez." I scowl. "Are my parents still on their date?"

"I guess. Why should I care?" She fills the copper teakettle with tap water and sets it down with more force than necessary. It shakes the stove.

"You had another fight," I say.

Norah doesn't respond, but the manner in which she roots through her cardboard box of tea is resentful and angry.

Her box of tea.

"No!" I jump up. "You're not reading my leaves."

"Nonsense. This is what you nee—"

"You don't know a thing about what I really need." The bitter words spit out before I can stop them.

She freezes. Her hair falls before her face like a shield. And then she tucks it behind her ears as if I didn't say anything, and she removes something from her box. "Fenghuang dancong oolong. Fenghuang means 'phoenix.' This is the one for you."

"No."

Norah opens our cabinet of drinking glasses and takes out a pink teacup. I don't recognize it, so it must be one of hers. My blood fires again. "You put your cups in our cabinets?"

"Just two." She pulls out another, the color of jade. "This one is mine."

"So where's your crystal ball? Beside the television? Will I find your turban in the laundry room?"

The empty cups rattle against their saucers as she sets them on the table. "You know I hate that crap. A costume doesn't signify meaning or experience. It's a lie."

"And what you do *isn't* lying?"

"Sit down," she says calmly.

"I've never let you read my leaves before, so why would I start now?"

Norah thinks for a moment. "Aren't you the least bit curious?"

"No." But I say it too quickly. She spots a waver as the back corners of my mind answer differently. Who isn't the least bit curious? I know fortune-telling is a deception, but my life has become such a struggle that I can't help but hope for an answer anyway. Maybe the fortune will tell me something about Cricket. Maybe it knows something I don't, or maybe it will make me think of something I wouldn't have otherwise realized.

Smugness on her lips. I sit back down but avert my eyes to show how much I dislike being here. The kettle whistles, and Norah scoops a spoonful of tea directly into it. The house creaks quietly while the oolong steeps. The longer we wait, the edgier I become. I almost get up to leave a dozen times, but curiosity has a strong hold on me.

"Drink," Norah says, when it's finished. "Leave about half a teaspoon of liquid."

I sip the tea, because it's hot. The flavor is light, and it tastes like a peach, but with something darker hidden inside. Like smoke. Norah doesn't mind the heat. She gulps hers down and pours another cup. I finally reach the bottom. I hold the pink cup close and frown at the brown-green leaves, looking for symbols. It's all lumped together.

"Now what?"

"Take the cup with your left hand."

"Is that my magic hand?"

She ignores this, too. "Now turn it three times, counter-clockwise—faster than that. Yes, good. Turn it over onto your saucer."

"Won't all the leaves run out?"

"Shh. Keep your hand on the bottom of the cup. And close your eyes and take a moment to think about what you'd like to know."

I feel stupid. THAT is what I think about. And . . . I think about Cricket Bell.

"Turn it back over. Carefully," she adds. I slow down and right my teacup. The leaves have used the last remaining droplets of liquid to stick to the sides. "I'll take that now." She's silent for many minutes. Her bony hands tilt the cup every which way, to gain different perspectives or perhaps just to see the shapes better in the dimmed kitchen light. "Well." Norah sets it down and gestures for me to scoot closer. I do. "Do you see this cloud here, close to the handle?"

"Sort of. Yeah."

"That means you're in a stage of confusion or trouble. But with me living here, we didn't need leaves to tell us that. And this triangle down here, that means you possess a natural talent for creativity. But we didn't need them to know that either."

I'm surprised by her frankness, as well as the rare compliment. I scoot a little closer.

"But do you see these dots, traveling around the edge of the cup?"

I nod.

"A path of dots means a journey. This one will be taken over the course of several months. If it circled all the way back around, it would have been at least a year," she explains. "But the journey ends here, into this shape. What does that look like to you?"

"Um. A moon, maybe? With a . . . stick coming out of it?"

"How about a cherry?"

"Yeah! I see that."

"Cherries represent first love. In other words, this path you're on leads to first love."

I jolt, and my legs smack the table. The way she doesn't startle makes me believe she expected this reaction. Does she know how I feel about Cricket? Or, should I say, how I felt about him in the past? She was certainly around, but how much did she observe?

Norah is messing with me.

She pauses. "Why don't you tell me what shapes you see in the cup?"

I stare into it for several minutes. I look for dogs or shoes or anything recognizable, but all I see are wet leaves. My eyes keep returning to the cherry. I set the cup down. "I don't know. There's a pile of sticks on that side. And a curlicue thing."

"Okay. The loop is near the rim, so that means you've been making—or you'll soon be making—impulsive actions."

"Good or bad?" I quickly ask.

She shrugs. "Could be either, but are things done on impulse ever really a good idea?"

"Is that something your therapist told you?" I snap.

Norah's tone darkens. "And see how the sticks are crossed, all on top of each other? That suggests a series of arguments. It usually leads to a parting." Her voice is short.

"A parting." I stand. "Yes, thank you. This was very educational."

Arguments, partings, impulses. Clouds of confusion. I thought fortunes were supposed to make people feel BETTER about their lives. I thought that's why people paid money to hear them. And a journey to first love? Just because Max insulted her doesn't mean she has to steer me into the arms of another guy.

Though it did look like a cherry.

I don't know why I'm giving any of this crap my consideration. Norah thinks my costumes are lies, that they lack meaning? She should look in the mirror. Her entire livelihood—what's left of it—lacks meaning. I'm steaming as I brush my teeth and get ready for bed. I turn off my lights just as a light behind my curtains flicks on.

So he's staying the night.

Has he been talking to Calliope? I wonder if he'll be able to complete his project for school, whatever it is. Probably not. I toss in my bedcovers, unable to sleep from the guilt over Cricket, from the caffeine in the tea, from that stupid freaking cherry. Maybe cherries don't mean first love. Maybe they mean the person you lose your virginity to. It would make more sense, and in that case, my path leads to Max.

Which means I'm on the right path?

I hear his window slide open.

And then . . . nothing more.

I don't know why, but I think he'll call my name. He doesn't. I grab my glasses and creep out of bed. I peer through the darkness. Cricket is looking up, staring at the sky. I watch him silently. He doesn't move. I reach for my curtain, that impulse I can't control, and open my window. "Hi," I say.

He looks directly at me. His eyes are deepened as if he's still staring at the stars.

"Is everything okay with your sister?"

Cricket nods slowly. "She'll survive."

"I'm sorry about your project."

"Don't worry about it."

"Will you get to make it up?"

"Maybe."

"Do . . . do you want those illustrations?"

A small smile. "Sure."

"Okay. Hold on." I dig through the piles on my floor until I find the binder of pictures printed from the internet and photocopies xeroxed from books—all of the inspiration for my dress that I've collected since I met Max at the beginning of summer. I return to my window, and Cricket is sitting in his, just like the first time I saw him again. At the end of summer. "Should I toss it to you?" I glance at Andy's compost pile below.

A split second of thought and he says, "I'll be right back."

He disappears, leaving me to observe his room. It's still bare, but traces of him have begun to appear—a science magazine by his bed, a pile of tangled rubber bands on his dresser, a half-filled juice glass on his desk, an unusual coat hanging on the back of his desk chair. Cricket returns a minute later with a broom and a metal basket of fruit. He removes the fruit, one by one, and sets them on his dresser.

I'm terrified he'll pull out a cherry.

He doesn't.

He places the empty basket on the wooden broom handle, raises the end, and the basket slides down to his hand. Cricket leans out his window and stretches out the broom handle. His arms are long enough that it reaches me with room to spare.

"Ready?"

I prepare for the catch. "Aye, Captain."

He tilts the broom, and the basket flies down the stick and into my arms. I laugh in delight. "You know, I really could have thrown it."

"Wouldn't want to take the chance. I might have missed it."

"You never miss a catch." I tuck the binder inside the basket. "It's kinda heavy."

"I've got it." Cricket holds the broom steady and up at an

angle. I stretch on my toes to slide the basket's handle onto the broom. I drop it. The weight lowers the broom, but he raises it in just enough time to send the basket flying back to him. "HA!" His belt buckle clicks against the window frame as he moves his body back inside, and I'm startled to recognize it. It's the same belt he's had for years—black, cracked leather. He pulls down his shirt, which has come up a bit. His torso is so long that shirts are always a little short on him. Another detail I'd forgotten.

I shake my head, trying to push away thoughts of his abdomen. But I'm smiling. "That was both ridiculously easy and way more complicated than it should have been."

He smiles back. "That's my specialty."

chapter nineteen

I'm ambushed as I pass the Bell house the next morning, but not by the preferred twin.

"We need to talk." Calliope's arms are crossed, and she's dressed in pale blue running clothes, the same shade of blue as her eyes. Cricket's eyes. The twins also share the same almost-black hair, although hers lies down neat and tidy. But their smiles are night and day. Cricket's looks as if it can't be helped, as if it can't *possibly* be contained, while Calliope's looks practiced. No doubt it is. I know how dedicated she is to practice.

She's clearly been waiting for me to come outside before beginning her daily run. To say that I'm unnerved would be a monumental understatement. "Talk about what?" I move today's schoolbag—a vintage glittery vinyl bowling bag—in front of my chest.

"What do you think you're doing?"

I glance around our street. "Um. Going to school?"

"With *my brother.*" Her voice grows even harder. "This stops now. I'm sick of watching you take advantage of him."

"Ex— excuse me?"

"Don't play dumb. You know exactly what I'm talking about. He's always been this total sucker for you; he'll do anything you say. So, tell me. Did you break up with your boyfriend last night before arriving home on Cricket's arm?"

My face reddens. "He offered to help me because my glasses broke. I couldn't see."

"And all of that flirting and pressing your chest into his arm? Did that also help?"

I'm too stunned to reply.

"My brother isn't like you," she continues. "He doesn't have a lot of experience. He's only had one girlfriend, and it wasn't for long, and she was barely that. I seriously doubt he's done anything more than kiss."

The blush grows deeper. The implication is that I *have* done more, which is *none* of her business.

"In other words, my brother is pretty freaking clueless when it comes to girls, and he can't tell when he's being had. But *I* can tell, so I'm telling you to BACK OFF."

My vision is blurring. I still can't find the words to speak.

Calliope takes a step closer. "The special trips home to see you, the crushing disappointment whenever he discovers you're out with Max. Stop jerking him around."

ENOUGH.

"You're mistaken." I straighten my spine, bone by bone. "Cricket and I are friends. Haven't you ever heard of friends?" I pause and then shake my head. "No, I guess not."

"I have a *best* friend. And you're messing with his head."

"Messing . . . *messing with his head*? What about you lying to him, two years ago? Telling him that I didn't want to come to his party?"

This time, she's the one who reddens.

"You're just worried you're losing him again. Now that he's gone to college, your life must be so *lonely*." I push past her. "It must be hard when your head cheerleader moves on and gets a life."

She grabs my coat to stop me. "This isn't about me."

"It's always about you." I shake her off, furious. "But just so you know, your brother has a life, too. He may not be performing for crowds, but he's just as talented. But you'd never notice it because your entire family is stuck in selfish Calliope world."

"Actually." The word is slow and venomous. "I have two talented brothers. And Cricket knows that we care about him."

"Does he? Are you sure about that?"

"He would say something." But suddenly she looks unsure.

"He does," I say through a clenched jaw. "To me, to *my* family. Now, if you don't mind, I'm going to be late for school."

Calliope's accusations hang over my head like black clouds. *Taking advantage of him.* I'm not doing anything on purpose—I would *never* intentionally hurt Cricket—but I was already aware that I haven't been doing him any favors. Hearing her point it out was awful, and I cringe every time I remember her mentioning the flirting.

More uncomfortable is the knowledge that Cricket had a girlfriend. Even if he is inexperienced, knowing he once dated someone shouldn't make me feel this way. Like my intestines are made of worms. I have Max, and Cricket should be allowed to have dated someone, too. To be dating someone now.

Oh God. The thought of Cricket with a new girlfriend makes me ill. *Please, please, please don't let him get a girlfriend until I become comfortable with this whole friendship thing.*

And then I feel worse, because jeez, what a selfish wish.

Max calls me after school to announce another Saturday night in Santa Monica. I knew the band had scheduled more shows down there, but the way he neglected to mention it earlier this week makes me paranoid that this is something additional, something booked to escape our brunch. I haven't seen him since that awful dinner. All I want to do is burrow into his arms and know that everything is still good between us.

He offers to take me out during my dinner break at work. We meet at a crappy Thai diner, and I can't keep my hands off him. I'm craving closeness. The owner shoots us dirty looks as we make out in the corner table.

"Come to my place after work?" he asks.

"Andy's picking me up, and I'm still grounded. What about tomorrow, before you leave? I can pretend like I have an early shift?"

"We're heading out early. There's a music store in L.A. we want to check out. Don't make that face, Lola-girl," he says when a pout slips onto my lips. He laces his fingers through mine. "I'll see you in a few days."

The weekend passes slowly without him. It also passes without Cricket. All I see of him is a sign, and not a sign like something in a teacup, but a sign written in black marker and taped to his window: SKATE AMERICA. SEE YOU NEXT WEEKEND. Why didn't he say earlier that he'd be out of town? Did Calliope tell him about our fight?

I want to call him, but I don't have his number. And I could ask Lindsey—I'm sure it's still saved in her phone—but it'd give the wrong impression for me to go out of my way like that. Calliope would probably bite me if she found out. So I do homework and stare at his sign instead.

Now it's Wednesday. It's still there.

And the more I've stared at his handwriting—very blocky, very boy—the more I want to prove to myself that we can be friends. I like Cricket. He likes me. It's not fair to let Calliope intimidate us out of even *trying*.

Which is, somehow, why I'm on a train to Berkeley. I think. In addition to the friendship thing, I've had increasingly distressing thoughts about my dress binder. I can't believe I gave it to him! THE WHOLE THING. Not, "Here are the relevant five pages." But six months of planning and daydreaming. What does he think when he looks at it? I recall each floofy, frilly, over-the-top picture, and my scribbled hearts and notes and doodles, and I want to die. He must think my brain is made of cake.

I have to get it back.

Besides, I'll also need my notes this week. I have a ton of work to do on the dress. So, really, it's practicality that led me onto a train as soon as school let out. The ones that run to the surrounding cities are sleeker than the ones that rumble through San Francisco. They rocket through the stations with fierce howls, but their passengers share the same tired and bored expressions. I fidget with my red, heart-shaped sunglasses and watch the dirty, industrial side of Oakland whiz by.

It's a lonely ride. It's only twenty minutes, but including the wait for the train at the station and the local train I took to get to *this* train, I've been traveling for over an hour. I can't believe St. Clair does this every day. Now I know when he does his homework. He travels an hour—two hours, since he has to return!—to see Anna. And she does this every weekend to see him.

What will Cricket say when I show up? He knows it's not a quick trip. Maybe I should tell him that I was vintage clothes shopping in the area, so I thought I'd drop by. Friends drop by, right? And then I can casually mention the binder and take it home. Yes, the friend thing and then the binder thing. Because that's why I'm going.

So why haven't you told Max?

I squirm in my seat and push away the question.

Apparently, I'm only grounded from things that involve my boyfriend. When I told Andy today that I was going to Lindsey's for a *Pushing Daisies* marathon, he didn't blink. He even gave me money to pick up a pizza. I think he feels guilty about Norah. It's been a week and a half, and there's still no sign of her leaving. Last night, one of her usuals even stopped by for a reading. My parents and I were already in bed when someone began pressing our doorbell like it was a panic button. I imagine that when Nathan gets home tonight, there'll be another hostile dispute. I bet Andy would rather be watching old television and eating pizza, too.

I'm not sure why I didn't tell him I'm visiting Cricket. I honestly don't think Andy would mind. Maybe I'm afraid my parents would mention it to Max. I mean, I *will* tell Max eventually, when it's really, really, really clear that Cricket and I are just friends.

When we're comfortable around each other.

I exit at the Downtown Berkeley station and head toward campus. Thanks to conversations with St. Clair, I know what dormitory Cricket lives in. I've printed out a map online. It shouldn't be too difficult to find, even though it's been a while. I used to drag Lindsey here sometimes on weekends to go shopping on Telegraph Avenue, but since last summer—and since Max—we haven't left the city together.

The buildings in this town look more California, less San Francisco. They're pretty, but they're newer and squarer. Instead of gingerbread Victorians with stained glass and peeling paint, they're made from stable brick. And there are beautiful trees everywhere, lining streets that are wider and cleaner and quieter.

It's busy enough, though, and everyone walking or bicycling around me is college-aged.

I push back my shoulders to appear more confident.

It's weird to think about Cricket living here. My memories of him are so connected to the lavender house in the Castro that it's difficult to picture him anywhere else. But that might be his drugstore. And that might be his taqueria. And that might be where he buys his Cal Golden Bears memorabilia!

No. It's impossible to picture Cricket in a T-shirt with a school mascot on it.

Which is why we are friends.

It takes another fifteen minutes to walk the long, sloping road to the Foothill Student Housing, and my mind can't help but add the time to St. Clair and Anna's tally. It's obscene how much time they spend getting to each other every day. And I've never heard them complain, not once. I can't even believe how often Cricket returns home. Lugging his laundry, no less!

An unsettling thought occurs to me.

His laundry bag. It's never full. Cricket has a large wardrobe for a guy; there's no way he's bringing *all* of his dirty clothes home. Which means he's doing some of his laundry here. Which means . . . what? The laundry is an excuse to come home? But he doesn't need an excuse to hang out with Calliope. She wants him there. So the excuse must have been crafted to strengthen a different reason for coming home.

Calliope's voice rings inside my head: *The special trips home to see you.*

An uncomfortable question lodges itself in the pit of my stomach. And what am I doing right now? *Making a special trip to see him.*

Oh, no—

I stop dead in my tracks. The Foothill Student Housing is TWO dormitories, on opposite sides of the street. I'd been expecting a high-rise. And I thought I'd be able to waltz in to some kind of . . . help desk. But I don't see anything resembling a help desk, and not only are there TWO dormitories, but each is made up of a series of labyrinth-like buildings shaped like Swiss chalets. Evil, evil Swiss chalets surrounded by tall gates.

WHAT AM I SUPPOSED TO DO?

Okay, calm down, Dolores. There's probably an easy solution. You can figure this out. No biggie. You've made it this far.

I try one of the gates. Locked.

ARRRRGHHHHHH.

Wait. Someone's coming! I pull out my cell and start chatting like crazy. "Ohmygod, I know. Did you see those spurs that urban cowboy was wearing at the gas station?" I pretend to reach for the gate just as the girl on the other side exits. She holds it open, and I give her a wave of thanks as I keep walking and chatting to no one.

I'm inside. I'M INSIDE.

Lindsey would be so proud! Okay, what would she do next? I examine the courtyard, and I'm dismayed to find the situation looks even worse from in here—endless buildings, floors, and hallways. Locks *everywhere*. On *everything*. It's a freaking fortress.

This was such a stupid idea. This was the stupidest idea of all of the stupid ideas I have ever had in my entire stupid life. I should go home. I'm still not even sure what I'd say to Cricket when I saw him. But I hate that I've already come this far. I crumple onto a bench and call Lindsey. "I need help."

"What kind of help?" She's suspicious.

"How do I find Cricket's building and room number?"

"And you need that information *why*?"

My voice grows tiny. "Because I'm in Berkeley?"

A long pause. "Oh, Lola." And then a sigh. "You want me to call him?"

"No!"

"So you're just gonna show up? What if he's not there?"

Crud. I hadn't thought about that.

"Forget it," Lindsey says. "Okay, call what's-his-name. St. Clair."

"Too embarrassing. Don't you have access to school records or something?"

"If I had access to something like that, don't you think I would have used it by now? No, you have to use a source. Your source is St. Clair."

"It's not you?"

"Bye, Lola."

"Wait! If my parents call, tell them I'm in the bathroom. We're eating pizza and watching *Pushing Daisies.*"

"I hate you."

"I love you."

She hangs up.

"All right," an English accent says to me. "(A) You're not in the toilets, (B) You're not eating pizza, and (C) Whom do you love?"

I jump up and throw my arms around him. "I don't believe it!"

St. Clair hugs me back before prying me off. "What are you doing at my dormitory?"

"I chose the right one? You live here? Which building?" I look around wildly as if it were about to light up.

"I don't know. Should I trust a lying girl wearing a yellow raincoat on a sunny day?"

I smile. "Why are you always in the right place at the right time?"

"It's a particular talent of mine." He shrugs. "Are you looking for Cricket?"

"Will you show me where he lives?"

"Does he know you're coming?" he asks.

I don't answer.

"Ah," he says.

"Do you think he'll mind?"

St. Clair shakes his head. "You're right. I sincerely doubt it. Come along, then." He leads me across the courtyard to a brown-shingled building in the back. We climb a set of stairs, and he unlocks another door, which puts us inside the building's second floor, in an ugly, battered hallway. He struts ahead of me, but his scuffed boots make heavy clomping noises on the carpet. Cricket doesn't make any noise when he moves.

Does Max make noise?

"Here's my room." St. Clair nods to a cheap-looking wooden door, and I laugh when I see the worn drawing taped to it. It's him wearing a Napoleon hat. "And here . . ." We walk down four more doors. ". . . is Monsieur Bell's room." There's also something taped to his door. It's an illustrated miniposter of a woman thrusting a battle-ax toward the heavens and straddling a white tiger. Naked.

St. Clair grins.

"Are you . . . sure this is his room?"

"Oh, I'm *quite* sure."

I stare at the naked tiger lady. She's skinny and blond and doesn't look anything like me. Not that it matters. Not that I should care for the opinion of someone who'd hang that on his door. But still. "And now I have a train to catch," St. Clair says. "Best of luck." He darts out the building.

If he's screwing with me, I'll kill him.

I take a deep breath. And then another.

And then I knock.

chapter twenty

"Lola?" Cricket looks astonished. "What are you doing here?"

"I—" Now that I'm standing before his door, my excuses sound ludicrous. *Hey, I was in the neighborhood, so I thought I'd drop by to hang out. Oh! And I wanted to get back that embarrassing binder, which I only lent to you because you were nice enough to offer to make something that would enable me to attend a dance with another guy.* "I came to see if you had any ideas for the panniers. I'm . . . in a bit of a time crunch."

Time crunch? I have never used the phrase time crunch before.

Cricket is still in shock.

"I mean, I came to see you, too. Of course."

"Well. You found me. Hi."

"Everything okay?" A girl pops out her head behind him. She's taller than me, and she's slender. And she has golden hair in natural waves and a glowing tan that says surfer girl rather than fake-and-bake.

And she looks totally pissed to see me here.

She places a hand possessively on his arm. His sleeve is pushed up so her bare skin is touching his. My stomach plummets. "S-sorry. It was rude of me to show up like this. I'll see you later, okay?" And then I'm speed-walking down the hall.

"LOLA!"

I stop. I slowly turn around.

He looks bewildered. "Where are you going?"

"I didn't mean to interrupt. I was in the neighborhood, um, shopping and . . . and of course you're busy." *Stop freaking out. He can date or make out with or—oh God—sleep with whomever he wants.*

"Is it raining?" The girl frowns at my raincoat and rain boots.

"Oh. No. They matched my dress." I unsnap the coat to expose a pretty dress in the same shade of yellow. Cricket startles like he's just noticed the girl's hand. He slides from her grasp and into the hall.

"This is my friend Jessica. We were working on our physics homework. Jess, this is Lola. The one . . . the one I told you about."

Jessica does not look pleased by this information.

HE TOLD HER ABOUT ME.

"So you came to work on the dress?" he asks.

"It's not a big deal." I move toward him. "We can do it later."

"No! You're here. You're never here." He glances at Jessica. "We'll finish tomorrow, okay?"

"Right." She fires me a death glare before storming away.

Cricket doesn't notice. He opens his door wide. "Come in. How did you find me?"

"St. Cla— OH."

"What? What is it?"

Two beds. Beside one, a constellation chart, a periodic table, and a desk crowded with papers and wires and small metal objects. Beside the other, more naked fantasy women, a gigantic television, and several gaming consoles.

"You have a roommate."

"Yeah." He sounds confused.

"The, um, picture on your door surprised me."

"NO. No. I prefer my women with . . . fewer carnivorous beasts and less weaponry." He pauses and smiles. "Naked is okay. What she needs are a golden retriever and a telescope. Maybe then it would do it for me."

I laugh.

"A squirrel and a laboratory beaker?"

"A bunny rabbit and a flip chart," I say.

"Only if the flip chart has mathematical equations on it."

I fake-swoon onto his bed. "Too much, too much!" He's laughing, but it fades as he watches me toss and turn. He looks pained. I sit up on my elbows. "What's the matter?"

"You're in my room," he says quietly. "You weren't in my room five minutes ago and now you are."

I pull myself up the rest of the way, suddenly conscious of both the bed and its lingering scent of bar soap and sweet mechanical oil. I glance at a space close to his head but not quite at it. "I shouldn't have barged in on you like this. I'm sorry."

"No. I'm glad you're here."

I find the courage to meet his eyes, but he's not looking at me anymore. He reaches for something on his desk. It's overflowing with towers of graphing paper and partially completed projects, but there's one area that's been cleared of everything. Everything except for my binder. "I did some sketches this weekend in Pennsylvania—"

"Oh, yeah." I looked up Skate America, and it was held in Reading this year. I ask the polite question. "How did Calliope do?"

"Good, good. First."

"She broke her second-place streak?"

He looks up. "What? Oh. No. She always gets first in these early seasonal competitions. Not to take anything away from her," he adds distractedly. Since he's not bothered by the mention, I gather that he doesn't know we spoke. Best to keep it that way. "Okay," he says. "Here's what I was working on."

Cricket sits beside me on his bed. He's in scientist inventor professional mode, so he's forgotten his self-imposed distance rule. He pulls out a few illustrations that he'd tucked inside, and he's rambling about materials and circumferences and other things I'm not thinking about, because all I see is how carefully he's cradling my binder in his lap.

Like it's fragile. Like it's important.

"So what do you think?"

"It looks wonderful," I say. "Thank you."

"It'll be big. I mean, you wanted big, right? Will you have enough fabric?"

Oops. I should have been paying closer attention. I study the dimensions. He hands me a calculator so I can punch in my numbers, and I'm surprised at how perfect it is. "Yeah. Wow, I'll even have the right amount of spare fabric, just in case."

"I'll collect the materials tomorrow so I can start it this weekend at my parents' house. I'll need . . ." His cheeks turn pink.

I smile. "My measurements?"

"Not all of them." Now red.

I write down what he needs. "I'm not one of *those* girls. I don't mind."

"You shouldn't. You're perfect, you look beautiful."

The words are out. He's been so careful.

"I shouldn't have said that." Cricket sets aside my binder and jolts up. He moves as far away from me as possible without stepping on his roommate's side. "I'm sorry." He rubs the back of his head and stares out his window.

"It's okay. Thank you."

We're quiet. It's grown dark outside.

"You know." I snap and unsnap my raincoat. "We spend a lot of time apologizing to each other. Maybe we should stop. Maybe we need to try harder to be friends. It's okay for friends to say things like that without it getting weird."

Cricket turns back around and looks at me. "Or to show up unannounced."

"Though if you gave me your number, I wouldn't have to."

He smiles, and I pull out my cell and toss it to him. He tosses his to me. We enter our digits into each other's phone. The act feels official. Cricket throws mine back and says, "I'm listed under 'Naked Tiger Woman.'"

I laugh. "Are you serious? Because I entered myself as 'Naked Tiger Lady.'"

"Really?"

I laugh harder. "No. I'm Lola."

"The one and only."

I walk his phone to him and place it in his open palm. "That's a mighty fine compliment coming from you, Cricket Bell."

His eyebrows rise slowly in a question.

And then the bedroom light flicks on.

"Whoops." A guy half the height of Cricket and twice as wide tosses a bag of Cool Ranch Doritos onto the other bed. "Sorry, man."

Cricket springs backward. "This is my roommate, Dustin. Dustin, this is Lola."

"Huh," Dustin says. "I thought you were gay."

"Um," Cricket says.

"You're always in the city, and you ignore Heather whenever she comes by."

Heather? There's another one?

"Guess I was wrong." Dustin shakes his head and flops down beside his chips. "Good. Now I don't have to worry about you looking at my junk anymore."

I tense. "How do you know he'd be interested in *your* junk? It's not like you're attracted to every girl in the world. Why would he be attracted to every boy?"

"Whoa." Dustin looks at Cricket. "What's the deal?"

Cricket throws on a coat. "We should go, Lola. You probably need to catch the train."

"You don't go here?" Dustin asks me.

"I attend school in the city." I slide my binder into my bag.

He looks me up and down. "One of those art students, huh?"

"No. I go to Harvey Milk Memorial."

"What's that?"

"A high school," I say.

Dustin's eyebrows shoot up. He turns to Cricket. "Is she legal?" His voice is tinged with appreciation and respect.

"Bye, Dustin." Cricket holds the door open for me.

"IS SHE LEGAL?" he says as Cricket slams the door shut behind us.

Cricket closes his eyes. "I'm sorry."

"Hey. No apologizing. Especially not for *him*." We head outside, and I shudder. No wonder Cricket comes home most weekends. "Besides," I continue, "I'm used to it. I get stuff like that alllll the—"

Cricket has stopped moving.

"—time." Crud.

"Right. Of course you do." With excruciating effort, he pushes through Max's ghost. Always present. Always haunting us. "So what's the boyfriend doing tonight?"

"I don't know. I haven't talked to him today."

"Do you usually talk to him? Every day?"

"Yeah," I say uncomfortably. I'm losing Cricket. His body is moving physically farther from mine as his mind rebuilds the barrier he built to protect us. "Do you want to get dinner or something?" I blurt. He doesn't answer. "Forget it, I'm sure you have things to do. Or whatever."

"No!" And then, with control, "Dinner would be good. Any particular craving?"

"Well . . . Andy gave me money for pizza."

Cricket tours me through his campus, pointing out the various buildings—all grand and immense and named Something-or-Other Hall—where he takes classes. He tells me about his teachers and the other students, and once again, I'm struck by how strange it is that he has this other life. This life I'm not a part of.

We wind up Telegraph Avenue, the busiest street in downtown Berkeley. It's the most San Francisco–like place here, with its bead stores, tattoo shops, bookstores, record stores, head shops, and Nepalese imports. But it's also overrun with street vendors selling cheaply made junk—ugly jewelry, tie-dyed shoelaces, bad art, and Bob Marley's face on everything. We have to walk through a group of dancing Hare Krishnas in sherbet-colored robes and finger cymbals, and I nearly run smack into a man wearing a fur hat and a cape. He's draping a supertiny table with velvet for tarot readings, right there on the street. I feel relieved that Norah's distaste for costumes means at least she doesn't look like this guy.

There are homeless everywhere. An older man with a weather-hardened face comes out of nowhere, limping and staggering in front of us like a zombie. I instinctively jolt backward and away.

"Hey," Cricket says gently, and I realize that he caught my reaction. It's comforting to know he understands why. To know I won't have to explain, and to know he's not judging me for it. He smiles. "We're here."

Inside Blondie's, I insist on paying with Andy's twenty. We sit at a countertop overlooking the street and eat one slice of pesto vegetarian (me) and three slices of beef pepperoni (him). Cricket sips a Cherry Coke. "Nice of Andy to give us dinner money," he says. "But why pizza?"

"Oh, the pizza place was on the way," I say. He looks confused. "On the way to Lindsey's house. They think I'm with Lindsey."

Cricket sets down his drink. "Please tell me you're joking."

"No. It was easier than explaining to Andy . . ." I trail off, unsure of what the rest of that sentence is.

"Explaining that you wanted to hang out with me?"

"No. Well, yeah. But I don't think my parents would mind," I add quickly.

He's exasperated. "So why didn't you tell them? Jeez, Lola. What if something happened to you? No one would know where you were!"

"I told Lindsey I was here." *Well, I told her later.* I push the Parmesan shaker away. "You know, you're starting to sound like my parents."

Cricket hangs his head and runs his hands through his dark hair. When he looks up again, it's sticking up even taller and crazier than usual. He stands. "Come on."

"What?"

"You have to go home."

"I'm eating. *You're* eating."

"You can't be here, Lola. I have to take you home."

"I don't believe it. You're serious?"

"YES. I'm not having this on my . . . permanent record."

"What the hell does that mean?"

"It means if your parents find out you've been here without their permission, they won't like me very much."

Now I stand. He's nearly a foot taller, but I try to make him feel as small as possible. "And why are you so concerned about my parents liking you? Is it necessary to remind you—AGAIN—that I have a boyfriend?"

The words are cruel, and I'm horrified as soon as they leave my mouth. Cricket's blue eyes become startlingly angry. "Then why are you here?"

I'm panicking. "Because you offered to help me."

"I *was* helping you, and then you just showed up. In my bedroom! You knew I was coming back next weekend—"

"You didn't come back last weekend!"

"And now I require your permission to go somewhere? Do you take pleasure in knowing I'm over there . . . *pining* for you?"

I throw my half-finished slice in the trash and flee. As always, he's on my heels. He grabs me. "Lola, wait. I don't know what I'm saying, this conversation is moving too fast. Let's try again."

I yank my arm from his grasp and resume my race toward the train station. He's beside every stride. "I'm going home, Cricket. Like you told me to."

"Please don't go." He's desperate. "Not like this."

"You can't have it both ways, don't you get it?" I jerk to a halt and sway. *I'm talking to myself, not to Cricket.*

"I'm trying," he says. "I'm trying so hard."

The words shatter my heart. "Yeah," I say. "Well. Me, too."

Confusion.

And then . . . "You're trying? Are you trying in the same way as me?" His words rush out, toppling over each other.

Life would be so much easier if I could say that I'm not interested, that he stands no chance with me. But something about the way Cricket Bell is looking at me—like nothing has ever mattered more to him than my answer—means that I can only speak the truth. "I don't know. Okay? I look at you, and I think about you, and . . . I don't know. No one has ever so completely confounded me the way you do."

His difficult equation face. "So what does that mean?"

"It means we're right back where we started. And I'm back at the train station. So I'm leaving now."

"I'll go with you—"

"No. You won't."

Cricket wants to argue. He wants to make sure I get home safely. But he knows if he comes with me, he'll cross a line that I don't want crossed. He'll lose me.

So he says goodbye. And I say goodbye.

And as the train pulls away, I feel like I've lost him again anyway.

chapter twenty-one

I love watching Max onstage. He's playing his current favorite cover. The first time he sang "I Saw Her Standing There"—*Well, she was just seventeen / You know what I mean*—with a mischievous glance in my direction, I thought I'd die. I was one of *those* girls. Girls who had songs dedicated to them.

It's still thrilling.

Lindsey and I are at Scare Francisco, an all-day, twelve-stage Halloween rock festival in Golden Gate Park. It's Saturday, and I'm still grounded, but we've had these tickets for months. Plus, Norah is inescapable. After being denied every low-income apartment in the city, she made arrangements to move in with her friend Ronnie Reagan. Ronnie stands for Veronica, and she is a he, and the only problem is that Ronnie's old roommate won't be moving out until *January.* My parents feel rotten and guilty about this. So they let me come today.

Per annual tradition, I'm wearing jeans, a nice blouse, a black wig with straight bangs, and red sneakers. Lindsey is wearing a fifties housewife dress, a vintage apron, four-inch heels, a blond wig with a flip, and large sparkly clip-on earrings.

We're dressed as each other, of course. I wear pretty much the same thing every year. She's always something new.

Amphetamine finishes on stage four, and they take apart their gear while the next band, Pot Kettle Black, sets up. I fan myself with a flyer for a haunted house, trying not to draw attention to the fact that I'm fanning my armpits more than my face. But I don't want to smell gross for Max. He hasn't seen me yet. The sun beats down, and my nose is burning, despite my SPF 25. The city tends to get its rare heat waves in the autumn.

"I can't wait until you're a detective, and I get to wear your badge," I say. "I'd totally arrest any girl who came here dressed as a sexy cat. Snooze."

"I can't wait until your podiatrist forbids you from wearing heels."

"But you look *fabulous,* darling."

"Lola?" a girl calls out from behind us.

I turn around to find Calliope, head tilted to the side. "That *is* you. You were right." She looks over her shoulder, and I follow her gaze as the other Bell twin appears from behind a monstrously large Hell's Angel. Or a guy dressed as a Hell's Angel. I fan my cheeks with the flyer, feeling hot again. I'm not sure which twin is more troubling "How could you tell?" Calliope continues. "She looks so . . . normal."

"I'll take that as a compliment," Lindsey whispers to me.

"She always looks like Lindsey on Halloween," Cricket says. Neither twin is costumed, but Cricket's hand *does* say BOO. "Cool outfit, Lindsey. You look great."

For all her I-don't-care-ness, Lindsey looks pleased by the compliment. "Thanks."

He's having trouble looking directly at me. Did he see Max's band? What did he think of them? The only contact I've had with him since Berkeley was that same night when I received a text from NAKED TIGER WOMAN asking if I'd made it home okay. If anyone else had done that after a fight, I would have found it insufferable. But Cricket seriously cannot help being a nice person.

I can't tell if Calliope knows that I visited him. I assume not, since she's speaking with me. Thank goodness for small miracles.

"Hey," I say, kinda sorta meeting Cricket's eyes. "What are you doing here?"

"Same thing you are." Calliope's voice is clipped. "Listening to music. Practice was canceled. Petro is sick."

"Petro?" Lindsey asks.

"My coach. Petro Petrov."

Lindsey and I stifle our laughter. Calliope doesn't notice. It's odd, but I suddenly realize that I haven't seen the twins stand beside each other in ages. They have a similar body shape, though Calliope is the petite version. This still means she's taller than her competitors. After her growth spurt, it took several years for her to adjust on the ice. Cricket once told me that when you're tall, your center of balance is also higher, and this accentuates mistakes. Which makes sense. But now her confidence and strength are forces to be reckoned with. She could kick my ass any day of the week.

I feel her noting the extra space and awkwardness between Cricket and me, and I have no doubt that she's considering it.

"Why didn't you guys dress up?" Lindsey asks.

"We did." Calliope cracks her first smile. "We're dressed as twins."

Lindsey grins back. "Hmm, I see it now. Fraternal or identical?"

"You'd be surprised how many people ask," Cricket says.

"What do you tell them?" Lindsey asks.

"That I have a penis."

Oh God. My cheeks burn as they all burst into laughter. *Think about something else, Dolores. ANYTHING else. Cucumbers. Bananas. Zucchini. AHHHH! NO NO NO NO NO NO NO.* I turn my face away from them as Calliope fakes a yakking sound.

"Definitely time to change the subject," she says.

"Hey, are you guys hungry?" I blurt. *SERIOUSLY?* I'm so thankful that mind readers aren't real.

"Starving," Cricket says.

"Says the guy who just ate three taco salads," Calliope says.

He rubs his stomach. His bracelets and rubber bands rattle. "Jealous."

"It's so unfair. Cricket eats all day long, the most horrendous things—"

"The most delicious," he says.

"—the most horrendous *and* delicious things, and he doesn't gain a pound. Meanwhile, I have to count calories every time I swallow an alfalfa sprout."

"What?" Lindsey says. She's as baffled as I am. "You're in perfect shape. Like, *perfect*."

Calliope rolls her eyes. "Tell that to my coach. And to the commentators."

"And Mom," Cricket says, and Calliope cuts him a glare. He glares back. It's spooky to see that they have the same glare.

And then they burst into laughter. "I win!" Cricket says.

"No way. You laughed first."

"Tie," Lindsey says authoritatively.

"Hey." Calliope turns to me, and the smile disappears. "Isn't that your boyfriend?"

Oh. Holy. Graveyards.

I've been so thrown that I forgot Max would be here any second. I want to shove Cricket back behind that Hell's Angel, and he looks like he wouldn't mind a disappearing act either. Max slinks through the crowd like a wolf on the prowl. I raise my hand in a weak wave. He nods back, but he's staring down Cricket.

Max pulls me into his tattooed arms. "How'd we sound?"

"Phenomenal," I say truthfully. His grip is tight, forcing me to point out the well-dressed elephant in the room. "This is my neighbor Cricket. Remember?" As if any of us could have forgotten.

"Hi," Cricket says, shrinking up.

"Hey," Max says in a bored voice. Which isn't even his regular bored voice. It's the mask of a bored voice that says, *See how much I don't care about you?*

"And this is his sister, Calliope."

"We saw your show," she says. "You were great."

Max looks her over. "Thanks," he says after a moment. It's polite but indifferent, and his coolness disconcerts her. He turns back to me and frowns. "What are you wearing?"

The way he says it makes me not want to answer.

"She's *me,*" Lindsey says.

Max finally acknowledges her presence. "So you must be Lola. Well. Can't say I'll be sorry when this holiday is over."

I'm aghast. Cricket's presence has made him reckless.

"I think they look terrific." Cricket straightens to his full height. He towers over my boyfriend. "I think it's cool that they do it every year."

Max leans over and speaks quietly so that only I can hear it. "I'm gonna load some stuff into the van." He kisses me, quickly at first, but then something changes in his mind. He slows down. And he REALLY kisses me. "I'll text you when I'm done." And he leaves without saying goodbye to anyone else.

I am so mortified. "Groups . . . make him uncomfortable."

Calliope looks disgusted, and my insides writhe, because I know she thinks I've been stringing along Cricket to keep dating *that*. But *that* was not my boyfriend. The disdain in Cricket's expression makes me feel even more humiliated. I imagine conversations in which Calliope uses this as proof that I'm shallow and not worthy of his friendship.

I turn to Lindsey. "I'm sorry. I'm sure he didn't mean it like that."

"Whatever." She rolls her eyes. "You know he hates me. I'm not crazy about him either."

I lower my voice. "Max doesn't hate you."

She shrugs. I can't bear for the twins to hear any more of this, so I take Lindsey's hand and lead her away. "We have to go, sorry. There's a band on stage six I've been dying to hear."

"Good, we'll follow," Calliope says. "You know these local bands better than us."

I'm howling on the inside as they follow a dead-silent Lindsey and me across the grass and through the skeletons, ghosts, and pirates to stage six, where a mediocre punk band is butchering "Thriller." I squint at the bass drum. My colored contacts are an old prescription. "The Flaming Olives?"

"The Evening Devils," Lindsey corrects, annoyed.

"That's a stupid name," I say.

"Olives would be worse," Calliope says. "I thought you were *dying* to hear them."

"I thought they were gonna be someone else," I grumble.

"Ah," Cricket says.

It's a disbelieving *ah,* and it furthers my shame. I stand my ground and try to lose myself in the band, but I can't believe my boyfriend just treated Lindsey like dirt. I can't believe Cricket just saw him treat Lindsey like dirt. And I'm glad he stepped in before Max could do further damage, but why did it have to be *him*? It should have been me. The orange sun beats down, and I'm sweating again. My wig is trapping heat. I wonder how bad my hair looks underneath, and if I can get away with removing it. At long last, I catch a break as a cloud passes over the sun. I release a tiny sigh.

"You're welcome," Cricket says.

And then I realize that he's standing behind me. Cricket is the cloud.

He gives an oddly grim smile. "You looked uncomfortable."

"This band blows, and my feet are killing me," Lindsey says. "Let's go."

My phone vibrates in my pocket. A text from Max:

@ marx meadow near first aid. where are you?

The plan was to hang out with Max and Lindsey for a few hours and then go home at dusk. I love Halloween. The Castro used to close off the streets and throw an insane party that attracted over a hundred thousand people, but a few years ago, someone died in the fray. The city stopped closing it off and urged people to stay in their own neighborhoods. Still. As far as places to be on October thirty-first, a crowd of drag queens can't be beat.

But now I don't want to hang out with Lindsey and Max together. And I want to stay with my friend, but I haven't been alone with Max in two weeks.

No. I should stay with Lindsey.

"Max?" she asks.

"Yeah. He's ready to meet up, but I'm gonna tell him we're going home early."

"He'll be pissed if you don't show."

"He won't be pissed," I say, with a nervous glance at Cricket. Even though Lindsey's right. But the way she said it makes it sound worse than it is.

"Yeah, well, you haven't seen him in forever. Don't let me stand in the way of your amorous pursuits."

I wish Lindsey would stop talking in front of Cricket.

"It's fine," she continues. "I'll hang out with them for a little while longer"—she gestures to the Bells—"and then I'll catch the bus home. I'm tired."

She's pushing me away out of spite. There's no good way of dealing with her when she's like this, except to give her what she wants. "So, um, talk to you tonight?"

"Go," she says.

I sneak another glimpse at Cricket before leaving. I wish I hadn't. He looks tortured. As if he'd do anything to stop me, but he's being held back by his own invisible demons. I mumble my goodbye. As I walk to the meadow, I take off the wig. I don't have a purse—Lindsey never carries one—so I drape it on the branch of a Japanese maple. Maybe someone will find it and add it to their costume. I shake out my hair, unbutton the top of my shirt, and roll up the sleeves. It's better, but I still don't look like me.

Actually, I look *more* like me. I feel exposed.

Max is leaning against the first-aid station, and his shoulders relax when he sees me. He's glad I'm alone. But when I lean up to kiss him, he hardens again, and it sends a chill down my spine. "Not now, Lola."

His rebuke stings. Is it because of how I look?

"You're still hanging out with him," he says.

No, it's because he's jealous. I'm sweating again. "Who?" I ask, buying time.

"Grasshopper. Centipede. Praying Mantis."

It makes me cringe to hear Max mock his name. "That's not funny. And that wasn't nice what you said to Lindsey earlier either."

He crosses his arms. "How long have you been seeing him?"

"I'm not seeing him. We just bumped into him and his sister, I promise." His silence intimidates me into blabbering. "I swear, Lindsey and I ran into them, like, three minutes before you showed up."

"I don't like the way he stares at you."

"He's just my neighbor, Max."

"How many times have you seen him since Amoeba?"

I hesitate and decide to go with a slant truth. "Sometimes I see him through my window on the weekend."

"Your window? Your *bedroom* window?"

I narrow my eyes. "And then I close my curtains. End of story."

"Lola, I don't believe—"

"You never believe me!"

"Because you lie your ass off all the time! Don't think I don't know you're still hiding things from me. What happened at Muir Woods, Lola?"

"What?"

"You heard me. Nathan was trying to get you to tell me

something at dinner. He was there, wasn't he? The neighbor boy."

"Ohmygod, you're crazy. It was a family picnic. You're getting paranoid, and you're making things up." I'm panicking. *How does he know?*

"Am I?"

"YES!"

"Because one of us is getting pretty worked up right now."

"Because you're accusing me of horrible things! I can't believe you think I'd lie to you about something like that." *Oh God, I'm going to hell.* I'm crying. "Why are you so convinced I'm ready to cheat on you?"

"I don't know. Maybe because I've never seen the same you twice. Nothing about you is real."

His words stop my heart.

Max sees he's taken it too far. He jerks forward as if a spell has broken. "I didn't mean that. You know I love the crazy outfits."

"You always say what you mean," I whisper.

He rubs his temples for a long moment. "I'm sorry. Come here." He wraps his arms around me. I hug him tightly, but it feels as if he's vanishing. I want to tell him that I'm sorry, too, but I'm scared to tell him the truth. I don't want to lose him.

When two people are in love, it's supposed to work. It *has* to work. No matter how difficult the circumstances are. I think about the sweet songs he's written, the ones he plays in his apartment, the ones for my ears only. I think about our future, when I'm no longer tied to my parents. Costumes by day, rock clubs by night. We'll both be a success, and it'll be because of each other.

Our love should make us a success.

Max kisses my neck. My chin. My lips. His kisses are hungry and possessive. Max is the one. We love each other, so he *has* to be the one.

He tears himself away. "This is the real me. Is this the real you?"

I'm dizzy. "This is me."

But it tastes like fear on my lips. It tastes like another lie.

chapter twenty-two

I'm discussing Max with the moon, but it's supremely unsatisfying. Her beams are casting an eerie luminescence on Cricket's window. "Max doesn't like it when I dress down, but he throws my usual appearance into my face when we fight. I'm never what he needs me to be."

The moon darkens by cloud cover.

"Okay, I've lied to him. But you saw how jealous he gets. It makes me feel like I *have* to. And I shouldn't have to defend my right to be friends with another guy."

I wait. The sky remains dark.

"Fine. The you-know-who situation is weird. Maybe . . . Max and Calliope aren't so far off. But if I'm never given Max's trust to begin with, how can he expect me to trust him in return? Do you see what I mean? Do you see how confusing it is?" I close my eyes. "Please, tell me. What do I do?"

The light behind my lids softly brightens. I open my eyes. The clouds have moved, and Cricket's window is illuminated by moonlight.

"You have a sick sense of humor," I say.

Her beams don't waver. And without knowing how it happens, I find myself removing a handful of bobby pins from my desk. I chuck them at his panes. *Dink! Dink! Dink dink!* Seven bobby pins later, Cricket opens his window.

"Trick-or-treat," I say.

"Is something wrong?" He's sleepy and disoriented. He's also only wearing his boxer briefs, and his bracelets and rubber bands.

OHMYGOD. HE'S ONLY WEARING BOXER BRIEFS.

"No."

Cricket rubs his eyes. "No?"

DON'T STARE AT HIS BODY. DO *NOT* STARE AT HIS BODY.

"Did you go anywhere fun tonight? I stayed in and handed out candy. Nathan bought good stuff, name-brand chocolate, not the cheapo mix he usually gets, you know with the Tootsie Pops and Dots and those tiny Tootsie Rolls flavored like lime, I guess you got a lot of kids at your house, too, huh?"

He stares at me blankly. "Did you wake me up . . . to talk about candy?"

"It's still so hot out, isn't it?" I blurt. AND THEN I WANT TO DIE.

Because Cricket has turned into stone, having realized the practically naked situation his body is in. Which I am not, not, not looking at. At all.

"Let's go for a walk!"

My exclamation unfreezes him. He edges out of sight, trying to play it cool. "Now?" he calls from the darkness. "It's . . . two forty-two in the morning."

"I could use someone to talk to."

Cricket pops back up. He has located his pants. He is wearing them.

I blush.

He considers me for a moment, pulls a T-shirt over his head, and then nods. I sneak downstairs, past my parents' bedroom and Norah's temporary bedroom, and I reach the street undetected. Cricket is already there. I'm wearing sushi-print pajama bottoms and a white camisole. Seeing him fully dressed again makes me feel *un*dressed, a feeling intensified when I notice him take in my bare skin. We walk up the hill to the corner of our street. Somehow, we both know where we're going.

The city is silent. The raucous spirit of Halloween has gone to sleep.

We reach the even bigger hill that separates us from Dolores Park. Eighty steps lead to the top. I've counted. About twenty up, he stops. "Are you gonna say what's on your mind, or are you gonna make me guess? Because I'm not good at guessing games. People should say what they mean to say and not make other people stumble around."

"Sorry."

He smiles for the first time in ages. "Hey. No apologizing."

I smile back, but it falters.

His disappears, too. "Is it Max?"

"Yes," I say quietly.

We walk slowly up the stairs again. "He seemed surprised to see me today. He doesn't know we hang out, does he?"

The sadness in his voice makes me climb slower. I wrap my arms around myself. "No. He didn't know."

Cricket stops. "Are you embarrassed by me?"

"Why would I be embarrassed by you?"

He puts his hands in his pockets. "Because I'm not cool."

I'm thrown. Cricket isn't cool in the same sense as Max, but he's the most *interesting* person I know. He's kind and intelligent and attractive. And he's well dressed. Cricket is REALLY well dressed. "How can you think that?"

"Come on. He's this sexy rock god, and I'm the boy next door. The stupid science geek, who's spent his life on the sidelines of figure-skating rinks. With his sister."

"You're not . . . you're not a geek, Cricket. And even if you were, what's wrong with that? And since when is science *stupid*?"

He looks unusually agitated.

"Oh, no," I say. "Please tell me this isn't about your great-great-whatever grandfather. Because that doesn't mean any—"

"It means *everything*. The inheritance that paid for our house, that pays for Calliope's training, that pays for my college education, that bought everything I've ever owned . . . it wasn't ours. Do you know what happened to Alexander Graham Bell after he became famous? He spent the rest of his life hiding in a remote part of Canada. In shame of what he'd done."

"So why did he do it?"

Cricket rakes a hand through his hair. "For the same reason everyone makes mistakes. He fell in love."

"Oh." That hurts. I'm not even sure why it hurts so much, but it does.

"Her father was wealthy and powerful. Alexander wasn't. He had *ideas* for the telephone, but he couldn't get them to work. Her father discovered that someone—Elisha Gray—was about to patent it, so they went to the patent office on the same day as Elisha, copied his idea, turned it in, and claimed they were there first. Alexander became one of the wealthiest men in America and was allowed to marry my great-great-great-grandmother. By the time Elisha realized he'd been had, it was too late."

I'm astounded. "That's terrible."

"History books are filled with lies. Whoever wins the war tells the story."

"But Alexander was still a smart man. He was still an inventor. You get *that* much honestly. Life isn't about what you get, it's about what you DO with what you get."

"I build things that have no use." His tone is flat. "It's just as bad. I should be creating something that makes a difference, something to . . . make up for the past."

I'm getting angry. "What do you think would happen if I believed genetics played that kind of role in my life? If I believed that because my birth parents made certain decisions, it meant that my life, my dreams were forfeit, too? Do you know what that would do to me? Do you have any idea what it HAS done to me?"

Cricket is devastated. "I wasn't thinking, I'm sorry—"

"You should be. You have a gift, and you're doubting it." I shake my head to clear my thoughts. "You can't let that kind of shame dictate who you are. You aren't your name. Your decisions are your own."

He stares at me.

I return the stare, and my senses surge. The energy between us ricochets so fiercely that it scares me.

I break our gaze.

We climb the rest of the way to the top, and the entire city stretches before us. The jutting houses, the golden hills, the high-rises, the glittering bay. It's stunning. We sit on an empty slab of asphalt overlooking the view. It's someone's driveway, but no one will see us. The eucalyptus tree dangling above us releases its soothing fragrance into the night air.

Cricket inhales, long and slow. He sighs his exhale. "I've missed that. Eucalyptus always reminds me of home."

And I fill with warmth because, even with his second life in Berkeley, he still thinks of this as home. "You know," I say. "When I was little, my parents were embarrassed by the way I dressed."

"Really? That's surprising."

"They were terrified that people would think THEY were dressing me like that. That THE GAYS were corrupting me with false eyelashes and glitter."

He laughs.

"But they learned it's who I am, and they accepted it. And their support gave me some confidence. And then, that summer, you taught me how to accept it for myself. To not worry about what other people said. And then . . . things weren't bad at all."

"*I* did?"

"Yeah, you. So I'm telling you this now. I will *never* forget that mechanical bird you made. The one that only sang when you opened its cage door?"

"You remember that?" He's mystified.

"Or the fifty-step Rube Goldberg machine that sharpened a pencil? Or that insane train of dominoes that took you two weeks to set up, but was over in a minute? It was incredible. Just because something isn't practical doesn't mean it's not worth creating. Sometimes beauty and real-life magic are enough."

I turn to face him, cross-legged. "It's like my Marie Antoinette dress. It's not practical, but . . . for that one moment, arriving at a dance in a beautiful, elaborate dress that no one else is wearing and that everyone will remember? I want that."

Cricket stares across the city lights toward the bay. "You will. You'll have it."

"Not without your help." I want to give him a friendly shove, but I settle for a verbal jab. "So are you gonna get started on my panniers tomorrow or what?"

"I already started them." He meets my eyes again. "I stayed in tonight, too. I didn't just hand out candy."

I'm touched. "Cricket Bell. You are the nicest guy I know."

"Yeah." He snorts. "The nice guy."

"What?"

"That was what my one-and-only girlfriend said when she broke up with me."

"Oh." I'm taken aback. The Girlfriend, at last. "That's . . . a really, *really* stupid reason."

Cricket scooches forward, and his knees almost bump mine. Almost. "It's not uncommon. Nice guys finish last and all."

There's a dig at Max amid his self-deprecation, but I ignore it. "Who was she?"

"One of Calliope's friends. Last year."

"A figure skater?"

"My social scene doesn't extend much further."

The news makes me unhappy. Skaters are *gorgeous.* And *talented.* And, like, *athletically gifted.* I stand, my heart pounding in my ears. "I need to get home."

He looks at his wrist, but he's not wearing his watch. "Yeah, I guess it's really late. Or really early."

We descend the eighty stairs to our street corner before Cricket unexpectedly halts. "Oh, no. You wanted to talk about Max. Do you—"

"I think we were supposed to talk tonight," I interrupt him with a glance toward the moon. She's a waxing gibbous, almost full. "And I thought it was supposed to be about Max, but I was wrong. We needed to talk about you." I point at my feet.

I'm standing over the word BELL.

It's imprinted on the grate for Pacific Bell, the phone company. They're everywhere, on every street. "See?" I say.

"Every time I see Dolores Street, I think of you." His words rush out. "Dolores Park. Dolores Mission. You're everywhere in this neighborhood, you *are* this neighborhood."

I close my eyes. He shouldn't say things like that, but I don't want him to stop. It's become impossible to deny he means something to me. I don't have the courage to name it. Not yet. But it's there. I open my eyes, and . . . he's gone.

He's walking swiftly up the stairs to his home.

Another vanished spirit on Halloween.

chapter twenty-three

I like to try new things. Like when I went vegan my freshman year. It only lasted three days, because I missed cheddar, but I tried it. And I'm constantly trying on hats in stores. They're the one item I can't make work for me, but I keep trying, because I'm positive that someday I'll find the right one. Maybe it'll be a vintage cloche dripping with faux peonies, or maybe it'll be a Stetson laced with a red bandanna.

I'll find it. I just have to keep trying them on.

So it annoys me when Lindsey suggests I'm not trying hard enough to find something to curl my hair. My fake hair. She's balancing chemistry equations while I borrow her parents' handheld steamer to bend my white hair into the appropriately sized curls. Later, I'll spray-glue them to my Marie Antoinette wig. But first I need to curl the stupid curls.

"Don't you have anything bigger? Or smaller?" I gesture to the cylindrical shapes—pens, markers, glassware, even a monocular spy scope—spread before me. None of them is the right size.

She flips a textbook page. "Got me. It's your wig. Try harder."

I search her room, but I know I won't find anything. Her bedroom is so well ordered that I would have already seen it if she had it. Lindsey's walls are painted classic Nancy Drew–spine yellow. Her complete collection of the novels is lined up in neat rows across the top shelves of her bookcase and below them, alphabetical by author, are titles like *History's Greatest Spies, Detecting for Dummies,* and *The Tao of Crime Fighting.* Beside her bed are meticulously organized magazine holders with four years' worth of back issues of *Eye Spy Intelligence Magazine* and a dozen *Spy Gear* catalogs tabbed with sticky notes marking wish-list items.

But her room is devoid of any further cylindrical objects.

"And in the closest race of the night, New York senator Joseph Wasserstein is still fighting to hold on to his seat," the toupee-d newsman says. It's Election Day, and since the Lims don't get cable, every channel is filled with boring coverage. The only reason the television is on is to drown out the sound of Mrs. Lim blasting Neil Diamond. He's this superold pop singer who wears sequined shirts. Even the sparkles aren't enough to sway me, though I'd never tell her that. When she's not cooking killer Korean barbecue at the restaurant, she blogs for his second-largest fansite.

I point at the newsman. "I bet that guy could help me. Does

he seriously think that rug on his head looks real?" It switches to a clip of Senator Wasserstein and his family waiting for the final tallies. His wife has that perfectly coiffed hair and that toothy political smile, but his teenage son looks uncomfortable and out of place. He's actually kinda cute. I say so, and Lindsey looks up at the screen. "God. You are so predictable."

"What?"

"He looks miserable. You only like guys who look pissed off."

"That's not true." I turn off the television, and Neil's vibrato shakes the floor.

Lindsey laughs. "Yeah, Max is known for his charming smile."

I frown. Two Sundays have passed, and we didn't have brunch on either one. Max called the morning after Halloween and told me he wouldn't be coming—that day or any Sunday after. I can't blame him for being tired of the scrutiny. I told my parents that he had more shows scheduled, and they're still too frazzled by Norah to inquire further. Truthfully, I hope my parents will just sort of *forget* that brunch was ever a requirement.

I've been seeing Max at odd times—before a weekend shift at the theater, during a dinner break, and once at his apartment after school. My parents thought I was at Lindsey's. But I've seen a lot of Cricket. It only took him one more night to finish the panniers, plus an afternoon at my house with final fittings. They're gigantic and amazing. It's like wearing the framework of a horizontal skyscraper.

And I've finished the stays, so I'm working on the best part now: the gown itself. Cricket helped measure and cut the fabric. It turns out that not only is he handy because of his math and science skills, but he also knows a little about sewing because of Calliope's costumes, which are in constant need of repair.

I've only had one more run-in with Calliope, another before-school incident, although this was accidental. She actually ran into me when she was leaving her house and didn't see me coming. At least, I think it was accidental. "You just can't stay away, can you?" she grumbled, before jogging away.

"I LIVE HERE!" I said, rubbing my bruised arm.

She ignored me.

But since Cricket and I have been busy with my project, it's been easier to be friends. There was only one awkward moment, when he came over the first time. I hadn't thought to clean up my room, and there was a hot pink bra thrown on the center of my floor. He turned the same shade of magenta when he saw it.

To be fair, I did, too.

Cricket. Wait a second.

I know EXACTLY what I need to curl my wig. "I'll be right back," I tell Lindsey, and I pop downstairs, where Mrs. Lim is at the family computer. I raise my voice above Neil's. "Where do you keep the broom?" Then I add, "I didn't break anything."

"In there." She gives a distracted gesture to the hall closet. "Troll on the message board. He's saying Wayne Newton is better than Neil Diamond. Do you believe?"

"Totally ridiculous." I grab the broom. It actually looks just like the one Cricket used to collect my binder. I race upstairs and thrust the handle at Lindsey. "Aha! The perfect circumference."

She smiles. "And plenty of room for us to steam multiple strands at once. Nice."

"You're gonna help?"

"Of course." And thank goodness she does, because it turns out to be a horrible, time-consuming job. "You're lucky I love you, Lola."

Another strand slips to the carpet before curling, and I stifle a scream. She laughs in an exhausted, slaphappy way, and it makes me laugh, too. "This really is one of the worst ideas I've ever had," I say.

"Not one of the worst. *The* worst." Her strand slips to the floor. "AHH!" she says, and we topple over with laughter. "Let's hope Cricket is right, and 'the beauty will be worth the effort.'"

It's like being hit by a train. "When did he say *that*?"

Lindsey's laughter fades. "Oh. Um. Sunday afternoon."

"Sunday? This last Sunday? You talked to Cricket on Sunday?"

She keeps her eyes on a new strand of white hair. "Yeah, um, we went out."

I drop the broom. "WHAT?"

"Not like that," she says quickly. "I mean, we hung out in a group. As friends."

My brain is fizzing and popping. "What group? Who?"

"He called to see if I wanted to go bowling with him and Calliope. And . . . with Charlie. You were at work, so you were busy. That's why we didn't ask."

I've lost the ability to speak. She lifts my side of the broom and puts it into my hands. I take it numbly. "I told them about Charlie at Scare Francisco, after you left to meet Max," she continues. "I don't know why. It just spilled out. Maybe I was bummed you were with Max again, and I was alone."

Guilt. Guilt, guilt, *guilt.*

"Anyway, Cricket thought it'd be a good idea if I hung out with Charlie as friends first, in a group. You know. To make it easier."

THAT WAS MY IDEA. MINE!

"So we went bowling, and . . . we had a fun time."

I'm not sure what hurts more: that she hadn't mentioned this until now, that she hung out with Cricket without me, that she hung out with Calliope *at all,* or that Cricket came up with the same brilliant idea that I did and got to take credit for it.

Okay, so my idea was a double date, and obviously Cricket isn't dating his sister. BUT STILL. It seems to have worked. And I wasn't there. And I'm supposed to be the best friend. "Oh. That's . . . that's great, Lindsey."

"I'm sorry. I should have told you sooner. But I didn't know how you'd feel about me hanging out with the twins, and I really wanted to go. And you were busy. You've been busy a lot in the last few months."

Since you met Max. She might as well have said it. I look back at my work. "No, I'm glad you went. I'm glad you had a nice time with Charlie." Half of that is true.

"I had a nice time with the twins, too," she says cautiously.

"Once Calliope relaxes, she's kinda fun. She's under an insane amount of pressure."

"Hmph. So people tell me."

"Honestly, Lo, I don't think she's the mean girl she once was. She's just protective."

I glare at her. "Her brother is in college. I think he can handle himself."

"And he does speak his mind now. However strangely it might come out," she adds. "You know that he never hurt you on purpose. And when you're not around, he asks a hundred questions about you. About Max, too. He likes you. He's *always liked you,* remember?"

I stop steaming curls.

"And I don't want you to bite my head off for saying this," she says rapidly, "but it's pretty clear you like Cricket Bell, too."

It's like something is caught in my throat. I swallow. "And why do you think that?"

She takes the steamer from me. "Because anyone with the power of observation can see you're still crazy about him."

I'm setting the dinner table when I discover a newspaper clipping tucked under the corner of my place mat. Andy strikes again. It's an article about an increase in STDs among teenagers. I shove it into the recycle bin. Do my parents know I'm having sex?

I know Max slept with many girls—many *women*—before me. But he's been tested. He's clean. Still, these mystery women haunt me. I picture Max in dark corners of bars, in his apartment, in beds across the city with glamorous succubi, intoxicated and infatuated. Max assures me the truth is far less exciting. I almost believe him.

It doesn't help that tonight, a night I have off from work, Amphetamine has a gig at the Honey Pot, a burlesque club that I'm not old enough to get into. I'm trying not to let it bother me. I know burlesque is an art, but it makes me uncomfortable. It makes me feel young. I hate feeling young.

But there are many things troubling me tonight.

It's Friday. Will Cricket come home this weekend?

Lindsey's words have been looping inside my head all week. How is it possible for me to feel this way? To be interested in Cricket and still be concerned about my relationship with Max? I want things to be okay with my boyfriend, I do. It's supposed to be simple. I don't want another complication. I don't *want* to be interested in Cricket.

During dinner, Andy and Nathan exchange worried looks over the veggie potpie. "Anything wrong, Lo?" Andy finally asks. "You seem distracted."

I tear my eyes from the window in our kitchen, from which I can barely see the Bell family's front porch. "Huh? Yeah. Everything's fine."

My parents look at me doubtfully as Norah comes in and sits at the table. "That was Chrysanthemum Bean, the one with the duck voice. She's coming over early tomorrow for a reading before buying her weekly scratch-offs."

Nathan winces and grinds more pepper on top of his potpie. And grinds. And grinds.

Andy shifts in his seat. He's always complaining that Nathan ruins his meals by adding too much pepper.

"Christ. Stop it, would you?" Norah says to her brother. "You're raising his blood pressure. You're raising MY blood pressure."

"It's fine," Andy says sharply. Even though I can see it's killing him.

We haven't had a relaxed meal since she—and her clients, none of whom should be spending their limited finances on tea-leaf readings or lottery scratch-offs—arrived. I turn away in time to catch a lanky figure running up the steps next door. And I sit up so fast that everyone stops bickering to see what's caused the disturbance. Cricket pats his pockets for his house key. His pants are tighter than usual. And the moment I notice this is the same moment that I'm knocked over by the truth of my feelings.

Lust.

He locates his key just as the front door opens. Calliope lets him inside. I sink back down in my chair. I didn't even realize that I'd partially risen out of it. Andy clears his throat. "Cricket looks good."

My face flames.

"I wonder if he has a girlfriend?" he asks. "Do you know?"

"No," I mumble.

Nathan laughs. "I remember when you two used to *accidentally* run into each other on walks—"

Andy cuts Nathan a quick look, and Nathan shuts his mouth.

Norah smirks. So it's true, our embarrassing crush was obvious to everyone. Fantastic.

I stand. "I'm going upstairs. I have homework."

"On a Friday night?" Andy asks as Nathan says, "Dishes first."

I take my plates to the sink. Will Cricket eat dinner with his family or go straight to his bedroom? I'm scrubbing the dishes so hard that I slice myself with a paring knife. I hiss under my breath.

"Are you okay?" All three ask at the same time.

"I cut myself. Not bad, though."

"Be careful," Nathan says.

Parents are excellent at stating the obvious. But I slow down and finish without further incident. The dishwasher is chugging as I race upstairs and burst into my room. My shoulders sag. His light is off.

Calm down, it's only Cricket.

I busy myself by sewing pleats into my Marie Antoinette dress. Twenty minutes pass. Thirty, forty, fifty, sixty.

What is he doing?

The Bells' downstairs lights are on, so for all I know, the entire family could be parked in front of the television watching eight hours of . . . something. Whatever. I can't concentrate, and now I'm angry. Angry at Cricket for not being here and angry at myself for caring. I wash off my makeup, remove my contacts, change into my pajamas—careful to close my curtains first—and flop into bed.

The clock reads 9:37. Max's band hasn't even started playing yet.

Just when I thought I couldn't feel like a bigger loser.

I toss and turn as images flash through my mind: Cricket, Max, burlesque dancers sitting in oyster shells. I'm finally drifting into a restless sleep when there's a faint *plink* against my window. My eyes shoot open. Did I dream it?

Plink, my window says again.

I leap out of bed and pull aside my curtains. Cricket Bell sits on his windowsill, feet swinging against his house. Something tiny is in one hand and the other is poised to throw something else. I open my window and a thousand bottled emotions explode inside of me at the full sight of him.

I like Cricket. Like *that.*

Again.

He lowers his hand. "I didn't have any pebbles."

My heart is stuck in my throat. I swallow. "What were you throwing?" I squint, but I can't make it out.

"Put on your glasses and see."

When I come back, he holds it up. He's smiling.

I smile back, self-conscious. "What are you doing with a box of toothpicks?"

"Making party trays of cubed cheese," he says with a straight face. "Why was your light off?"

"I was sleeping."

"It's not even ten-thirty." His legs stop swinging. "No hot date?"

I don't want to go there. "You know"—I point at his legs—"if you stretch those out, I bet they could touch my house."

He tries. They fall a few feet short, and I smile again. "They looked long enough."

"Ah, yes. Cricket and his monstrously long legs. His *monstrously* long body."

I laugh, and his eyes twinkle back. "Our houses just need to be closer together," I say. "Your proportions are perfect."

He releases his legs and stares at me carefully. The moment lasts so long that I have to look away. Cricket once said he thought my body was perfect, too. I blush at the memory and for revealing something unintentionally. At last, he speaks. "This isn't working for me." He throws his legs inside and disappears into his room, out of view.

I'm startled. "Cricket?"

I hear him rustling around. "Five minutes. Take a bathroom break or something."

It's not a bad idea. I'm not sure how much he can see in the darkness, but a little makeup wouldn't hurt. I'm raising the mascara wand to my lashes when I'm struck by how . . . not smart this is. Applying makeup. For someone who isn't my boyfriend. I settle for just a cherry-flavored lip gloss, but as soon as the scent hits me, I'm shaking.

Cherry flavored. Tea leaves. First love.

I return to my bedroom, wiping the gloss off on my hand, as there's a *CLANG* against my window. And then I see what he's about to do. "Oh God! No, Cricket, don't!"

"It'll hold my weight. Just grab onto that side, okay? Just in case?"

I clutch it tightly. He's removed one of his closet shelves, the thick wire kind that's coated in a white plastic, and he's using it as a bridge between our bedrooms.

"Careful!" I shout too loudly, and the bridge shakes.

But he smiles. "It's okay. I've got it."

And he does. Cricket scoots across quickly, right to where I'm holding it. His face is against mine. "You can let go now," he whispers.

My hands throb from gripping it so hard. I step back, allowing him room to enter. He slides down, and his legs brush against mine lengthwise. My body jolts. It's the first time we've touched in ages. He's so tall that his heart beats against my cheek.

His *heart*.

I falter backward. "What were you thinking?" I hiss, feeling all kinds of anxious. "You could have fallen and broken your neck."

"I thought it'd be easier to talk face-to-face." He keeps his voice low.

"We could've met on the sidewalk, gone for another walk."

He hesitates. "Should I go back?"

"No! I mean . . . no. You're already here."

A knock on my door startles us even farther apart. "Lola?" Nathan says. "I heard a crash. Are you all right?"

My eyes widen in panic. My parents will KILL me if they find an unexpected boy in my room. Even if it is Cricket! I push him on the floor behind my bed, where he can't be seen from my door. I jump in and pray Nathan doesn't question the sound of bedsprings. "I fell out of bed," I say groggily. "I was exhausted. I was having a nightmare."

"A nightmare?" The door opens, and Nathan peeks his head in. "It's been a long time since you've had one of those. Do you want to talk about it?"

"No, it was . . . stupid. A wolverine was chasing me. Or a werewolf. I dunno, you know how dreams are. I'm fine now." *Pleeeeease go away.* The longer my dad stands there, the more likely he is to see the bridge.

"Are you sure you're okay? You were so distant at dinner, and then when you cut yourself—"

"I'm fine, Dad. Good night."

He pauses and then, resigned, begins to shut the door. "Good night. I love you."

"Love you, too."

And he's almost gone, when . . . "Why are you wearing your glasses in bed?"

"I—I am?" I fumble and pat my face. "Oh. Wow. I must have been more tired than I thought."

Nathan frowns. "I'm worried about you, Lo. You haven't been yourself lately."

I *really* don't want to have this conversation in front of Cricket. "Dad—"

"Is it Norah? I know things haven't been easy since she got here, but—"

"I'm fine, Dad. Good night."

"Is it Max? Or Cricket? You turned strange when you saw him tonight, and I didn't mean to embarrass you when I said—"

"Good night, Dad."

PLEASE STOP TALKING.

He sighs. "Okay, Lola-doodle. But take off your glasses. I don't want you to crush them." I set them on my bedside table, and he leaves. Cricket waits until the footsteps hit the landing below. His head pops up beside my own, and even though I know he's there, it makes me jump.

"My dad was talking about . . ." I struggle for a nonincriminating answer. "I saw you come home, and it was at the same time Norah was telling us about this awful client. I must have been making a terrible face."

I hate myself.

He's quiet.

"So . . . now what?" I ask.

Cricket turns away from me. He leans his back against the side of my bed. "If you want me to go, I will."

Sadness. Desire. An ache inside of me so strong that I don't know how I believed it had ever left. I stare at the back of his head, and it's like the oxygen has disappeared from my room. My heart has turned to water. I'm drowning.

"No," I whisper at last. "You just got here."

I want to touch him again. I *have* to touch him again. If I don't touch him again, I'll die. I reach toward his hair. He won't even notice. But just as my fingertips are about to make contact, he turns around.

And his head jerks backward as I nearly poke out an eye.

"Sorry! I'm sorry!" I whisper.

"What are you doing?" But he grins as he lunges to poke out mine. I grab his finger, and then—just like that—I'm holding on to him. My hand is wrapped around his index finger. But he zeros in on my rainbow Band-Aid. "Is that where you cut yourself?"

"It was nothing." I let go of him, self-conscious again. "I was doing the dishes."

He watches me wring my hands. "Cool nails," he finally says.

They're black with a pink stripe down the center of each nail. And then . . . I know how I can touch him. "Hey. Let me paint yours." I'm already getting up for my favorite dark blue polish. Somehow, I know he won't protest.

I carry it to the floor, where he's still leaning against my bed. He sits up straight. "Will this hurt?" he asks.

"Badly." I shake the bottle. "But try to keep your screams low, I don't want Nathan coming back."

Cricket smiles as I reach for my chemistry textbook. "Put this on your lap, I'll need a steady surface. Now place your hands on it." We're close to each other, much closer than we've been while working on my dress. "I'm going to take your left hand now."

He swallows. "Okay."

Cricket holds it up slightly. Tonight the back of his hand has a star drawn on it. I wonder what it means as I slide my hand underneath his fingers. His hand twitches violently. "You'll have to hold it steady," I say. But I'm smiling. *Contact.*

I paint his nails Opening Night blue by the light of the moon. Our grips relax as I focus on my work. Slow, careful strokes. We don't talk. My skin and his skin. Only a book between my hand and his lap. I feel him watch me the entire time—not my hands, but my face—and his gaze burns like an African sun.

When I finish, I lift my eyes to his. He stares back. The moon moves across the sky. Her beams hit his eyelashes, and I'm struck anew that I'm alone, in the dark, with a boy who once shattered my heart. Who would kiss me, if I didn't have a boyfriend. Who I would kiss, if I didn't have a boyfriend.

Who I want to kiss anyway.

I bite my bottom lip. He's hypnotized. I lean forward, moving the curves of my body into the slender shadow of his. The air between us is physically hot, painfully so. He glances down my shirt. It is very, very close to his line of vision.

I part my lips.

And then he's stumbling away. "I want to," he croaks. "You know I *want* to."

He tests the bridge for firmness and springs onto it. Cricket Bell doesn't look back, so he doesn't see the tears spilling down my face. The only thing he leaves behind is a smudge of blue polish on my window frame.

chapter twenty-four

"Loooo-laaaa. Beautiful Lola." Franko's eyes are red and dilated. As usual.

I dig through the box-office drawers, throwing dry pens and dusty instruction manuals to the floor. "Have you seen the ink cartridges for the tickets?"

"No, but have you seen the popcorn today? It's so . . . aerodynamically inclined. I think I might've eaten some. Do I have kernels in my teeth?"

"No kernels," I snap.

"I think I have kernels in my teeth. Like, right between my front teeth." He stands, and his tongue explores his own mouth in a disgusting form of self–French kissing. "The strings are beautiful tonight."

"Sure. The strings."

"I mean, I wouldn't cut one, but if I did, I'd say . . . *that's a beautiful string.*"

Seriously, if he doesn't shut up soon, I'm strangling him. My patience is at an all-time low. I wave my arms at St. Clair, who is ripping tickets tonight. There's no one around, so he strolls over. "For the love of God, you two have to switch jobs," I say.

"You're beautiful, St. Clair," Franko says.

"Everyone is beautiful to you when you're high." He sits in Franko's seat. "Scat."

Franko lumbers away.

"Thank you," I say. "I just . . . can't handle that right now."

He gives me a full-bodied shrug. "Right now or for the entire month of November?"

"Don't even," I warn. But it's true. Since my complete and total humiliation with Cricket two weeks ago—and his subsequent disappearance from my life—I've been extremely unpleasant. I'm hurt, and I'm angry. No, I'm furious, because it's my stupid fault. I *threw* myself at him. What does he think of me now? Obviously, not much. I've called him twice and sent three apology texts, but he's ignored them all.

So much for Mr. Nice Guy.

"Mr. Nice Guy?" St. Clair asks. "Who's that?"

Oh, no. I'm talking out loud again. "Me," I lie. "Mr. Nice Guy is gone."

He sighs and checks the clock on the wall. "Fantastic."

"I'm sorry." And I mean it. My friends—Lindsey, Anna, and St. Clair—have all been patient with me. More than I deserve.

I told Lindsey what happened, but St. Clair, and through him, Anna, must have heard some version of something from Cricket. I'm not sure what. "Thank you for taking Franko's place. I appreciate it."

The European shrug again.

We work quietly for the next hour. As the minutes tick by, I feel more and more guilty. It's time to change my attitude. At least around my friends. "So," I say during the next customer lull. "How did it go with Anna's family? Didn't her mom and brother visit for Thanksgiving?"

He smiles for the first time since coming in here. "I wooed them off their feet. It was an excellent visit."

I grin and then give him a nod with exaggerated formality. "Congratulations."

"Thank you," he says with equal formality. "They stayed with my mum."

"That's . . . weird."

"Not really. Mum is cool, easy to get along with."

I raise a teasing eyebrow. "So where did YOU guys stay?"

"Where we always stay." He stares back solemnly. "In our *very* separate dormitories."

I snort.

"What about you?" he asks. "Did you spend Thanksgiving with the boyfriend?"

"Uh, no." I stumble through an explanation about Norah being difficult and Max being busy, but it sounds hollow and forced. We're silent for a minute. "How do you . . ." I'm struggling to find the right words. "How do you and Anna make it work? You make it seem easy."

"Being with Anna *is* easy. She's the one."

The one. It stops my heart. I thought Max was the one, but . . . there's that *other* one.

The first one.

"Do you believe in that?" I ask quietly. "In one person for everyone?"

Something changes in St. Clair's eyes. Maybe sadness. "I can't speak for anyone but myself," he says. "But, for me, yes. I have to be with Anna. But this is something you have to figure out on your own. I can't answer that for you, no one can."

"Oh."

"Lola." He rolls his chair over to my side. "I know things are shite right now. And in the name of friendship and full disclosure, I went through something similar last year. When I met Anna, I was with someone else. And it took a long time before I found the courage to do the hard thing. But you have to do the hard thing."

I swallow. "And what's the hard thing?"

"You have to be honest with yourself."

"Lola. You look . . . different."

The next afternoon and I'm on Max's doorstep, sans wig and fancy makeup. I'm wearing an understated skirt and a simple blouse, and my natural hair is loose around my shoulders. "Can I come in?" I'm nervous.

"Of course." He moves aside, and I enter.

"Is Johnny here?"

"No, I'm alone." Max pauses. "Do your dads know you're here?"

"They don't have to know where I am *all the time.*"

He shakes his head. "Right."

I wander toward his couch, pick up the Noam Chomsky book on his coffee table, flip through the pages, and set it back down. I don't know where to begin. I'm here for answers. I'm here to find out if he's the one.

Max is staring at me strangely, about something other than my sudden presence. It makes me even more uncomfortable. "What?" I ask. "What's that look?"

"Sorry. You . . . look a little young today."

My heart wrenches. "Is that bad?"

"No. You look beautiful." And he gives me that gorgeous half smile. "Come here." Max collapses onto his beat-up couch, and I climb into his arms. We sit in silence. He waits for me to speak again, aware that I'm here for a reason. But I can't form the words. I thought being here would be enough. I thought I'd know when I saw him.

Why is the truth so hard to see?

I trace his spiderwebs. Max closes his eyes. I lightly brush the boy in the wolf suit in the crook of his elbow. He releases a moan, and our lips find each other. He pulls me onto his lap. I'm helpless against the current.

"Lolita," he whispers.

And my entire body freezes.

Max doesn't notice. He lifts the edge of my shirt, and it's enough to wake me up. I yank it back down. He startles. "What? What's the matter?"

I can barely keep my voice steady. "Which one, Max?"

"Which one, what?" He's unusually dazed. "What are we talking about?"

"Which Dolores Nolan are you in love with? Are you in love with me, Lola? Or are you in love with Lolita?"

"And what is *that* supposed to mean?"

"You know exactly what it means. You call me Lolita, but you get weird when I'm not dressed up, when I look my age. So which one? Do you like the older me or the younger me?" A worse thought occurs. "Or do you only like me *because* I'm young?"

Max is furious. He pushes me off his lap and stands up. "You really want to have this conversation? Right now?"

"When would be a better time? When, Max?"

He swipes up his lighter from the side table. "I thought we'd been over the age thing. I thought it was something that bothered *other* people."

"I just want the truth. Do you love me? Or do you love my age?"

"How the HELL can you say that?" Max throws his lighter across the room. "In case you've forgotten, let me remind you. You chased ME down. I didn't want this."

"What you mean you 'didn't want this'? You didn't want *me*?"

"That's not what I said!" he bursts out. "Oh, I wanted you.

But guys like me aren't supposed to go after girls like you, remember? Isn't that what we're talking about? Jesus. I don't know what you want me to say. It sounds like every answer I give you will be the wrong one."

The truth hits me with a vicious punch to the gut. *Every answer is the wrong one.*

"You're right," I whisper.

"Damn right, I'm right." A pause. "Wait. Right about what?"

"There's no right answer. It doesn't exist. There's no way this can end well."

He stares me down. For several moments, neither of us speaks.

"You're not serious," he says at last.

I force myself to stand. "I think I am."

"You *think* you are." His jaw hardens. "After your parents. After *Sunday brunch*? Do you have any idea what I've put up with to be with you?"

"But that's just it! You shouldn't have to 'put up' with—"

"Did I have a choice?" Max closes the distance between us.

"Yes. No! I don't know . . ." I'm shaking. "I'm just trying to be honest."

"Oh." His nose is an inch from mine. "You're ready to be honest."

I swallow hard.

"Honestly," he says, "I don't know who you are. Every time I see you, you're someone different. You're a liar, and you're a fake. Despite what you think, despite what your dads have told you, there is nothing *special* about you. You're just a little girl with a lot of issues. *That* is what I think about you."

And then . . . my world goes black.

"Love," I blurt. "I thought you loved me."

"I thought I did, too. Thank you for making things so clear."

I stumble backward in horror. For one crazy moment, I want to throw myself at his feet and beg for his forgiveness. Promise to be someone else, promise to be *one* person.

Max crosses his arms.

And then . . . I want to hurt him.

I step back into him, *my* nose against *his*. "Guess what?" I hiss back. "I am a liar. I do like Cricket Bell. You're right. I've been hanging out with him this whole time! And he's been in my bedroom, and I've been in his. And I want him, Max. I *want* him."

He's shaking with rage. "Get. Out."

I grab my purse and throw open his front door.

"I never want to see you again." His voice is deathly low. "You are nothing to me. Do you understand?"

"Yes," I say. "Thank you for making things so clear."

chapter twenty-five

I'm dizzy. Seeing spots. Stumbling. Walk or bus? Walk or bus? I'm walking. Yes, I'll walk home. But then I see the bus and somehow I'm on the bus and I'm sobbing my guts out. A hipster with an ironic mustache shifts down a row. An elderly man in a baseball cap knits his brows at me, and the woman with the quilted jacket looks as if she actually wants to say something. I twist away and continue weeping.

And then I'm pulling the cord and I'm off the bus and I'm staggering uphill. Toward home. It feels like someone is clawing at my stomach, my chest, my heart. Like my insides are being ripped from my body and stitched to my skin for the world to ridicule.

How could he? How could he say those things?

How could my life change so drastically, so quickly? One minute we were fine. The next . . . oh God. *It's over.* I want to crawl into bed and disappear. I don't want to see anyone. I don't want to talk to anyone. I don't want to think or do anything.

Max. I clutch my chest. I can't breathe.

Get inside, Dolores. You're almost there.

I'm only two houses away when I see them. The Bell family. They're wrapped in a heated discussion in the center of their small driveway. Mr. Bell—tall and slender like the twins, but with sandy hair—is shaking his head and gesturing at the road. Mrs. Bell—shorter, but with the twins' same dark hair—is rubbing her fingers against her temples. Calliope's back is to me, hands on her hips. And Cricket . . . he's staring straight at me. He seems shaken, no doubt by both my sudden appearance and how I actually appear. The rest of his body turns to face me, which reveals another surprise.

There's a baby on his hip.

I hide my face with a curtain of hair and run up the stairs to my house. The Bells have stopped talking. They're watching me and listening to my choked sobs. I glance over as I'm opening the front door. Alexander is there, too. The twins' older brother. I didn't see him because he's standing behind Cricket, several inches shorter.

The baby. Right. Aleck's daughter, Abigail.

Max. His name strikes again like whiplash, and the Bells are forgotten, and I'm slamming the door and racing into my bedroom. Nathan hears my pounding footsteps and chases after me. "What is it, Lola? What's going on, what happened?"

I lock my door and fall against it. I collapse. Nathan is knocking and shouting questions and soon Andy and Norah have joined him. Betsy's tail thumps rapidly against the wall.

"MAX AND I BROKE UP, OKAY? LEAVE ME ALONE." The last word is cut off as my throat swells and blocks it. There's an agitated murmuring on the other side. It sounds like Norah is pulling away my parents, and I hear Betsy's jingling dog tags follow everyone back downstairs.

The hall is quiet.

I'm alone now. I'm actually *alone.*

I throw myself into bed, shoes and all. How could Max be so cruel? How could I be so cruel back? He's right. I'm a liar, and I'm a fake, and . . . I'm not special. *There's nothing special about me.* I'm a stupid little girl crying on her bed. Why does my life keep cycling back to this moment? After Cricket, two years ago. After Norah, almost two months ago. And now, after Max. I'll *always* be the little girl crying on her bed.

The thought makes me cry harder.

"Lola?" I'm not sure how much time has passed when I hear the faint voice outside my window. "Lola?" Louder. He tries a third time, a minute later, but I don't get up. How convenient of Cricket to appear *now,* when I haven't seen him in two weeks. When he hasn't returned my calls. When my soul is bluer than blue, blacker than black.

I'm a bad person.

No, Max is a bad person. He's difficult, he's condescending, he's jealous.

But I'm worse. I'm a child playing dress-up, who can't even recognize herself under her own costume.

chapter twenty-six

The rational side of me knows that I need some kind of release. But I can't cry anymore. I'm empty. I'm drained. And I can't move.

Not that I'd want to.

Because that's the thing about depression. When I feel it deeply, I don't *want* to let it go. It becomes a comfort. I want to cloak myself under its heavy weight and breathe it into my lungs. I want to nurture it, grow it, cultivate it. It's mine. I want to check out with it, drift asleep wrapped in its arms and not wake up for a long, long time.

I've been spending a lot of time in bed this week.

When you're asleep, no one asks you to do anything. No one expects anything of you. And you don't have to face any of your troubles. So I've been dragging myself to school, and I've been dragging myself to work. And I've been sleeping.

Max is gone. And not just gone as in he's not my boyfriend anymore, but gone as in he's *gone.* I asked Lindsey to retrieve a textbook I'd left at his apartment, and his roommate said he left the city on Tuesday. Johnny wouldn't say where Max went.

He finally ran away. Without me.

I wish it didn't hurt to think about him. And I'm not upset because I want to be with him, I don't, but he was so much to me for so long. He was my future. And now he's nothing. I gave him *everything,* and now he's nothing. He was my first, which means I'll never be able to forget him, but I'll fade from his memory. Soon I'll just be another notch on his bedpost.

I didn't know it was possible to simultaneously hate and ache for someone. I thought Max and I would be together forever. No one believed me. We were going to prove them wrong, but we were the ones who were wrong. Or maybe I'm the only one who was wrong. Did Max think of me as forever?

The question is too painful, either way, to consider.

My parents are worried, but they've been leaving me alone so that I can heal. As if it were possible to ever heal from heartbreak.

It's around midnight—not quite Friday, not quite Saturday—and the moon is full again. Traditionally, farmers called the December full moon the Cold Moon or the Long Nights Moon. Both feel appropriate tonight. I opened my window to better absorb her coldness and longness, to use it feed it to my own, but it was a dumb mistake. I'm freezing. And I had another long shift at the theater, and I'm exhausted, and I can't find the energy to shut it.

But I can't sleep.

The silk fabric of my Marie Antoinette gown, draped across my sewing table, shimmers with a pale blue glow in the moonlight. It's so close to completion. The winter formal is still a month and a half away, there was plenty of time.

It doesn't matter anymore. I'm not going.

And I don't even care about not having a date. It's the idea of showing up in something so ridiculous, that's what hurts. Max was right. The dance is stupid. My classmates wouldn't be impressed by my dress; they'd be merciless. I don't know how long I've been staring at its folds when a yellow light flicks on outside my window.

"Lola?" A call through the night.

I close my eyes. I can't speak.

"I know you're in there. I'm coming over, okay?"

I stiffen as the *CLUNK* of his closet-bridge hits my window. He called out to me once more last weekend, but I pretended that I didn't hear him. I listen to the creak of his weight against the bridge, and a moment later, he drops quietly onto my floor. "Lola?" Cricket is on his knees at the side of my bed. I feel it. "I'm here," he whispers. "You can talk to me or not talk to me, but I'm here."

I close my eyes tighter.

"St. Clair told me what happened. With Max." Cricket waits

for me to say something. When I don't, he continues. "I'm—I'm sorry I didn't call you back. I was angry. I told Cal about that night in your bedroom, and she went ballistic. She said she'd warned you to stay away from me, and we got into this huge fight. I was angry with her for talking behind my back, and I was angry with you for not telling me. Like . . . you didn't think I could handle it."

I cringe and curl into a ball. Why *didn't* I tell him? Because I didn't want him to realize that her accusations were true? Because I was afraid that he'd listen to her words over mine? I'm such a jerk. As fearful of Calliope as she is of me.

"But . . . this is coming out backward." I hear him shift on his knees, agitated. "What I was trying to say—what I was getting at—is that I've been thinking a lot about everything, and I'm not actually angry with you at all. I'm angry with myself. I'm the one who keeps climbing in your window. I'm the one who can't stay away. All of this weirdness is my fault."

"Cricket. This is *not* your fault." It comes out in a croak.

He's silent. I open my eyes, and he's watching me. I watch him back. "The moon is bright tonight," he says at last.

"But it's cold." The tears have found me again. They fall.

Cricket reaches out and brushes my neck. He traces upward, along my jaw, and then my cheek. I close my eyes at the unbearable sensation of his thumb drying my tears. He presses down gently. I turn my head, and it becomes cradled in his hand. He holds the weight for several minutes.

"I'm sorry I didn't tell you that I talked with Calliope," I whisper.

He pulls away, carefully, and I notice another star drawn on the back of his hand. "I'm only upset that she spoke with you in the first place. It wasn't any of her business."

"She was just worried about you." As the words spill out, I realize that I believe them. "And she had every right to be worried. I'm not exactly a good person."

"That's not true," he says. "Why would you say that?"

"I was a terrible girlfriend to Max."

There's a long pause. "Did you love him?" he asks quietly.

I swallow. "Yes."

Cricket looks unhappy. "And do you still love him?" he asks. But before I can answer, he says in one great breath, "Forget it, I don't want to know." And suddenly Cricket Bell is inside my bed, and his torso is flattening against mine, and his pelvis is pressing against mine, and his lips are moving toward mine.

My senses are detonating. I've wanted him for so long.

And I need to wait a little longer.

I slide my hand between our mouths, just in time. His lips are soft against my palm. I slowly, slowly remove it. "No, I don't love Max anymore. But I don't want to give you this broken, empty me. I want you to have me when I'm *full,* when I can give something *back* to you. I don't have much to give right now."

Cricket's limbs are still, but his chest is pounding hard against my own. "But you'll want me someday? That feeling you once had for me . . . that hasn't left either?"

Our hearts beat the same wild rhythm. They're playing the same song.

"It never left," I say.

—

Cricket stays through the night. And even though we don't talk anymore, and even though we don't do anything *more* than talk, it's what I need. The calming presence of a body I trust. And when we fall asleep, we sleep heavily.

In fact, we sleep so heavily that we don't see the sun rise.

We don't hear the coffeepot brewing downstairs.

And we don't hear Nathan until he's right above us.

chapter twenty-seven

Nathan grabs Cricket by the shoulders and throws him off my bed. Cricket scrambles into a corner while I flounder for my closest eyeglasses. My skin is on fire.

"What the hell is going on in here? Did he sneak in while—" Nathan cuts himself off. He's noticed the bridge. He stalks up to Cricket, who shrinks so low that he almost becomes Nathan's height. "So you've been climbing into my daughter's bedroom for how long now? Days? Weeks? *Months?*"

Cricket is so mortified he can hardly speak. "No. Oh God, no. Sir. I'm sorry, sir."

Andy runs into the room, sleep disheveled and frenzied. "What's happening?" He sees Cricket cowering beneath Nathan. *"Oh."*

"Do something!" I tell Andy. "He'll kill him!"

Murder flashes across Andy's face, and I'm reminded of what Max said ages ago, about how much worse it was dealing with *two* protective fathers. But it disappears, and he takes a tentative step closer to Nathan. "Honey. I want to kill him, too. But let's talk to Lola first."

Nathan is terrifyingly still. He's so angry that his mouth barely moves. "You. Out."

Cricket lunges for the window. Andy's eyes bulge when he sees the bridge, but all he says is, "The front door, Cricket. Out the *front* door."

Cricket holds up both hands, and in the daylight, it's the first time I see that there are still scattered shreds of blue paint on his nails. "I just want you to know that we didn't do anything but talk and sleep—*sleep* sleep," he quickly adds. "Like with eyes closed and hands to oneself and dreaming. *Innocent* dreams. I would never do anything behind your back. I mean, never anything dishonorable. I mean—"

"Cricket," I plead.

He looks at me miserably. "I'm sorry." And then he tears downstairs and out the front door. Nathan storms out of my room, and the master bedroom door slams shut.

Andy is silent for a long time. At last, he sighs. "Care to explain why there was a boy in your bed this morning?"

"We didn't do anything. You have to believe me! He came over because he knew I was sad. He only wanted to make sure I was okay."

"Dolores, that's how boys take advantage of girls. Or other

boys," he adds. "They attack when your guard is down, when you're feeling vulnerable."

The implication makes me angry. "Cricket would never take advantage of me."

"He climbed into your bed fully aware that you're hurting over someone else."

"And we didn't do anything but talk."

Andy crosses his arms. "How long has this been going on?"

I tell the truth. I want him to believe me so that he'll also believe Cricket is innocent. "There was only one other time. But he didn't stay the night."

He closes his eyes. "Was this before or after you broke up with Max?"

My head sinks into my shoulders. "Before."

"And did you tell Max?"

It sinks farther. "No."

"And that didn't make you wonder if there was something wrong with it?"

I'm crying. "We're friends, Dad."

Andy looks pained as he sits on the edge of my bed. "Lola. Everyone and their grandmother knows that boy is in love with you. *You* know that boy is in love with you. But as wrong as it was for him to be here, it's so much worse for you to have led him on. You had a boyfriend. What were you thinking? You don't treat someone like that. You shouldn't have treated either one of them like that."

I didn't know it was possible to feel any worse than I already did.

"Listen." The look on Andy's face means he'd rather eat glass than say what he's about to say. "I know you're growing up. And as hard as it is, I have to accept that there are certain . . . *things* you're doing. But you're an intelligent young woman, and we've had the talk, and I know—from this point on—you'll make the right decisions."

Oh God. I can't look at him.

"But you have to understand this part is difficult for us, especially for Nathan. Norah was your age when she ran away and got pregnant. But you can talk to me. I *want* you to talk to me."

"Okay." I can barely get the word out.

"And I *don't* want to find a boy in your room again, you hear me?" He waits until I nod before standing. "All right. I'll talk to Nathan and see what I can do. But don't for a second think you're getting out of this easily."

"I know."

He walks to the door. "Never. Again. Understand?"

"What . . . what about when I'm married?"

"We'll buy a cot. Your husband can sleep on that when he visits."

I can't help it. I let out a tiny snort of laughter. He comes back and hugs me.

"I'm not kidding," he says.

The punishment arrives in the afternoon. I'm grounded through the end of my upcoming winter break from school. Another month of grounding. But, honestly, I don't even care. It's the other half of the punishment—the unspoken half—that makes me feel terrible.

My parents no longer trust me. I have to earn it back.

Throughout the day, I try to catch Cricket at our windows, but he never goes inside his bedroom. Around three o'clock, I see his figure dart past his kitchen window, so I know he's still at home. Why is he avoiding me? Is he embarrassed? Is he angry? Did my parents call his parents? I'll die if they called Mr. and Mrs. Bell, but I can't ask, because if they haven't, it might give them the idea.

I'm a wreck by the time Cricket's light turns on. It's just after eight. I throw aside my English homework and run to my window, and he's already at his. We open them at the same time, and the misty night air explodes . . . with *wailing.*

Cricket is holding Aleck's daughter again.

"I'm sorry!" he shouts. "She won't let me put her down!"

"It's okay!" I shout back.

And then I realize something. I slam my window shut. Cricket looks startled, but I hold up a finger and mouth *ONE SECOND.* I rip out a page from my spiral notebook and scribble on it with a fat purple marker. I hold the message against my window.

MY PARENTS!!! TALK LATER? WHEN NO BABY!!!

He looks relieved. And then panicked as he slams his own window shut. The next minute is rife with tension as we wait for my parents to tear into my bedroom. They don't. But even with our windows closed, I hear Abigail's cries. Cricket bounces her on his hip, pleading with her, but her face remains contorted in misery.

Where is Aleck? Or Aleck's wife? Shouldn't they be taking care of this?

Calliope bursts through Cricket's door. She takes Abigail from him, and Abigail screams harder. Both of the twins wince as Calliope thrusts her back into Cricket's arms. The baby grows quieter, but she's still crying. Calliope glances in my direction. She freezes, and I give a weak wave. She scowls.

Cricket sees her expression and says something that causes her to stalk away. Her bedroom light turns on seconds later. He's turning back toward me, still bouncing Abigail, when Mrs. Bell enters. I yank my curtains closed. Whatever is going on over there, I don't want his mom to think I'm spying on it.

I sit back down with my five-paragraph essay for English, but I can't concentrate. That familiar, nauseating feeling of guilt. When I saw the Bells in their driveway last week, they were clearly in distress about *something*. And I never asked Cricket what it was about. He was in my bedroom for an entire night, and I didn't even think to ask. And he's always concerned about what's happening in my life. I'm so selfish.

A new kind of truth hits me: *I'm not worthy of him.*

His light turns off, and the sudden darkness acts as a confirmation of my fears. He's too good for me. He's sweet and kind and honest. Cricket Bell has integrity. And I don't deserve him. But . . . I want him anyway.

Is it possible to earn someone?

He doesn't return for nearly two hours. The moment he's back, I raise my window again. Cricket raises his. Exhaustion has settled between his brows, and his shoulders are sagging. Even a lock of hair has flopped onto his forehead. I've *never* seen Cricket's hair fall down. "I'm sorry." His voice is tired. He keeps it low, conscious that the parental threat has not passed. "For last night. For this morning, for tonight. Your parents didn't come up, did they? I'm such an id—"

"Stop, please. You don't have to apologize."

"I know. Our rule." He's glum.

"No. I mean, don't apologize for last night. Or this morning. I wanted you there."

He raises his head. Once again, the intensity of his eyes makes my heart stutter.

"I—I'm the one who's sorry," I continue. "I knew something was going on with your family, and I didn't ask. It didn't even cross my mind."

"Lola." His brow deepens farther. "You're going through a difficult time. I would never expect you to be thinking about my family right now. That would be crazy."

Even when I'm in the wrong, he puts me in the right. *I don't deserve him.*

I hesitate.

Earn him.

"So . . . what's going on? Unless you don't want to tell me. I'd understand."

Cricket leans his elbows against his windowsill and looks into the night sky. The star on his left hand has faded from washing, but it's still there. He waits so long to answer that I wonder if he heard me. A foghorn bleats in the distance. Mist creeps into my room, carrying the scent of eucalyptus. "My brother left his wife last week. Aleck took Abby, and they're staying here until he figures out what to do next. He's not in great shape, so we're kinda taking care of them both right now."

"Where's his wife? Why did he take the baby?"

"She's still at their apartment. She's going through . . . a lifestyle crisis."

I wrap my arms around myself. "What does that mean? She's a lesbian?"

"No." Cricket pries his eyes from the sky to glance at me, and I see that he's uncomfortable. "She's much younger than Aleck. They married, got pregnant, and now she's rebelling against it. This new life. She stays out late, parties. Last weekend . . . my brother found out that she'd cheated on him."

"I'm so sorry." I think about Max. About Cricket in my bedroom. "That's awful."

He shrugs and looks away. "It's why I finally came back. You know, to help out."

"Does that mean you're still fighting with Calliope?"

"Maybe. I don't know." Cricket runs his fingers through his dark hair, and the part that had flopped down sticks back up. "Sometimes she makes things so difficult, more than they have to be. But I guess I'm doing the same thing right now."

I allow the thought to hang, and my mind returns to Max. It

fills with shameful, retired fantasies about our future. "Do you think . . . did Aleck's wife do that because she got married too young?"

"No, they got married too *wrong*. The only person in my family who thought it would last was Aleck, but it was clear she wasn't the one."

The one. There it is again.

"How did you know? That she wasn't the one for him?"

Now he's staring at his hands, slowing rubbing them together. "They just didn't have that . . . natural magic. You know? It never seemed easy."

My voice grows tiny. "Do you think things have to be easy? For it to work?"

Cricket's head shoots up, his eyes bulging as they grasp my meaning. "NO. I mean, yes, but . . . sometimes there are . . . extenuating circumstances. That prevent it from being easy. For a while. But then people overcome those . . . circumstances . . . and . . ."

"So you believe in second chances?" I bite my lip.

"Second, third, fourth. Whatever it takes. However long it takes. If the person is right," he adds.

"If the person is . . . Lola?"

This time, he holds my gaze. "Only if the other person is Cricket."

chapter twenty-eight

Cricket isn't the only thing I have to earn. I have to earn back my parents' trust.

I'm a good daughter, *I am*. I have plenty of faults, but I keep up with my homework, I do my chores, I rarely talk back, and I like them. I'm one of the few people my age who actually cares what her parents think. So I'm dressing like someone responsible (all black, very serious), and I studied like crazy for my finals, and I'm doing whatever they ask. Even when it's awful. Like taking Heavens to Betsy for her late-night walk when it's forty degrees outside, which, by the way, I have done every night this week.

I want my parents to remember that I'm good, so they'll also remember that Cricket is good. Better than good. He came over to formally apologize to them, though I don't think it helped.

His name is still banned from our household. Even after Mrs. Bell told Andy what was happening with Aleck, and my parents were tut-tutting for the family over dinner, they skipped over Cricket's name. It was, "Calliope and . . . *hmph*."

At least Mr. and Mrs. Bell don't know what happened. My parents didn't call them. I probably have Andy to thank for that, maybe even Norah. She's been surprisingly cool about all of this. "Give them time," she says. "Don't rush anything."

Which is what I know I need anyway. Time.

The memory of Max is still bitter and strong. I didn't realize it was possible to have such an ugly breakup when you were the one who did the breaking up. And I'm pretty sure I'm the one who did the breaking up. At least, I did it first.

And then he did it better.

I feel terrible about how it ended, and I feel terrible for not being honest with him while we were together. I want to apologize. Maybe it would get rid of these bad feelings, and I'd be able to move on. Maybe then it wouldn't sting whenever my mind summons his name. I've left several messages on his voice mail, but he hasn't called me back. And he's still gone from the city. I even went to Amoeba to ask Johnny.

Max's last words haunt me. *Am* I nothing to him? Already?

I'm not ready for Cricket, and his hands are full anyway. With Aleck too depressed to give Abigail his attention, she's decided that Cricket is the next best thing. He's home for winter break—we're both on winter break—and I rarely see him without Abby hanging from his arms or wrapped around his legs. I recognize that feeling, that *need,* inside of her. I wish there was someone I could hold on to.

Lindsey helps. She calls every day, and we talk about . . . not Max. Not Cricket. Though she did guiltily announce that she's attending the winter formal. She asked Charlie, and of course he said yes. I'm happy for her.

A person can be sad and happy at the same time.

I've moved my Marie Antoinette dress and wig and panniers into Nathan's office, aka Norah's room. I don't like looking at them. Maybe I'll finish the dress later, for Halloween next year. Lindsey can wear it. But I'm still not going to the dance, and at least I know *that* was the right decision. The last few weeks of school were miserable.

"Who died and turned you Goth?" Marta sneered, turning up her nose at my all-black ensemble. Her friends, the trendiest clique at Harvey Milk Memorial, joined in, and soon everyone was accusing me of being a Goth, which—even though it's not true—would have been fine. Except then the Goth kids accused me of being a poseur.

"I'm not a Goth. And I'm not in mourning," I insisted.

At least my new wardrobe helps me blend into my neighborhood. In the winter, the Castro turns into a sea of trendy black clothing. Black helps me disappear, and I don't want to be seen right now. It's amazing how clothing affects how people see—or *don't* see—you. The other day I waited for the bus beside Malcolm from Hot Cookie. He's served me dozens of rainbow M&M cookies, and we're always debating the merits of Lady Gaga versus Madonna, but he didn't recognize me.

It's odd. Me, the *real* me, and I'm unknown.

The few people who do recognize me always ask if I'm feeling okay. And it's not that I feel great, but why does everyone assume something is wrong because I'm not costumed? Our usual bank teller went so far as to mention his concern to Nathan. Dad came home worried, and I had to assure him, again and again, that I'm fine.

I am fine.

I'm not fine.

What am I?

The blinking Christmas lights and flickering menorahs in the windows of the houses, hardware store, bars and clubs and restaurants . . . they seem false. Forced. And I'm unnaturally aggravated by the man dressed as sexy Mrs. Claus handing out candy canes in front of the Walgreens and collecting money for charity.

I spend my break working at the theater—I take extra shifts to fill my spare time—and watching Cricket. Throughout the day, I can usually spot him through one of the Bells' windows, playing with Abigail. Abby has sandy-colored hair like her father and grandfather, but there's something sweet and pure about her smile that reminds me of her uncle. He bundles her up and takes her on walks every day.

Sometimes, I grab a coat and run after them. I've gone with them to the park for the swings, to the library for picture books, and to Spike's for espresso (Cricket and me) and an organic gingerbread man (Abby). I try to be helpful. I want to earn him, deserve him. He always bursts into a smile when he sees me, but it's impossible to mistake the silent examination that follows. As if he's wondering if *now* I'm okay. If today is the day. And I can tell by his expression, always a little confused and sad, that he knows it's not.

I wish he wouldn't look at me like that. I've become his difficult equation face again.

In the evenings, after Abby has gone to bed, I'll see him tinkering in his bedroom. I can't tell what he's making, it must be something small, but the telltale signs of mechanical bits and pieces—including objects opened and stripped for parts—remain scattered about his desk. *That's* making me happy.

Christmas passes like Thanksgiving, without a bang. I go to work—movie theaters are always packed on Christmas Day—and Anna and St. Clair are both there. They try to cheer me up by playing this game where we get a point every time someone complains about the ticket price or yells at us because a show is sold out. Whoever has the most points at the end of the day gets the unopened bag of gummy lychee candy St. Clair found in theater twelve. It's not a great prize. But it helps.

The managers bought Santa hats for everyone to wear. Mine is the only one that's hot pink. I appreciate the thought, but I feel ridiculous.

I get yelled at the most. I win the lychee candy.

New Year's Day. It's cold, but the sun is out, so I take Betsy to Dolores Park. She's sniffing out places on the hillside to leave her mark when I hear a tiny, "O-la!"

It's Abby. I'm flattered she spoke my name. At one and a half years old, her vocabulary isn't immense. She tears toward me from the playground. She's dressed in a tiny purple tutu. Cricket walks in long strides behind her, hands in his pockets, smiling.

I get on my knees to hug Abby, and she collapses into my arms, the way really little kids do. "Hi, you," I say. She lunges for the turquoise rhinestone barrette in my hair. I'd forgotten to take it out. Norah—NORAH, of all people—snapped it in at breakfast. "It's the New Year," she said. "Sparkles won't kill you today."

Cricket pulls off Abby before she can rip out the barrette. "All right, all right. Abigail Bell, that's *enough*." But he's grinning at her. She grins back.

"You've made quite the new best friend," I say.

His expression turns to regret. "Children do have questionable taste."

I laugh. It's the first time I can remember laughing this week.

"Though she has great taste in hair accessories," he continues. Betsy rolls onto her stomach for him, and he scratches her belly. His rainbow bracelets and rubber bands shake against her black fur. The back of his entire left hand, including fingers, is crammed with mathematical symbols and calculations. Abby leans over hesitantly to pet my dog. "It's nice to see you in something sparkly again," he adds.

My laughter stops, and my cheeks redden. "Oh. It's stupid, I know. It's New Year's, so Norah thought . . ."

Cricket frowns and stands back up. His shadow stretches, tall and slender, out for infinity behind him. "I was being serious.

It's nice to see a little bit of Lola shining through." The frown turns into a gentle smile. "It gives me hope."

And I can't explain it, but I'm on verge of tears. "But I *have* been me. I've been trying hard to be me. A better me."

He raises his eyebrows. "On what planet does Lola Nolan not wear . . . color?"

I gesture at my outfit. "I have this in white, too, you know."

The joke falls flat. He's struggling not to say something. Abby bumps into his left leg and grips it with all of her might. He picks her up and sets her on his hip.

"Just say it," I tell him. "Whatever it is."

Cricket nods slowly. "Okay." He collects his thoughts before continuing. He speaks carefully. "Being a good person, or a better person, or whatever it is you're worried about and trying to fix? It shouldn't change who you are. It means you become *more* like yourself. But . . . I don't know this Lola."

My heart stops. I feel faint. It's just like what Max used to say.

"What?" Cricket is alarmed. "When did he say that?"

I flush again and look down at the grass. I wish I didn't talk out loud when I'm distressed. "I haven't seen him again, if that's what you mean. But he said . . . before . . . that because I dressed in costume, he didn't know who I really was."

Cricket closes his eyes. He's shaking. It takes me a moment to realize that he's shaking with *anger*. Abby squirms in his arms. It's upsetting her. "Lola, do you remember when you told me that I had a gift?"

I gulp. "Yes."

His eyes open and lock on mine. "You have one, too. And maybe some people think that wearing a costume means you're trying to hide your real identity, but I think a costume is more truthful than regular clothing could ever be. It actually says something about the person wearing it. I knew that Lola, because she expressed her desires and wishes and dreams for the entire city to see. For *me* to see."

My heart is beating in my ears, my lungs, my throat.

"I miss that Lola," he says.

I take a step toward him. His breath catches.

And then he takes a step toward me.

"Ohhhh," Abby says.

We look down, startled to discover that she's still on his hip, but she's pointing into the winter-white sky. San Francisco's famous flock of wild parrots bursts across Dolores Park in a flurry of green feathers. The air is filled with beating wings and boisterous screeching, and everyone in the park stops to watch the spectacle. The surprising whirl disappears over the buildings as swiftly as it arrived.

I turn back to Abby. The unexpected explosion of color and noise and beauty in her world has left her awed.

chapter twenty-nine

It's the Sunday night before school resumes, and my parents are on a date. I'm hanging out with Norah. We're watching a marathon of home decorating shows, rolling our eyes for different reasons. Norah thinks the redesigned houses look bourgeois and, therefore, boring. I think they look boring, too, but only because each designer seems to be working from the same tired manual of modern decorating.

"It's nice to see you looking like yourself again," she says during a commercial break.

I'm wearing a blue wig, a ruffled Swiss Heidi dress, and the arms from a glittery golden thrift-store sweater. I've cut them off, and I'm using them as glittery golden leg warmers. I snort. "Yeah, I know how much you like the way I dress."

She keeps her eyes on the television, but that familiar Norah edge returns to her voice. "It's not how *I* would dress, but that doesn't mean I don't appreciate it. It doesn't mean I don't like you for who you are."

I keep my eyes on the television, too, but my chest tightens.

"So," I say a few minutes later as the show recaps what we've already seen. "What's happening with the apartment? Has Ronnie set a move-in date yet?"

"Yep. I'll be gone by the end of the week."

"Oh. That's really . . . soon."

She snorts. *Her snort sounds like mine.* "Soon can't come soon enough. Nathan's been suffocating me from the moment I arrived."

And there's the ungrateful Norah I know. Suddenly her impending departure is welcome. But I only shake my head, and we watch the rest of the episode in discontented silence. Another commercial break begins.

"Do you know the secret to fortune-telling?" she asks, out of the blue.

I sink into the couch cushions. Here we go.

Norah turns to look at me. "The secret is that I don't read leaves. And palm readers don't read palms, and tarot readers don't read cards. We read people. A good fortune-teller reads the person sitting across from them. I study the signs in their leaves, and I use them to give an interpretation of what I know that person wants to hear." She leans in closer. "People prefer paying when they hear what they want to hear."

I cringe, sure that I don't want to hear whatever's coming next.

"Say a woman comes in," she continues. "No wedding ring, tight shirt, cleavage up to her chin. Asks about her future. This is a woman who wants me to say that she's about to meet someone. And, usually, if the shirt is tight enough and with confidence gained from a good fortune, guess what? She'll probably meet someone. Now, it may not be the *right* someone, but it still means her fortune came true."

My frown deepens. I stare at the television screen, but the flashing commercials are making it hard to focus. "So . . . when you looked at me, you saw someone who wanted arguments and confusion and partings? And you wanted it to come true?"

"No." Norah scoots even closer. "You were different. I don't have many chances to talk to you when you might actually listen to what I have to say. Reading your leaves was an opportunity. I didn't tell you what you wanted to hear. I told you what you *needed* to hear."

I'm confused and hurt. "I needed to hear bad things?"

She places a hand on mine. It's bony, but somehow it's also warm. I turn to her, and her gaze is sympathetic. "Your relationship with Max was waning," she says, using her fortune-teller voice. "And I saw that you had a much more special one waiting right behind it."

"The cherry. You *did* know how I felt about Cricket back then."

She removes her hand. "Christ, the mailman knew how you felt about him. And he's a good kid, Lola. It was stupid of you to get caught with him in bed—you know your parents are strict as hell about that shit—but I know he's good. They'll come around to it, too. And I know *you're* good."

I'm quiet. She thinks I'm a good person.

"Do you know my biggest regret?" she asks. "That you turned into this bright, beautiful, fascinating person . . . and I can't take credit for any of it."

There's a lump in my throat.

Norah crosses her arms and looks away. "Your fathers piss me off, but they're great parents. I'm lucky they're yours."

"They care about you, too, you know. *I* care about you."

She's silent and stiff. I take a chance and, for the first time since I was a little girl, burrow into her side. Her hard shoulders melt against me.

"Come back and visit," I say. "Once you've moved."

The lights of the commercials flash.

Flash.

Flash.

"Okay," she says.

I'm in my bedroom later that night when my phone rings. It's Lindsey. "On second thought," she begins, "maybe I shouldn't tell you."

"What?" Her unnaturally disturbed tone gives me an instant chill. "Tell me what?"

A long, deep breath. "Max is back."

The blood drains from my face. "What do you mean? How do you know?"

"I just saw him. My mom and I were shopping in the Mission, and there he was, walking down Valencia."

"Did he see you? Did you talk to him? What did he look like?"

"No. Hell no. And like he always does."

I'm stupefied. How long has he been back? Why hasn't he called? His continued silence means that he must have been telling the truth: *I'm nothing to him anymore.*

Lately, I've gone several hours—once, an entire day—without thinking of him. This is a fresh dig into my wounds, but somehow . . . the blow isn't as crushing as I thought it would be. Perhaps I'm becoming okay with being nothing to Max.

"Can you breathe?" Lindsey asks. "Are you breathing?"

"I'm breathing." And I am. An idea is quickly mushrooming inside of me. "Listen, I have to go. There's something I need to do." I grab a faux-fur coat and my wallet, and I'm racing out my door when I hear a faint *plink.*

I stop.

Plink, my window says again. *Plink. Plink.*

My heart leaps. I throw open the panes, and Cricket sets down his box of toothpicks. He's wearing a red scarf and some sort of blue military jacket. And then I notice the leather satchel slung over his shoulder, and this blow *is* crushing. His break is over. He's going back to Berkeley.

His arms slacken. "You look incredible."

Oh. Right. It's been a month since he's seen me in anything other than black. I give him a shy smile. "Thank you."

Cricket points at my coat. "Going somewhere?"

"Yeah, I was on my way out."

"Meet me on the sidewalk first? Would your parents would mind?"

"They're not home."

"Okay. See you in a minute?"

I nod and hurry downstairs. "I'll be back in an hour," I tell Norah. "There's something I have to do. Tonight."

She mutes the television and raises an eyebrow in my direction. "Does this mysterious errand have to do with a certain guy?"

I'm not sure which one she means, but . . . either is correct. "Yeah."

She studies me for several excruciating seconds. But then she un-mutes the television. "Just get back here before your parents do. I don't wanna have to explain."

Cricket is waiting at the bottom of my stairs. His willowy figure looks exquisite in the moonlight. Our gazes are fixed on each other as I walk down the twenty-one steps to my sidewalk. "I'm going back to school," he says.

I nod at his bag. "I guessed as much."

"I just wanted to say goodbye. Before I left."

"Thank you." I shake my head, flustered. "I mean . . . I'm glad. Not that you're going. But that you found me before leaving."

He puts his hands in his pockets. "Yeah?"

"Yeah."

We're quiet for a minute. Once more, I smell the faintest trace of bar soap and sweet mechanical oil, and my insides nervously stir.

"So . . . which way?" He gestures in both directions down the sidewalk. "Where are you going?"

I point in the opposite direction from where he'll go to catch his train. "That way. There's, uh, some unfinished business I have to attend to."

Cricket knows, from my hesitation, what I'm talking about. I'm afraid he'll tell me not to go—or, worse, ask to escort me—but he only pauses. And then he says, "Okay."

Trust.

"You'll come home soon?" I ask.

The question makes him smile. "Promise you won't forget me while I'm gone?"

I smile back. "I promise."

And as I walk away, I realize that I have no idea how I'll manage to *stop* thinking about him.

The dread doesn't hit until I arrive at his apartment and see the familiar brown stucco walls and pink oleander bush. I glance up at Max's apartment. The light is on and there's movement behind the curtain. Doubt creeps in like a poisonous fog. Was it wrong of me to come here? Is it selfish for me to want to apologize if he doesn't want to hear it?

I climb the dark stairwell that leads to his front door. I'm relieved when he opens it, and not Johnny, but my relief is short-lived. Max's amber eyes glare at me, and the scent of cigarettes is strong. No spearmint tonight.

"I—I heard you were back."

Max remains silent.

I force myself to hold his stony gaze. "I just I wanted to tell you that I'm sorry. I'm sorry for lying, and I'm sorry for the way things ended. I didn't treat you fairly."

Nothing.

"Okay. Well. That was it. Bye, Max."

I'm on the first step back down when he calls out, "Did you sleep with him?"

I stop.

"While we were together," he adds.

I turn and look him in the eye. "No. And that's the truth. We didn't even kiss."

"Are you sleeping with him now?"

I blush. "God, Max."

"Are you?"

"*No.* And I'm leaving now." But I don't move. This is my last chance to know. "Where have you been for the last month? I called. I wanted to talk with you."

"I was staying with a friend."

"Where?"

"Santa Monica." Something about the way he says it. As if he wants me to ask.

"A . . . girl?"

"A woman. And I *did* sleep with her." Max slams his door.

chapter thirty

Max has always known what to say—and when to say it—to make it hurt the worst. His words stung, but it only took a moment for me to realize why. It's not because I care that he's been with another woman. It's because I can't believe that I ever loved him. I viewed Max in such a willfully blind way. How could I have ignored his vindictive side? How could I have committed myself to someone whose knee-jerk reaction was always anger and cruelty?

I apologized. He reacted in his typical fashion. I went to his apartment for absolution, and I got it.

Good riddance.

Winter break comes to an end, and with it, so does my grounding. School resumes. I'm surprised when three of my classmates—three people I don't know well—approach me the first day and say that they're happy to see I'm dressing like myself again.

It makes me feel . . . gratified. Appreciated.

Even Lindsey sits taller and prouder, a combination of Charlie and his friends (who have joined us at lunch) and seeing me colorful again. It's nice to have more people around. The hard part is waiting for the weekend. I miss that *chance* of seeing Cricket at any moment. The pale blue glass of my window looks dull without him on the other side.

Friday is the longest school day in the history of time. I watch the clock with eyeballs like Ping-Pong balls, driving Lindsey crazy. "It'll come," she says. "Patience, Ned." But as the last bell rings, my phone does, too. A text from NAKED TIGER WOMAN:

> Not coming home this weekend. Unexpected project. On the first week! This sucks.

My world caves in. But then a second text appears:

> I miss you.

And then a third:

> I hope that's ok to say now.

My heart is cartwheeling as I text back:

Miss you, too. Miss you even more this weekend.

!!!!!!!!! = chirping crickets + ringing bells

We text for my entire walk home, and I'm floating like a pink fluffy cloud. I let him go so that he can work, and he protests for several texts, which makes me even happier. Throughout the night, my phone blinks with new messages—about his roommate Dustin's hideous friends, about being hungry, about not being able to read his own notes. I fill his phone with messages about Norah repacking her boxes, about Andy's seasonal clementine pie, about accidently leaving my math book in my locker.

In the morning, my parents are taken aback when I wake up early and materialize downstairs while they're still eating breakfast. Andy examines the calendar. "I thought your shift didn't start until four."

"I'd like to go to Berkeley. Just for a few hours before work."

My parents trade an unsettled glance as Norah shuffles into the room behind me. "Oh, for God's sake, let her go. She'll go anyway."

They give me permission. Hourly phone-call check-ins, but I gladly accept. I'm bouncing out the door when a split-second decision has me returning for something tiny that I keep stashed away in my sock drawer. I slip it into my purse.

I stop by New Seoul Garden, and Lindsey packs a bag of

takeout, which causes the entire car—on both of the trains it takes to get to Berkeley—to smell. Whoops. I decide to be brave this time and call him when I reach his dormitory gates, but someone is leaving as I'm arriving, and it's not necessary. I pass through the landscaped courtyard and the other doors just as easily.

And then I'm at *his* door.

I lift my hand to knock as a girl laughs on the other side. My knuckles land against the wood in a tremble. Is that Jessica? Again?

The door pops open, and . . . it's Anna.

"Hey, space cowgirl!" She's already taken in the silver fringe dress and my red cowboy boots. For one nightmarish second, I'm consumed by suspicion, but the door swings back and reveals St. Clair. Of course. He and Cricket are sitting against the side of Cricket's bed. And then Cricket Bell sees me, and the atmosphere *lights up.*

My soul lights up in response.

"Hi." He springs to his feet. "Hi," he says again.

"I was worried that you wouldn't have time to eat lunch today." I hold up the takeout as I notice a spread of empty Chinese boxes on the floor. "Oh."

Anna gives me a gap-toothed grin. "Don't worry. He'll eat what you've brought, too."

"His stomach is quite tall," St. Clair says.

"And yours is so wee," Anna says. He shoves her legs from his place on the floor, and she shoves his back. They're like puppies.

Cricket gestures me forward with both arms. "Here, come in, sit down."

I glance around. Every surface is covered.

"Uh, hold on," he says. There's a mound of school papers spread across the surface of his bed, which he bulldozes aside. "Here. Sit here."

"We should go," Anna says. "We just stopped by to feed Cricket and grill him about the Olympics. Did you know they're in France this year?" She sighs. "I'm dying for a visit."

Her boyfriend bites a pinkie nail. "And I'm trying to convince her that if Calliope makes the team, we should consider it a sign and take the holiday."

I smile at Anna. "Lucky you."

St. Clair turns toward Cricket and points an accusing finger. "I'm counting on you to ensure your sister wins at Nationals next weekend, all right?"

My heart selfishly plummets. Next weekend. More time away from Cricket.

"She only has to get one of the top three spots," Cricket says. "But I'll take out an opponent's kneecap if I have to."

Anna prods St. Clair's shoulder. "Come on. Weren't you gonna show me that thing?"

"What thing?"

She stares at him. He stares back. She cocks her head toward Cricket and me.

"Ah, yes." St. Clair stands. "That thing."

They rush out. The door shuts, and St. Clair shouts, "Lola,

Cricket wants to show you his thing, too-oo!" They're laughing as their feet echo down the hall.

Cricket hastily looks away from me and places the carton of Bibimbap in his microwave.

"Oh. I got something beef-y for you," I say, because he's heating the vegetarian dish first.

He shrugs and smiles. "I know. I saw."

I smile, too, and sit on the edge of his bed. "So all three of you are going to France, and I'm staying here? Talk about unfair." I'm only half kidding.

"You should come."

I snort. "Yeah, my parents would definitely be cool with that."

But Cricket looks thoughtful. "You know, Andy loves figure skating. If you had a free ticket, he might bite."

"And where, exactly, would I find a free ticket?"

He sits beside me. "Courtesy of my great-great-great-grandfather Alexander Graham Bell, the world's richest liar?"

I stop smiling. "Cricket. I could never accept that."

He nudges one of my cowboy boots with one of his pointy wingtips. "Think about it."

My foot tingles from the shoe-on-shoe contact. I nudge his shoe back. He nudges mine. The microwave beeps, and he hesitates, unsure if he should get up. I reach out and take his wrist, over his rubber bands and bracelets. "I'm not that hungry," I say.

Cricket looks down at my hand.

I slide my index finger underneath a red bracelet. My finger brushes the skin of his inner wrist, and he releases a small sound.

His eyes close. I twine my finger in and out of his bracelets, tying myself against him. I close my eyes, too. My finger guides us onto our backs, and we lie beside each other, quietly attached, for several minutes.

"Where's Dustin?" I finally ask.

"He'll be back soon. Unfortunately."

I open my eyes, and he's staring me. I wonder how long his eyes have been open. "That's okay," I say. "I came here to give you a late Christmas present."

His eyebrows raise.

I smile. "Not *that* kind of present." I untangle my finger from his wrist and roll over to grab my purse from his floor. I rummage through it until I find the tiny something taken from my sock drawer. "Actually, it's more like a late birthday present."

"How . . . belated of you?"

I roll back toward him. "Hold out your hand."

He's smiling. He does.

"I'm sure you don't remember anymore, but several birthdays ago, you needed this." And I place a tiny wrench into his palm. "Lindsey and I went everywhere to find it, but then . . . I couldn't give it to you."

His expression falls. "Lola."

I close his fingers around the gift. "I threw away your bottle cap, because it killed me to look at. But I never could throw away this. I've been waiting to give it to you for two and a half years."

"I don't know what to say," he whispers.

"I'm almost full," I say. "Thank you for waiting for me, too."

chapter thirty-one

The doorbell rings early the next Saturday. It wakes me from a deep slumber, but I immediately fall back asleep. I'm surprised when I'm being shaken awake moments later. "You're needed downstairs," Andy says. "Now."

I sit up. "Norah? She was kicked out already?"

"Calliope. It's an emergency."

I tear out of bed. An emergency with Calliope can only mean one thing: an emergency with Cricket. We've been texting, so I know he planned to come home before leaving for Nationals. But his light was off when I got back from work last night. I couldn't tell if he was there. What if he *tried* to come home, and something happened along the way? "Oh God, oh God, oh God, oh God, oh God." I throw on a kimono and race downstairs, where Calliope is pacing our living room. Her normally smooth hair is unwashed and disheveled, and her complexion is puffy and red.

"Is he okay? What happened? Where is he?"

Calliope stops. She cocks her head, muddled and confused. "Who?"

"CRICKET!"

"No." She's momentarily thrown. "It's not Cricket, it's me. It's . . . this." Her hands tremble as she holds out a large brown paper bag.

I'm so relieved that nothing is wrong with Cricket—and I'm so upset for thinking that something *was* wrong—that I snatch the bag a bit too harshly. I peer inside. It's filled with shredded red gauze.

And then I gasp with understanding. "Your costume!"

Calliope bursts into tears. "It's for my long program."

I carefully remove one of the shimmering strips of torn fabric. "What happened?"

"Abby. You'd think she was a dog, not a child. When Mom came down for breakfast, she discovered her playing in . . . *this.* I'd left my costume downstairs for cleaning. Who would've thought she could rip it?" Calliope's panic grows. "I didn't even know she was strong enough. And we're leaving tomorrow! And my seamstress is out of town, and I know you can't stand the sight of me, but you're my only hope. Can you fix it in time?"

As intriguing as it is to be her only hope, there's no hope to be had. "I'm sorry," I say. "But I can't fix this *period*. It's ruined."

"But you HAVE to do something. There has to be something you can do!"

I hold up a handful of shreds. "These are barely big enough to blow your nose on. If I sewed them back together—even if I could, which I can't—it'd look terrible. You wouldn't be able to compete in it."

"Why can't you wear one of your old costumes?" Nathan interrupts.

Andy looks horrified. "She can't do that."

"Why not?" Nathan asks. "It's not the outfit that wins competitions."

Calliope shudders, and that's when I remember her second-place curse. She must have already been racked by nerves, and then to add this on top of it? I do feel sorry for her. "No," she says. The word barely comes out. "I can't do that." She turns to me with her entire body, an eerily familiar gesture. "Please."

I feel helpless. "I'd have to make a new one. There's no—"

"You could make a new one?" she asks desperately.

"No!" I say. "There's not enough time."

"Please," she says. "Please, Lola."

I'm feeling frantic. I want her to know that I'm a good person, that I'm not worthless, that I deserve her brother. "Okay. Okay," I repeat. Everyone stares at me as I stare at the tatters. If only I had bigger pieces to work with. These are so small that they wouldn't even make a full costume anymore.

It hits me. "About those old costumes—"

Calliope moans.

"No, listen," I say. "How many do you have?"

She gives me another familiar gesture, the parted mouth and

furrowed brow. The difficult equation face. "I don't know. A lot. A dozen, at least."

"Bring them over."

"They don't all fit anymore! I can't wear them, I won't—"

"You won't have to," I reassure her. "We'll use the parts to make something new."

She's on the verge of hysterics again. "You're Frankenstein-ing me?"

But I feel calm now that I have a plan. "I won't Frankenstein you. I'll revamp you."

She's back in five minutes, and she returns with . . . Cricket. Their arms are piled high with stretchy fabric and sparkly beads. His hair is still sleep-tousled, and he's not wearing his bracelets. His wrists look naked. Our eyes meet, and his thoughts are just as exposed: gratitude for helping his sister and the unmistakable ache of longing.

The ache is reciprocated.

I lead them upstairs to my bedroom. Cricket hesitates at the bottom, unsure if he's allowed to go up. Andy gives him a prod on the back, and I'm relieved. "We'll definitely find something in all of this," I tell Calliope.

She's still on edge. "I can't believe my stupid niece did this to me."

My facial muscles twinge, but I'd say the same thing if I were in her situation. "Let's spread out the costumes and see what we have."

"Spread them out *where?*"

I almost lose my cool, when I look at my floor and realize she has a point. "Oh. Right." I shove the piles of discarded shoes and clothing into corners, and Andy and Cricket join in. Nathan waits in the doorway, eyeing the situation—and Cricket—warily. When my floor is clear enough, we lay out her costumes.

Everyone stares at the spread. It's a little overwhelming.

"What's your music?" Andy asks.

Our heads snap to look at him.

"What?" He shrugs. "We need to know what she's skating to before Lo can design the right costume. What's her inspiration?"

Nathan blinks.

I smile. "He's right. What are you skating to, Calliope?"

"It's a selection from 1968's *Romeo and Juliet*."

"No idea what that sounds like." I point her to my laptop. "Download it."

"I can do better than that." She sits in my chair and types her own name into a search engine. One of the first entries is a video from her last competition. "Watch this."

We gather around my computer. Her music is haunting and romantic. Fraught with drama and strung with tension, it collapses into sorrow, and ends with a powerful crescendo into redemption. It's beautiful. *Calliope* is beautiful. It's been a while since I've seen her perform, and I had no idea what she'd become. Or I'd forgotten.

Or I'd forced myself to forget.

Calliope moves with passion, grace, and confidence. She's a prima ballerina. And it's not only the way she skates—it's the expressions on her face, which she carries into her arms, hands, fingers. She acts every emotion of the music. She *feels* every emotion of the music. No wonder Cricket believes in his sister. No wonder he's sacrificed so much of his own life to see her succeed. She's extraordinary.

The clip ends, and everyone is silent. Even Nathan is awed. And I'm filled with the overwhelming sensation of Calliope's presence—this power, this beauty—in the room.

And then . . . I'm aware of another presence.

Cricket stands behind me. The faintest touch of a finger against the back of my silk kimono. I close my eyes. I understand his compulsion, his need to touch. As my parents burst into congratulating Calliope, I slide one hand behind my back. I feel him jerk away in surprise, but I find his hand, and I take it into mine. And I stroke the tender skin down the center of his palm. Just once.

He doesn't make a sound. But he is still, so still.

I let go, and suddenly *my* hand is in *his*. He repeats the action back. One finger, slowly, down the center of my palm.

I cannot stay silent. I gasp.

It's the same moment Mrs. Bell explodes into my bedroom, and, thankfully, everyone turns to her and not me. Everyone except for Cricket. The weight of his stare against my body is heavy and intense.

"What's the progress?" Mrs. Bell asks.

Calliope sighs. "We're just getting started."

I spring forward, trying to shake away what has to be the

most inappropriate feeling in the world to have when three out of our four parents are present. "Hi, Mrs. Bell," I say. "It's good to see you again."

She tucks her cropped hair behind her ears and launches into a heated discussion with Calliope. It's like I don't even exist, and I'm embarrassed that this hurts. I want her to like me. Cricket speaks for the first time since entering our house. "Mom, isn't it great that Lola is helping us?" His fingers grasp at his wrists for rubber bands that aren't there.

Mrs. Bell looks up, startled at his awkward intrusion, and then scrutinizes me with a severe eye. I make her uncomfortable. She knows how I feel about her son, or how he feels about me. Or both. I wish I were wearing something respectable. My just-rolled-out-of-bed look makes me feel trashy.

This is not how I would choose to represent myself to her.

Mrs. Bell nods. "It is. Thank you." And she turns back to Calliope.

Cricket glances at me in shame, but I give him an encouraging smile. Okay, so we need to work on our parents. We'll get there. I turn around to grab a notebook, and that's when I catch Nathan and Andy exchanging a private look. I'm not sure what it means, but, perhaps, it holds some remorse.

I feel a surge of hope. Strength.

I step forward to work, and things become crazy. Everyone has an opinion, and Mrs. Bell's turns out to be even stronger than her daughter's. The next half hour is hectic as arguments are had, fabric is trod upon, and garments are ripped. I'm trying to measure Calliope when Andy bumps into me, and I crunch against the sharp edge of my desk.

"OUT," I say. "Everybody out!"

They freeze.

"I'm serious, everyone except Calliope. I can't work like this."

"GO," Calliope says, and they scatter away. But Cricket lingers behind. I give him a coquettish smile. "You, too."

His smile back is dazed.

Nathan clears his throat from the hallway. "Technically, you aren't even allowed in my daughter's room."

"Sorry, sir." Cricket tucks his hands in his pockets. "Call me if you need anything." He glances at Calliope, but his eyes return to mine. "If either of you need anything."

He leaves, and I'm grinning all the way down to my glittery toenail polish as I resume taking her measurements. She picks up an eyelash curler from my desktop and taps it against her hand. "Why isn't my brother allowed in your room?"

"Oh. Um, I'm not allowed to have any guys in here."

"Please. Did Nathan catch you doing something? NO. Yuck. Don't tell me."

I yank the measuring tape around her waist a little too hard.

"Ow."

I don't apologize. I finish my work in silence. Calliope clears her throat as I write down the remaining measurements. "I'm sorry," she says. "It's nice of you to do this for me. I know I don't deserve it."

I stop mid-scratch.

She slams down my eyelash curler. "You were right. I thought he knew, but he didn't."

I'm confused. "Knew what?"

"That he's important to our family." She crosses her arms. "When Cricket was accepted into Berkeley, that was when I decided to return to my old coach. I wanted to move back here so that I could stay close to him. Our parents did, too."

It looks like Calliope has more to say, so I wait for her to continue. She lowers herself into my desk chair. "Listen, it's not a secret that I've made my family's life difficult. There are things that Cricket hasn't had or experienced because of me. And I haven't had them either, and I've hated it, but it was my choice. He didn't have a choice. And he's accepted everything with this . . . exuberance and good nature. It would've been impossible for our family to hold it together if we didn't have Cricket doing the hardest part. Keeping us happy." She raises her eyes to meet mine. "I want you to know that I feel *terrible* about what I've done to my brother."

"Calliope . . . I don't think . . . Cricket doesn't feel that way. You know he doesn't."

"Are you sure?" Her voice catches. "How can you be sure?"

"I'm sure. He loves you. He's proud of you."

She's silent for a minute. Seeing such a strong person struggle to hold it together is heartbreaking. "My family should tell him more often how remarkable he is."

"Yes, he is. And, yes, you should."

"He thinks you are, too. He always has." Calliope looks at me again. "I'm sorry I've held that against you."

And I'm too astonished by this admission to reply.

She rests her hand on the ruffled costume beside her. "Just answer this one question. My brother never got over you. Did you ever get over him?"

I swallow. "There are some people in life that you *can't* get over."

"Good." Calliope stands and gives me a grim smile. "But break Cricket's heart? I'll break your face."

We work together for a half hour, picking out pieces, throwing ideas back and forth. She knows what she wants, but I'm pleased to discover that she respects my opinion. We settle on a design using only her black costumes, and she collects the others to take home.

"So where's your dress?" she asks.

I have no idea what she's talking about. "What dress?"

"The Marie Antoinette dress. I saw your binder."

"You *what?*"

"Cricket was carrying it around at one of my competitions, practically fondling the damn thing. I teased him mercilessly, of course, but . . . it was interesting. You put a lot of work into those pages. He said you'd put a lot of work into the real thing, too." She looks around my room. "I didn't think it was possible to hide a giant-ass ball gown, but apparently I was wrong."

"Oh. Uh, it's not in here. I stopped working on it. I'm not going to the dance."

"What? WHY? You've been working on it for a half a year."

"Yeah, but . . . it's lame, right? To show up alone?"

She looks at me like I'm an idiot. "So show up with my brother."

I'm thrilled by her suggestion—*permission!*—but I've already considered it. "The dance is next weekend. He'll still be on the other side of the country for Nationals."

Nationals are a full week. Practice sessions, acclimation to the ice and rink, interviews with the media, two programs, plus an additional exhibition if she medals. Cricket will be staying with her the entire time for support.

"Oh," she says.

"Besides, it's stupid anyway." I stare at the notes for her costume, and I tug on a strand of hair. "You know, big dance. Big dress. What's the point?"

"Lola." Her tone is flat. "It's not stupid to want to go to a dance. It's not stupid to want to put on a pretty dress and feel beautiful for a night. And you don't need a date for that."

I'm quiet.

She shakes her head. "If you don't go, then you *are* stupid. And you *don't* deserve my brother."

chapter thirty-two

I work all day and night on Calliope's costume—seam-ripping the old ones, stitching new pieces together, adding flourishes from my own stashes—only stopping for a quick break at my window around midnight. Cricket joins me. He leans forward, elbows resting against his windowsill. The position looks remarkably *insectlike* with his long arms and long fingers. It's cute. Very cute.

"Thank you for helping my sister," he says.

I lean forward, mimicking his position. "I'm happy to."

Calliope leans out her window. "STOP FLIRTING AND GET BACK TO WORK."

So much for my break.

"Hey, Cal," he calls. She looks over as he removes a green

rubber band from his wrist and shoots it at her head. It hits her nose with a tight *snap* and falls between our houses.

"Really mature." She slams her window shut.

He grins at me. "That never gets old."

"I knew you wore those for a reason."

"What color would you like?"

I grin back. "Blue. But try not to aim for my face."

"I would never." And he swiftly flicks one into the space beside me.

It lands on my rug, and I slide it onto my wrist. "You're good with your fingers." And I give him a pointed look that means, *I am not talking about rubber bands.*

His elbows slide out from underneath him.

"Good night, Cricket Bell." I close my curtains, smiling.

"Good night, Lola Nolan," he calls out.

The rubber band is still warm from his skin. I work for the rest of the night, finishing the costume as the moon is setting. I collapse into bed and fall asleep with my other hand clasped around the blue rubber band. And I dream about blue eyes and blue nails and first-kiss lips dusted with blue sugar crystals.

"Where is it?"

"Mmph?!" I wake up to the frightening vision of Calliope and her mother hovering above my bed. People have GOT to stop doing this to me.

"Did you finish? Where is it?" Calliope asks again.

I glance at my clock. I've only been asleep for two hours. I roll out of bed and onto my floor. "Iss in my closet," I mumble, crawling for the closet door. "Needed to hang it up pretty."

Mrs. Bell reaches the closet first. She throws open the door and gasps.

"What? What is it?" Calliope asks.

Mrs. Bell takes it out and holds it up for her to see. "Oh, Lola. It's *gorgeous.*"

Calliope grabs it from the hanger and strips down in that way only beautiful, athletic girls can do—without shame and with a crowd. I look away, embarrassed.

"Ohhh," she says.

I look back over. She's standing before my full-length mirror. The black costume has long, slender, gossamer sleeves—delicate and shimmering and seductive—but they're almost more like fingerless evening gloves, because they stop at the top of her arms, allowing for an elegant showing of shoulder skin. The body has a skirt to echo this feeling, but the top ends in a halter, and I added a thin layer to peek out from underneath, so it's multistrapped and sequined and sexy.

The overall effect is romantic but . . . daring.

Calliope is in awe. "I was afraid you'd give me something crazy, something Lola. But this is me. This is my song, this is my program."

And even with the insult thrown in, I glow with happiness.

"It's better than your original," Mrs. Bell says to Calliope.

"You really think?" I ask.

"Yes," they both say.

I pick myself up from the floor and inspect the costume. "It could use some altering, here and here"—I point to two loose places—"but . . . yeah. This should work."

Mrs. Bell smiles, warm and relieved. "You have a special talent, Lola. Thank you."

She likes me! Or at least my sewing skills, but I'll take it.

For now.

There's a knock on my door, and I let in my parents. They *ooh* and *aah,* and Calliope and I are both beaming. I mark the costume for quick alterations, which I can do in an hour. Which I *have* to do in an hour, because that's when they leave for the airport. I shoo everyone away, and as I'm stitching, I glance again and again at Cricket's window. He's not there. I pray to an invisible moon that I'll see him before he leaves.

Sixty-five minutes later, I run into the Bells' driveway. Calliope and her parents are loading the last suitcases. Aleck is there with Abby on his hip. He looks as sleep-deprived as I feel, but he jokingly offers out Abby's hand to hold the new costume.

Calliope does not find the joke funny.

Aleck and Abby are staying while everyone else goes. The time alone will hopefully force him back into motion, but Andy and I have secret plans to check up on them. Just in case. I'm opening my mouth to ask about Cricket, when he races from the house. "I'm here, I'm here!" He comes to an abrupt halt six inches from me, when he finally notices there's someone else in the driveway.

I look up. And up again, until I meet his gaze.

"Get in the car," Calliope says. "We're leaving. Now."

"You're still wearing the rubber band," he says.

"I'm still wearing everything you last saw me in." And then I want to kick myself, because I don't want it to sound like I *forgot* I was wearing it. I am very, very aware of wearing his rubber band.

"CRICKET." This time, Mr. Bell.

I'm filled with a hundred things I want to say to Cricket, but I'm conscious of his entire family watching us. So is he. "Um, see you next week?" he asks.

"Good luck. To your sister. And you. For . . . whatever."

"CRICKET!" Everyone in the car.

"Bye," we blurt. He's climbing in when Aleck leans down and whispers something in his ear. Cricket glances at me and turns red. Aleck laughs. Cricket slams his car door, and Mr. Bell is already pulling away. I wave. Cricket holds up his hand in goodbye until the car turns the corner and out of sight.

"So." Aleck ducks his head out of reach from Abby's grabbing hands. "You and my brother, huh?"

My cheeks flame. "What did you say to him?"

"I told him your loins were clearly burning, and he should man up and make a move."

"You did not!"

"I did. And if he doesn't, then I suggest you jump *his* bones. My brother, in case you haven't noticed, is kind of an idiot about these things."

—

Cricket has left a new message for me in his window. It's written in his usual black marker but with one addition—a crayon rubbing of my name, imprinted from the sidewalk corners on Dolores Street.

The sign reads: GO TO THE DANCE DOLORES

I am going to the dance.

"I heard about Calliope," Norah says on Friday night. "Sixth place?"

I sigh. "Yep." In her post-short-program interview, Calliope was quiet but poised. A professional. "I'm disappointed," she said, "but I'm grateful to have another chance."

"That's a shame," Norah says.

"It's not over yet." My voice is sharp. "She still has a shot."

Norah gives me a wary look. "You think I don't know that? Nothing is ever over."

My family, Lindsey, and I are gathered around the television. Everyone is working on my Marie Antoinette gown. The last few decorative details are all that remain, and I appreciate the help as we wait for Calliope's long program to begin.

The ladies' short program was two nights ago. We saw the end from the beginning, in the moment the camera cut to Calliope's first position. It was in her eyes and underneath her smile. *Fear.* The music started, and it was clear that something was wrong.

It happened so quickly.

Her most difficult sequences were in the beginning—they usually are, so that a skater has full strength to perform them—and the commentators were in a tizzy over her triple jump, which she hadn't been landing in practice.

Calliope landed it, but she fell on the combination.

The expression on her face—only for a moment, she picked herself up instantly—was terrible. The commentators made pitying noises as she bravely skated to the other end of the rink, but our living room was silent. An entire season's worth of training. For nothing.

And then she fell *again*.

"It's not all about talent," the male commentator said. "It's also about your head. She's not been able to do what people have expected of her, and it's taken its toll."

"There's no greater burden than potential," the female commenter added.

But as if Calliope heard them, as if she said *enough,* determination grew in every twist of her muscles, every push of her skates. She nailed an extra jump and earned additional points. Her last two-thirds were solid. It's not impossible for her to make the Olympic team, but she'll need a flawless long program tonight.

"I can't watch." Andy sets down his corner of my Marie Antoinette dress. "What if she doesn't medal? In Lola's costume?"

This has been bothering me, too, but I don't want to make

Andy even more nervous, so I give him a shrug. "Then it won't be my fault. I only made the outfit. She's the one who has to skate in it."

The rest of us abandon my dress as the camera cuts to her coach Petro Petrov, an older gentleman with white hair and a grizzled face. He's talking with her at the edge of the rink. She's nodding and nodding and nodding. The cameraman can't get a good shot of her face, but . . . her costume looks *great.*

I'm on TV! Sort of!

"You made that in one day?" Norah asks.

Nathan leans over and squeezes my arm. "It's phenomenal. I'm so proud of you."

Lindsey grins. "Maybe you should have made my dress."

We went shopping earlier this week for the dance. I'm the one who found her dress. It's simple—a flattering cut for her petite figure—and it's the same shade of red as her Chuck Taylors. She and Charlie have decided to wear their matching shoes.

"You're going to the dance?" Norah is surprised. "I thought you didn't date."

"I don't," Lindsey says. "Charlie is merely a friend."

"A cute friend," I say. "Whom she hangs out with on a regular basis."

She smiles. "We're keeping things casual. My educational agenda comes first."

The commentators begin rehashing Calliope's journey. About how it's a shame someone with such *natural talent* always *chokes.* They criticize her constant switching of coaches and make a bold statement about a misguided strive for perfection. We boo the television. I feel sadness for her again, for having to live with such constant criticism. But also admiration, for continuing to strive. No wonder she's built such a hard shell.

I'm yearning for the network to show her family, which they didn't do AT ALL during the short program. Shouldn't a twin be notable? I called him yesterday, because he's still too shy to call me. He was understandably stressed, but I got him laughing. And then he was the one who encouraged me to invite Norah today.

"She's family," he said. "You should show encouragement whenever you can. People try harder when they know that someone cares about them."

"Cricket Bell." I smiled into my phone. "How did you get so wise?"

He laughed again. "Many, many hours of familial observation."

As if the cameramen heard me . . . HIM. It's him! Cricket is wearing a gray woolen coat with a striped scarf wrapped loosely around his neck. His hair is dusted with snow and his cheeks are pink; he must have just arrived at the arena. He is winter personified. He's the most beautiful thing I've ever seen.

The camera cuts to Calliope, and I have to bite my tongue to keep from shouting at the television to go back to Cricket. Petro takes ones of Calliope's clenched hands, shakes it gently, and then she glides onto the ice to the roar of thousands of spectators, cheering and waving banners. Everyone in my living room holds their breath as we wait for the first clear shot of her expression.

"And would you look at that," the male commentator says. "Calliope Bell is here to fight!"

It's in the fierceness of her eyes and the strength of her posture as she waits for her music to begin. Her skin is pale, her lips are red, and her dark hair is pulled into a sleek twist. She's stunning and ferocious. The music starts, and she melts into the romance of it, and she *is* the song. Calliope *is* Juliet.

"Opening with a triple lutz/double toe," the female says. "She fell on this at World's last year . . ."

She lands it.

"And the triple salchow . . . watch how she leans, let's see if she can get enough height to finish the rotation . . ."

She lands it.

The commentators drift into a mesmerized hush. Calliope isn't just landing the jumps, she's performing them. Her body ripples with intensity and emotion. I imagine young girls across America dreaming of becoming her someday like I once did. A gorgeous spiral sequence leads into a dazzling combination spin. And soon Calliope is punching her arms in triumph, and it's over.

A flawless long program.

The camera pans across the celebrating crowd. It cuts to her family. The Bell parents are hugging and laughing and crying. And beside them, Calliope's crazy-haired twin is whooping at the top of his lungs. My heart sings. The camera returns to Calliope, who hollers and fist-pumps the air.

No! Go back to her brother!

The commentators laugh. "Exquisite," the man says. "Her positions, her extensions. There's no one like Calliope Bell when she's on fire."

"Yes, but will this be enough to overcome her disastrous short program?"

"Well, the curse remains," he replies. "She couldn't pull off two clean programs, but talk about redemption. Calliope can hold her head high. This was the best performance of her career."

She puts on her skate guards and walks to the kiss-and-cry, the appropriately nicknamed area where scores are announced. People are throwing flowers and teddy bears, and she high-fives several people's hands. Petro puts his arm around her shoulders, and they laugh happily and nervously as they wait for her scores.

They're announced, and Calliope's eyes grow as large as saucers.

Calliope Bell is in second place.

And she's ecstatic to be there.

chapter thirty-three

The wig comes on, and I'm . . . almost happy.

There's something wrong with my reflection.

It's not my costume, which would make Marie Antoinette proud. The pale blue gown is girly and outrageous and gigantic. There are skirts and overskirts, ribbons and trim, beads and lace. The bodice is lovely, and the stays fit snugly underneath, giving me a flattering figure—the correct body parts are either more slender or more round. My neck is draped in a crystalline necklace like diamonds, and my ears in shimmery earrings like chandeliers. I sparkle with reflected light.

Is it the makeup?

I'm wearing white face powder, red blush, and clear red lip gloss. Marie Antoinette didn't have mascara, so I felt compelled to cheat there. I've brushed on quite a bit over a pair of false eyelashes. My gaze travels upward. The white wig towers at two feet tall, and it's adorned with blue ribbons and pink roses and pink feathers and a single blue songbird. It's beautiful. A work of art. I spent a *really long time* making it.

And . . . it's not right.

"I don't see me," I say. "I'm gone."

Andy is unlacing my buckled platform combat boots, preparing to help me step inside of them. He gestures in a wide circle. "What do you mean? ALL I can see is you."

"No." I swallow. "There's too much Marie, not enough Lola."

His brow furrows. "I thought that was the point."

"I thought so, too, but . . . I'm lost. I'm hidden. I look like a Halloween costume."

"When *don't* you look like a Halloween costume?"

"Dad! I'm serious." My panic rapidly intensifies. "I can't go to the dance like this, it's too much. Way too much."

"Honey," he shouts to Nathan. "You'd better get in here. Lola is using new words."

Nathan appears in my doorway, and he grins when he sees me.

"Our daughter said"—Andy pauses for dramatic effect—*"it's too much."*

They burst into laughter.

"IT'S NOT FUNNY." And then I gasp. My stays crush my rib cage, making the outburst labored and painful.

"Whoa." Nathan is suddenly beside me, his hand on my back. "Breathe. Breathe."

I was already nervous about going to the dance and seeing my classmates. At least I won't be alone—I'm meeting Lindsey and Charlie there—but I can't go like this. It'd be humiliating. I need Lindsey here; she'd take control. But she's in the middle of a murder-mystery dinner party, and Charlie has wagered a month of school lunches that he'll solve the mystery before she does. It's important to Lindsey that she wins.

"Phone," I pant. "Give me my phone."

Andy hands it to me, and I dial Cricket instead. I'm sent directly to his voice mail, like I have been all afternoon. He called this morning to make sure I was going to the dance, but we haven't talked since. I keep fantasizing that we can't get in touch because he's on an airplane, planning to surprise me by magically appearing at my school during the first slow song, but it's most likely a snowstorm wreaking havoc with his connection. Tonight is the Exhibition of Champions, and Calliope is performing in it. He has to be there.

But tomorrow . . . he'll be home.

The thought temporarily calms me. And then I see my reflection again, and I realize that tomorrow helps nothing about *tonight*.

"O-kaaaay." Andy pries the phone from my death grip. "We need a plan."

"I have a plan." I tear at the pins holding the wig to my head. "I'll take it apart. I'll do a modern reinterpretation of it in my own hair." I'm flinging the pins to the floor like darts, and my parents step back nervously.

"That sounds . . ." Nathan says.

"Complicated," Andy says.

I rip off the wig and throw it onto my desk.

"Are you sure you want to—" Nathan's words die as I wrench the pink roses from the wig. Half of them tear, and Andy clamps a hand over his mouth. The songbird is yanked off next. "It's fine," I say. "I'll put them in my own hair, it'll be fine." I push the rest of the wig to the floor, look up, and cry out. My hair is matted and tangled, bushy and flattened. It's every bad thing that can happen to someone's head, all at once.

Andy gingerly removes another stray pin as I try to tug a brush through the disaster. "Careful!" he says.

"I'M BEING CAREFUL." The brush snags in my hair, and I explode into tears.

Andy spins around to Nathan. "Who do we call? Who do we know who does hair?"

"I don't know!" Nathan looks blindsided. "That queen with the big order last week?"

"No, she'd be working. What about Luis?"

"You hate Luis. What about—"

"I'll wear the wig! I'll just wear the wig, forget it!" I feel my black mascara trailing through my white face powder as I trip backward, and my right foot lands on the wig. The chicken wire structure underneath it smashes flat.

My parents gasp. And the last remaining vision I had of entering my winter formal as Marie Antoinette disappears.

I pull at my stays, forcing room to get air inside my chest. "It's over."

There's a *thud* beside my window as someone drops into the room. "Only the wig is over."

I lunge toward him instinctively, but my dress is so heavy that I crumple face-first into my rug. My gown falls around me like a deflated accordion. I didn't realize it was possible to die of embarrassment. But I think it might actually happen.

"Are you okay? Are you hurt?" Cricket drops to his knees. His grip is strong as he helps me sit up. I want to collapse into his arms, but he carefully lets go of me.

"What . . . what are you . . . ?"

"I left Nationals early. I know how important the dance is to you, and I wanted to surprise you. I didn't want you to have to walk in alone. Not that you couldn't handle it," he adds. Which is gracious of him, considering my current status. "But I wanted to be there, too. For your big entrance."

I'm wiping rug burn and mascara from my cheeks. "My big entrance."

My parents are frozen dumbstruck by the sudden appearance. Cricket turns to them apologetically. "I would have used the front door, but I didn't think you'd hear me. And the window was open."

"You've always been . . . full of surprises," Andy says.

Cricket smiles at him before swiveling back around to me. "Come on. Let's get you ready for the dance."

I turn my head. "I'm not going."

"You have to go." He nudges my elbow. "I came back so that I could take you, remember?"

I can't meet his eyes. "I look stupid."

"Hey. No," he says softly. "You look beautiful."

"You're lying." I lift my gaze, but I have to bite my lip for a moment to keep it from quivering. "I have mascara clown face. My hair screams child-eating storybook witch."

Cricket looks amused. "I'm not lying. But . . . we should clean you up," he adds.

He takes my arms and begins to help me stand. Nathan steps forward, but Andy grabs one of his shoulders. My parents watch Cricket rearrange the skirt of my dress to get me safely to my feet. He leads me to the bathroom attached to my bedroom. Nathan and Andy follow at a careful distance. Cricket turns on the sink's tap and searches the bottles and tubes on my countertop until he finds what he's looking for. "Aha!"

It's makeup remover.

"Calliope uses the same kind," he explains. "She's been known to need this after particularly brutal performances. For the, uh,"—he gestures in a general way toward my face—"same reason."

"Oh God." I blink at the mirror. "It looks like I've been vomited on by an inkwell."

He grins. "A little bit. Come on, the water is warm."

We scoot around awkwardly until I'm positioned in front of the sink, and then he drapes a towel over the front of my dress. I—very difficultly—lean over. His fingers slide through my hair and hold it back while I scrub. His physical presence against me is soothing. The face powder, mascara, false eyelashes, and blush disappear. I dry my face, and my eyes find his in the mirror. My skin is bare and pink.

He stares back with unguarded desire.

Nathan clears his throat from the doorway, and we startle. "So what are we going to do about your hair?" he asks.

My heart falls. "I guess I'll wear a different wig. Something simple."

"Maybe . . . maybe I can help," Cricket says. "I do have some experience. With hair."

I frown. "Cricket. You've had that same hair your entire life. Don't tell me you style it that way yourself."

"No, but . . ." He rubs the back of his neck. "Sometimes I help Cal with hers before competitions."

My eyebrows raise.

"If you'd asked me yesterday, I would have said it was a seriously embarrassing skill for a straight guy."

"You're the *best,*" I say.

"Only you would think that." But he looks pleased.

It's in this moment that I finally register what he's wearing. It's a handsome skinny black suit with a shiny sheen. The pants are too short—on purpose, of course—exposing his usual pointy shoes and a pair of pale blue socks that match my dress *exactly.*

And I totally want to jump him.

"Tick tock," Nathan says.

I scooch past Cricket, back into my bedroom. He gestures to my desk chair, so I lift my skirts up and around the back, and I find a way to sit down. And then he finger-combs my hair. His hands are gentle and quick, the movements smooth and assured. I close my eyes. The room is silent as his fingertips untangle the strands from roots to tips and run loose throughout my hair. I lean back into him. It feels like my entire body is blossoming.

He leans over and whispers in my ear, "They've gone."

I look up, and, sure enough, my parents have left the door ajar. But they're gone. We smile. Cricket resumes his work, and I nestle into his hands. My eyes close again. After a few minutes, he clears his throat. "I, um, have something to tell you."

My eyes remain shut, but my eyebrows lift in curiosity. "What kind of something?"

"A story," he says.

His words become dreamlike, almost hypnotic, as if he's told this to himself a hundred times before. "Once upon a time, there was a girl who talked to the moon. And she was mysterious and she was perfect, in that way that girls who talk to moons are. In the house next door, there lived a boy. And the boy watched the girl grow more and more perfect, more and more beautiful with each passing year. He watched her watch the moon. And he began to wonder if the moon would help him unravel the mystery of the beautiful girl. So the boy looked into the sky.

"But he couldn't concentrate on the moon. He was too distracted by the stars."

I hear Cricket remove a rubber band from his wrist, which he uses to hold a twist of my hair.

"Go on," I say.

I hear the smile in his voice. "And it didn't matter how many songs or poems had already been written about them, because whenever he thought about the girl, *the stars shone brighter.* As if she were the one keeping them illuminated.

"One day, the boy had to move away. He couldn't bring the girl with him, so he brought the stars. When he'd look out his window at night, he would start with one. One star. And the boy would make a wish on it, and the wish would be her name.

"At the sound of her name, a second star would appear. And then he'd wish her name again, and the stars would double into four. And four became eight, and eight became sixteen, and so on, in the greatest mathematical equation the universe had ever seen. And by the time an hour had passed, the sky would be filled with so many stars that it would wake his neighbors. People wondered who'd turned on the floodlights.

"The boy did. By thinking about the girl."

My eyes open, and my heart is in my throat. "Cricket . . . I'm not *that*."

He stops pinning my hair. "What do you mean?"

"You've built up this idea about me, this *ideal,* but I'm not that person. I'm not perfect. I am far from perfect. I'm not worth such a beautiful story."

"Lola. You are the story."

"But a story is just that. It isn't the truth."

Cricket returns to his work. The pink roses are added. "I know you aren't perfect. But it's a person's imperfections that make them perfect for someone else."

Another pin slides into place as I catch sight of the back of his hand. A star. Every star he's drawn onto his skin has been for *me*. I glance at my doorway to make sure it's still empty, and I grab his hand.

He looks at it.

I trace my thumb around the star.

He looks at me. His eyes are so painfully, exquisitely blue.

And I pull him down into me, and I plant my lips against his, which are loose with surprise and shock. And I kiss Cricket Bell with everything that's been building inside of me, everything since he moved back, everything since that summer, everything since our childhood. I kiss him like I've never kissed anyone before.

He doesn't move. *His lips aren't moving.*

My head jerks back in alarm. I've acted rashly, I've pushed him too quickly—

He collapses to his knees and yanks me back to his lips.

His kiss isn't even remotely innocent. There's passion, but there's also an urgency verging on panic. He pulls me closer, as close as my dress and my chair allow, and he's gripping me so tightly that I feel his fingers press through the back of my stays.

I pull back, gasping for breath. Reeling. His breath is ragged, and I place my hands on his cheeks to steady him. "Is this okay?" I whisper. "Are you okay?"

His reply is anguished. Honest. "I love you."

chapter thirty-four

Moonlight shines into my bedroom and reveals his fragile state. "I didn't say it so you'd say it back," he says. "Please don't say it if you don't mean it. I can wait."

I rise and detach my gown from the chair. And then I help him stand, and I place his hands around my waist. I lean onto my tiptoes, rest my fingers against the back of his neck, and kiss him gently. Slowly. His tongue finds mine. Our hearts beat faster and faster, and our kisses grow hotter and hotter, until we burst apart from breathlessness.

I smile, dizzily, and touch my swollen lips. These are *not* the kisses of a sweet, wholesome boy next door. I draw him closer by his tie and whisper into his ear, "Cricket Bell, I have been in love with you for my entire life."

He doesn't say anything. But his fingers tighten against the back of my bodice. I ache to press my body into his, but my dress is making full contact impossible. I wiggle into a slightly better position. He glances down and notices that I'm still wearing a certain blue something, and, this time, it's *his* index finger that wraps underneath *my* rubber band.

I shiver wonderfully. "I'm never taking it off."

Cricket brushes the delicate skin of my wrist. "It'll fall off."

"I'll ask you for another one."

"I'll give you another one." He smiles and touches his nose to mine.

And then he spasms violently and pushes me away.

Someone is coming upstairs. Cricket grabs the songbird off my desk and shoves it into my hair as Andy pops his head in. My dad gives us a look. "Just making sure everything is okay. It's getting late. You should get going."

"We'll be down in a minute," I say.

"You're not even wearing shoes. Or makeup."

"Five minutes."

"I'm timing it." Andy disappears. "And it'll be Nathan up here next," he calls out.

"So what do you think?" Cricket asks.

"You're good. Very, very good." I poke his chest, giddy with the knowledge that I can touch him now whenever I want. "How did you get so good?"

"It's safe to say that you're the one who brings it out of me." He pokes my stomach. "But I meant your hair."

I'm beaming as I turn toward the mirror, and . . . "OH."

The updo looks professional. It's tall and splendid and elaborate, but it doesn't overwhelm me. It complements me. "This is . . . it's . . . perfect."

"You will never tell anyone I did that on pain of death." But he's grinning.

"Thank you." I pause, and then I look down at my pale blue fingernails. "You know that thing you said about someone being perfect for someone else?"

"Yeah?"

My eyes lift back to his. "I think you're perfect, too. Perfect for me. And . . . you look amazing tonight. You always do."

Cricket blinks. And then again. "Did I black out? Because I've daydreamed those words a thousand times, but I never thought you'd *actually* say them."

"THREE MINUTES," Andy calls from downstairs.

We break into nervous laughter. Cricket shakes his head to refocus. "Boots," he says. "Socks."

I point them out, and while he finishes prepping them, I mascara my lashes, powder my face, and gloss my lips. The makeup is dropped into my purse. I have a feeling I'll need retouching before I come home. Cricket sweeps me up by my waist and carries me to the bed, and I'm lifting my skirts as he sets me down on the edge. His eyes widen, but it turns into more laughter when he sees how many layers are underneath.

I grin. "There's more than panniers under here."

"Just give me your foot."

From downstairs: "ONE MINUTE."

Cricket kneels and takes my left foot into his hands. The sock comes on too fast. My boot squeaks as he slides it over my leg. His careful, quick fingers lace it all the way up to my knee, where they linger ever so slightly. I close my eyes, praying for the clock to stop. He tugs and tightens the buckles. And then he repeats everything on the other side.

Somehow, this is the sexiest thing that has ever happened to me.

"I wish I had more feet," I say.

"We can do this again." He tightens the last buckle. "Anytime."

There's a knock against my door frame as Betsy eagerly bounds toward us. My parents are both here. Cricket helps me stand.

Nathan's expression softens into astonishment. "Wow."

I hesitate. "Good wow?"

"Standing ovation wow," Cricket says.

The way everyone is staring makes me nervous again. I turn toward the mirror, and I see . . . a magnificent gown and beautiful hair and a glowing face. And the reflection smiling back at me is *Lola*.

"One more," Andy says. "From the side, so we can see the bird in your hair."

I turn my head to pose for another picture. "This is the last one."

"Did you get a shot with the boots?" Nathan asks. "Show us the boots."

I lift my hem and smile. "Tick tock."

"I am trying *really* hard not to use the word 'fabulous' right now," Andy says.

But I feel fabulous. My parents take two more rounds of pictures—one with both of us and one with just Cricket—before we make our escape into the foggy night. Getting to the sidewalk requires folding the panniers, lifting my skirts, and stepping sideways down the stairs. We're walking to my school, because it's close.

Also, because I can't fit into a car.

"Hey! There they are!"

Aleck appears on the porch next door. Abby is on his hip. I wave, and her eyes grow HUGE like when she saw the wild green parrots in the park. "Ohhhh," she says.

"You guys look great," Aleck calls down. "Crazy. But great."

We grin our thanks and say goodbye. Unsurprisingly, the dress makes it difficult to maneuver down the sidewalk—I frequently have to turn to the side, and hand-holding is tricky—but we make our way down the first block.

"Are they still watching?" I ask.

Cricket looks back. "All four of them."

My stomach is fluttering, but the butterflies are happy and anticipatory. We're both waiting for the same moment. We finally turn a corner, and Cricket pulls me into the purple-black shadows of the first house. Our mouths crush against each other. My hands rake through his hair, tugging him closer. He tries to back me against the wall, but I bounce off it. Our lips are still touching as we laugh.

"Hold on." I hoist up the structure of my dress, but I fold it the other way this time, so that the lifted, flat surface is in the back. "Okay. Try again."

He does it slowly this time, pushing his entire figure against mine, using his hips to press me against the house. It doesn't matter how much fabric is between us, the solid strength of his body against mine is electric. Charged. And then our arms are enveloping and our fingers are digging and our mouths are searching and our bodies find this *lock*.

And if I'm the stars, Cricket Bell is entire galaxies.

The winter wind spirals around us, cold and bitter, but the space between us is hot and sweet. His scent makes me ravenous. I kiss his neck in a downward trail, and I can't hear it over the wind, but I feel him moan. His fingers easily, gracefully slide through the laces of my stays and work their way around the chemise underneath. They stroke only the smallest square of my back, but the tremor runs the full length of my spine.

Our mouths clasp again. We press against each other harder. His fingers slip out of my stays. They move from my back to my front, and for the first time ever, I wish this dress were less complicated. My next one will be much smaller, a single layer, with a thin silk that will allow me to feel *everything*.

Cricket breaks away, his eyes wild. "We have to stop. If we don't stop now . . ."

"I know." Even though all I want to do is keep going.

But he wraps his arms around me, and he holds me as if I were about to fly away with the wind. He holds me until our hearts stop pounding so furiously. He holds me until we can breathe again.

The fog is still heavy, and the sidewalks are packed, but everyone sees us coming. They part aside with claps and cheers. Our smiles as are full as our hearts. As we promenade down the glittery sidewalks of the Castro, I feel as if we're in a music video. A woman with a pompadour gives Cricket a fist pump, and the man with the Care Bears tattoo who owns the environmentally friendly dry cleaners gives us both wolf whistles.

Or maybe just Cricket. He *does* look hot.

We turn the last corner toward my school, and he pulls me into the privacy of another gap between houses. I look up at him teasingly through my eyelashes. "You know, I just reapplied my lip gloss."

But Cricket is suddenly nervous. Very nervous.

His expression fills me with apprehension. "Is . . . everything okay?" I ask.

He places a hand inside the inner pocket of his suit jacket. "I wanted to give you this for Christmas, and then for New Year's. But I couldn't get it ready in time. And then I thought it'd make a better gift for tonight anyway, assuming, of course, that you'd come with me to the dance. But then I couldn't give it to you in your bedroom, because it was too bright inside, so I had to wait until we were outside, because it's dark outside—"

"Cricket! What is it?"

He swallows. "Sohereitis, Ihopeyoulikeit."

And he removes his hand from his pocket and thrusts a slender golden object into my palm. The disk is warm from his body heat. It's round like a makeup compact, and there's a tiny button to open it, but it's deeper than a compact.

And the metal has been etched with stars.

The sound of my heart is loud inside my ears. "I'm almost afraid to open it. It's perfect as it is."

Cricket takes it and holds it at my eye level. "Press the button."

I extend a shaky index finger.

Click.

And then . . . the most wondrous thing appears. The lid pops back, and a miniature, luminous universe rises up and unfolds. A small round moon glows in the center, surrounded by tiny twinkling stars. I gasp. It's intricate and alive. Cricket places the automaton back into my palm. I cradle it, enchanted, and the stars wink at me lazily.

"The moon is what took so long. I had trouble getting the cycle correct."

I look up, mystified. "The cycle?"

He points to the real moon. She's a waxing gibbous—a slice of her left side is dark. I look back down. The little moon is *almost* entirely illuminated. A slice of its left side is dark. I'm stunned into silence.

"So you won't forget me when I'm gone," he says.

I raise my eyes in alarm.

Cricket reacts quickly. "Not gone-gone. I meant during

the week, when I'm at school. No more moving. I'm here. I'm wherever you are."

I let out a relieved breath, one hand clutching my tight stays.

"You haven't said anything." He plucks at a rubber band. "Do you like it?"

"Cricket . . . this is the most extraordinary thing I've ever seen."

His expression melts. He enfolds me into his arms, and I rise on my platform tiptoes to reach his lips again. I want to kiss him for the rest of the night, for the rest of our lives. *The one.* He tastes salty like sea fog. But he tastes sweet, too, like . . .

"Cherries," he says.

Yes. Wait. Was I talking out loud?

"You taste like cherries. Your hair smells like cherries. You've always smelled like cherries to me." Cricket presses his nose against the top of my head and inhales. "I can't believe I'm allowed to do that now. You have no idea how long I've wanted to do that."

I bury my face against his chest and smile. Someday I'll tell him about my teacup.

The sound of laughter and music floats through the night air, swirling and ephemeral. It's beckoning us. I look up and deep into his eyes. "Are you sure you want to do this? A high school dance? You don't think it's . . . kind of lame?"

"Sure, but aren't they supposed to be?" Cricket smiles. "I don't know. I've never been to one. And I'm happy. I'm *really* hap—"

And I interrupt his words with another ecstatic kiss. "Thank you."

"Are you ready?" he asks.

"I am."

"Are you scared?"

"I'm not."

He takes my hand and squeezes it. With my other, I hitch up the bottom of my dress. My platform combat boots lead the way. And I hold my head high toward my big entrance, hand in hand with the boy who gave me the moon and the stars.

acknowledgments

This novel should have two sets of acknowledgments: one for Kiersten White and one for everybody else.

Oh, Kiersten! Thank you for the backyard pirate games, the English seaside, the Gothic orchid mysteries, the Icelandic dancing, the French cafés, and for every other adventure we took while I was writing this book. Thank you for keeping me sane, despite the questionable sanity of that last sentence. Thank you for gently, persistently guiding me to The End. (Again and again and again.) And—most of all—thank you for being my friend. I am so grateful to have you in my life.

Kate Schafer Testerman: Remember that whole thing about you being my Dream Agent? I'm happy to announce that the reality is even sweeter. Thank you for being both kind and kick-ass.

Julie Strauss-Gabel: I want to draw glittery hearts around your name. My novels are so much better, so much stronger because of you. Thank you for your guidance, for your patience, and for uncovering the story that I've always wanted to tell. Working with you is a pleasure and an honor.

Further thanks to the entire Penguin Young Readers Group. Standing ovations for: Scottie Bowditch, Kristina Duewell, Ashley Fedor, Jeanine Henderson, Lauri Hornik, Anna Jarzab, Liza Kaplan, Doni Kay, Eileen Kreit, Katie Kurtzman, Rosanne Lauer, Linda McCarthy, Irene Vandervoort, and Lisa Yoskowitz.

Thank you to my family, my most enthusiastic cheerleaders: Mom, Dad, Kara, Chris, Beckham, J.D., Fay, and Roger. I am lucky to have you. I love you.

Thank you to the following authors for friendship, for critiquing drafts, and for understanding absolutely *everything*: Paula Davis, Gayle Forman, Lisa Madigan, Laini Taylor, Natalie Whipple, and Daisy Whitney. You are all goddesses.

Thank you to my amazing blog readers. Thank you to John Green, Nerdfighteria, and Wizard Rock for not forgetting to be awesome. Thank you to Lauren Biehl, Natalie Payne, Lisa Pressley, and Michelle Wolf for that crazy-good vegan brunch. Thank you to Manning Krull and Marjorie Mesnis for the transcontinental hospitality, terrible horror films, and exquisite wine. Thank you to Chris Lane for living on the right street in the right neighborhood in the right city, to Anna Pfaff for letting me borrow her future dog's name, and to anyone working for LGBT equality.

Finally, thank you to Jarrod Perkins. Who recognized the importance of a high school dance. Who flew across the country, swept me off to prom, and wore the matching Chuck Taylors. Who always makes me feel beautiful. You are beautiful, too. Thank you for ten dazzling years of marriage and for many, many more to come. Let's ask Elvis to renew our vows, okay? We'll wear our Chucks.